Brooklyn
Secrets

Brooklyn Secrets

An Erica Donato Mystery

Triss Stein

Poisoned Pen Press

First Edition 2015

10 9 8 7 6 5 4 3 2 1

Library of Congress Catalog Card Number: 2014958050

ISBN: 9781464204104   Hardcover
        9781464204128   Trade Paperback

Poisoned Pen Press
6962 E. First Ave., Ste. 103
Scottsdale, AZ 85251
www.poisonedpenpress.com
info@poisonedpenpress.com

Printed in the United States of America

"To absent friends...."

For Diane Parker and Janet Barnett,
real Brooklyn girls, real readers, and real friends,
who never knew they helped inspire Erica.

Acknowledgments

Thanks to authors Eric Dezenhall and Joseph Trigoboff for their insights; to Marco Conelli and Bernard Whalen for answering questions about law enforcement process; Marty Leventhal and Anne Osnato for Brownsville stories; Sylvia Kossar, Director of Municipal Archives, New York, for graciously answering questions about her work; Susan Chalfin for a verifying a detail; and Harriet Engle and especially my cousin Edna Stewart, for crucial medical information.

Any errors that have crept in are my own.

For ongoing support and encouragement, Jane Olson and Mary Darby; and for tech support, legal advice, and proofreading, Bob Stein, as always.

Chapter One

These are words to live by: no parent of a teenager really knows what her child is up to. Any parent who believes she does has either dangerously forgotten her own teenage years or is in for a big surprise one day. Maybe both.

So when my fifteen-year-old said, "Mom, we have to talk," it chilled my blood. Did she want to attend a three-day music festival? Or go on birth control? Or drop Chemistry? Or did she merely want new and expensive boots?

It was a Sunday. No school for her. I was having a rushed lunch while she ate a leisurely breakfast. Her words could start a discussion that could go on forever, wrecking all my plans and derailing all responsibilities for the afternoon.

I took a deep breath, stopped my simultaneous gathering up of research papers and dirty dishes. I sat down, ready to listen. Ready, if not entirely enthusiastic.

"I've been thinking it over and I've decided it's time for you to start dating again."

"What? What are you talking about?" I had been blindsided.

"When I was little you never dated. I get that. But now that I have a boyfriend I think you need more life of your own."

"Thank you very much, but my life is too damn full as it is. I don't think I have energy for one more thing in it. And I do have fun, and I do date."

She gave me that know-it-all-teen look. "Really? Your life is full? You go to work at a museum. You go to grad school. You work on your dissertation. You take care of me. Once in awhile you and Darcy do girlfriend things. That is not a life. And Mike the cop is nice enough, but I don't see you being all that excited when he calls."

My daughter is way too observant for a child. Or a teen. It was indeed becoming clear to me that occasional dinners with Mike, whose brother was a high school friend, was like dating a relative. We share too many memories of the old days in the old neighborhood and too little of…something.

"So I have the perfect solution."

"Oh?" I was seriously torn between listening to her and killing her.

"Date Joe. You know he likes you." The smug delivery of her words of wisdom merited something extreme.

I laughed at her.

"Joe is a player, in case you did not know that. A new girl every few months. You met the last one, that redhead. Now there's a different one. And I know him even better than Mike. He's just a good friend."

"Seriously? You think of him as a friend? Seriously? When he comes over to fix things any time you ask? And even my friends see he is pretty hot for an older guy?"

"You know what? Seriously? I am not taking romantic advice from someone who is not old enough to drive."

"Humph. I'm only a year younger than you were when you met Dad. And you were old enough."

She grinned—mockingly—when she saw I could not answer that. "Just think about it, okay?"

I stood up. "I have work to do today. I can't laze around thinking about romance, like some people."

"Laze around? If only. I have a practice college essay to write for Guidance, a chapter of Chem to read, and half of *Hamlet* for English. Plus an art project to plan. And Mel is coming over so we can do each other's nails. She has these tiny decals…"

I was half listening, half looking for a book I needed, half thinking about grocery supplies. Too many halves? Well, I am a historian-to-be, not a mathematician.

"I'll be back for dinner."

"Uh, Mom? Party at Dani's tonight. There will be food."

"Party on a school night?"

"No school tomorrow. It's teacher workshops, remember? I told you."

"Right, you did. Jared coming down for the party?"

"All the way from Riverdale. Yes." She suddenly smiled, and I saw the little girl I remembered. It was a birthday candles, riding the carousel smile. "His dad will come get him after."

"Okay, kiddo." Quick kiss on the top of her head. "Gotta run. I can't use my phone in the library, but you can leave me a message. I'll check in later."

In some ways, Chris is always the most important thing on my mind. I've been a single parent since she was three and I was twenty-four, so it's become a habit.

Otherwise, what was on my mind that morning, more urgent than my anemic social life, was crime. I'd reached the point in my dissertation on how neighborhoods changed in Brooklyn—it seemed like a good idea at the time—where I needed to discuss crime and how it changed, or didn't, as waves of immigration changed a neighborhood. I had a long afternoon in the library ahead of me.

I began with my least scholarly source, a book of photographs, the catalogue of a new museum exhibit. They turned out to be raw, ugly, often badly printed, but they were full of the drama of the moment. They were mid-twentieth-century tabloid newspaper photos, taken by the first famous crime scene photographer. They called him Espy for what seemed like his extra-sensory ability to find a crime scene every single time he went out.

He was a man obsessed with the city and the night, Espy was. Dark streets, street lamp reflections off the dark pavement, dark deeds. I found myself humming a song from *Guys and Dolls*, courtesy of my mom's old records, the one about his time of night, when the street belongs to the cop and the janitor with a mop. And it belonged to Espy. But he looked at the real thing, not the Broadway version.

I saw victims, both the quick and the dead, and criminals, both the weeping and the grinning, and bystanders from appalled to curious to indifferent. There was no makeup, no Photoshop, no flattering lighting. They all looked like scenes from a noir film, captured in real time.

And, aha. Here is where he would be most useful to me. His earliest beat was Brownsville, where he grew up and the very area I was studying. I recognized the name on a candy shop sign; it was the headquarters of a notorious Brownsville gang. Here was a photo of Pitkin Avenue, the main shopping street, bustling with shoppers and pushcarts, and here was a portrait of three nattily dressed men in playful poses. I knew their names. Back in the day, the Brooklyn DA, the local cops, and the tabloid editors knew them too.

These were his first published photos. He was only fifteen when he began documenting the rough life around him. Looking at his photos, I was seeing his world, through his eyes.

Then I began the slog through my library work. The book of photos was so much more interesting, so much more immediate, than the dry reports I was analyzing. My dissertation had come to feel like a dark tunnel with no light in sight at the moment.

Perhaps the prospect of a Sunday night alone while my daughter was out partying contributed to my mood. I thought I was used to it. I was certainly used to it. At least I usually was.

Maybe what Chris said had gotten to me after all.

At home I dozed off on the couch watching a bad movie and dreamed about streetlamps on wet pavement, with the flashing lights of cop cars and a voice-over by Edward G. Robinson. It wasn't restful. Not at all.

The next day I was going to explore Brownsville in the here and now. My guidebook was a memoir by a once-famous literary critic, Maurice Cohen, who had also grown up there in the 1920s and '30s, when it was Jewish, crime-ridden, and poor. Now it was African-American, crime-ridden, and poor.

It was the first book I read when I started this part of my work, and the best. Espy showed me how it looked; Cohen told me how it felt. They would be my guides to the time and place, walking there with me even if only in my mind.

And how horrified my adviser would be, to hear something so frivolous.

I wanted to duplicate Cohen's walk around his old neighborhood if I could, see what it looked like now, compare some then-and-now photos. If the result was not academic enough for dissertation use, there might be an article in it. I had to think about those things now.

I figured I could handle Brownsville, a high-crime neighborhood though it was. Sure I could. I grew up in blue-collar Brooklyn and though it wasn't quite as tough, there certainly were rough types out and around. I learned plenty of street smarts.

Attitude was key. Put on my game face. Walk fast, with purpose. Stay alert to everything around me, but don't look nervous. Don't wear diamonds and pearls. Not that I had any. Wear jeans and my old jacket. That part was easy; I didn't have too much else in my closet. No purse; carry my wallet and phone in my jacket. My ancient Civic would certainly not attract any attention.

Anyone who noticed me, a small white woman in her thirties, would assume I was a social worker or a teacher and not worth bothering.

I could use my phone for photos and not carry a camera. I knew what I was doing. I was prepared. However, I had carefully not told my father anything about this excursion. He'd have a lot to say and I was not going to listen.

As I drove I tried to keep the old photos in my head but it was not easy because the streets looked so different. Then, they were lined with ramshackle tenements, individual houses, and duplexes. Now, projects, low-income public housing, rose everywhere. Cohen wrote about it. They were just being built at the end of his book—clean, new apartments with modern kitchens and shiny bathrooms.

Any urban historian knows they turned out to be an experiment that failed, high-rise slums. And Brownsville was the most "projected" neighborhood in New York, maybe the country.

Pitkin Avenue, once a low-end but bustling main street, was still low end but not bustling. Not many people were out on this blustery April morning. A few women in office clothes, walking quickly and deep in conversation. Probably they really were teachers or social workers. A team of sanitation workers with a noisy truck. Scattered young men, hanging around, looking furtive. Were they up to no good, or watching out for potential problems? Or just killing time, waiting for some excitement? A man in a doorway. Urinating. Eww. A white man slouching along looking like a derelict. Only his whiteness made him noticeable.

But what was this? The famous local movie palace, the Loews Pitkin, had been a crumbling, deserted wreck for decades—I'd seen the photos—but now was under renovation for a new school and retail strip. I wondered if this was a sign of hope.

Here was the corner of Livonia and Saratoga, where the Moonlight Min candy store once stood. Its back room was the home office of the mob's killers-for-hire squad. The irony of using a candy store was not lost on me, though I suspected it was on the actual mobsters involved. They weren't exactly subtle thinkers.

I pulled over and snapped a few photos from the safety of the car. Now it was a shabby corner grocery/newsstand/deli/ smoke shop just like the others all over New York, most of the windows covered with security gates. I wondered what they used the back room for now.

Looking for more landmarks, I was startled to pass one that still stood unchanged. I double-parked again and leafed through my books. Yes, it was the former Brownsville Children's Library, unique in the city. This used to be Stone Avenue; now the street signs said Mother Gaston Boulevard. No wonder I was surprised.

There it was in its entire, original splendor, a solid brick building with a tower-like entrance and elaborately carved, ornamental limestone trimmed around the windows. It looked like a small bank, and like the old banks, was intended to say, "Something that matters takes place in here."

Maybe it mattered even more than money, I thought. Then again, maybe it didn't in this impoverished piece of New York. In those days, children stood in long lines here, waiting to get in. Were they the ones who grew up to become Maurice Cohen, Aaron Copland, Al Capp, Henry Roth, Joseph Papp? And the ones who liked money more than books became the local gangsters, Lepke Buchalter, Gurrah Shapiro, and their associates, squeezing their already impoverished neighbors for protection payoffs. Some children of Brownsville went to Hollywood; some went to the mob.

Neatly put, I thought to myself, but maybe too neat. And who used this library now? A parking space opened up right around the corner. I could go in and ask.

I was so busy thinking, I forgot to be alert to what was happening around me, my own rule number three. There is not appearing nervous, and then there is relaxing into stupidity.

As I turned to lock the car door, suddenly four teenage boys surrounded me.

"What this?" one said. "White lady in the hood? We waiting around for our girl Savanna to come out and look what we find."

"What you want here, little lady?"

They were smiling but not in a friendly way. Unless you would call sharks friendly.

I put on my own fierce face and suppressed any shakiness in my voice. "I need to leave. Please let me pass."

"That your car? I'd be 'shamed to drive that piece a shit car. White lady got no pride. You agree, bros?"

The responses were obscene variants of "Hell, yeah."

"So we could mess it up, just for fun? Do the little lady a favor, get her some insurance cash?"

I thought they were teenagers, but they were big. At that moment they all seemed very big. And I didn't have insurance on my old piece-of-crap car.

"Okay, enough fun." I snapped it out, sounding authoritative. I hoped. "Now let's all go on about our business."

"Bossy little lady." He smiled a little more. "You think you know our business? Naah. Maybe it's you is our business. We see you don't have no purse, but maybe you got something good in that bag you carrying. Maybe money? Maybe one of them little computers? Worth something on the street?"

"A nice phone? Maybe she got money hidden somewhere else. They all got money. Maybe we got to take her somewhere and search her."

He put out his hand and rubbed my arm. Now I was really scared.

"Naah, she too old to be fun for that."

What? Who was he calling old? That puff of anger blew away the fear, but just for a moment.

Then the fear came back. There were four of them. A kick might disable the nearest, but what then? If I ran, I could not get past all four. If I screamed, who was there to hear me on this empty street on this cold spring day?

Up the street, at the corner, a side door opened at the library and someone came out. I could see the blue of a uniform and the flare of a cigarette lighter. This was the moment to make some noise.

"Get out of my way." I said it as loud as I could. Louder, actually, than I thought I could.

They were laughing at me. My shouting amused them in their cat-and-mouse game, but it kept them from noticing the man running toward them, yelling at them obscenely to move along and that a patrol car was on the way.

They were way too cool to run, or panic, or even act concerned, but they were suddenly drifting off down the street. The leader turned back just for a second and waved a mocking farewell.

Chapter Two

"Are you all right, ma'am? Those kids. They always hanging around here, annoying all of us. They been trying to follow one of our pages home."

My voice trembled. "I'm okay, just kind of shaky. Nothing really happened."

"This time." He came down hard on those two words. "Nothing happened this time. Do you want to come into the library, have a glass of water or whatever?"

"I was planning to do exactly that, come into the library. And thank you for coming to the rescue."

He smiled. "What I'm here for. You know, most of the time it's a boring job, library security. Most exciting thing I do is tell kids to behave or leave."

"I'll be happy to let your boss know what you did. How's that?"

"'Preciate it." He checked to make sure the car doors were locked. "You come along now. My name is Wilson."

The library instantly felt like a refuge from the street outside. It was calm and quiet and pretty. Shabby, perhaps, but welcoming. It wasn't a bit like the library in my own childhood neighborhood, a building with all the charm of an airplane hangar.

"Ms. Talbot," he said to the tall, gray-haired woman at the desk, "this young lady was coming for a visit right here and had a little run-in with those boys been bothering Savanna. You know the ones."

"They're back? My word, what a nuisance. Would you let Savanna know you'll walk her home?" She turned to me. "Are you all right? Did they hurt you?"

"I'm fine. Really. It was just a little scary there for a minute. It's not like I scare easily but there were more of them than me. Um, Mr. Wilson came to my rescue, actually."

"I know all them boys." He shook his head. "Two of them already done some time. Not one of them goes to school or works, neither one. They'd rob their own grandmother if she had anything worth taking. One of their good dads threw him out 'cause he a bad influence on the littler ones."

Ms. Talbot said, "You were on your way here? What can I do for you?"

She was surprised by my explanation. "Not much happens to write about here, except the bad things," she said. "Around here we have gangs and guns and most people are just struggling. I'll certainly help if I can." Her manner was forthright but warm.

"Well, I know some of the history of this building." I showed her Espy's photo of the same building, perfectly recognizable.

"That's when this place was brand-spanking new. Poor old thing, it's worse for wear now. Well, I'm not what I once was either." She chuckled. "In fact, we're closing soon for a renovation that's way overdue. I mean decades. I'm happy to show you around.

"This has not been a special children's library for I don't know how many decades. It wasn't even when I was growing up around here, anyway. Now we have the children's section over here on the right. Look around you."

The fireplace presented an elaborate fairy tale scene with a castle painted on the tile surround. There were very old, Gothic-style benches with rabbit heads carved on the armrests.

"Yes." She smiled. "We have a few original items. They have promised me—in blood, mind you!—that they will still be here after the renovation."

"Even the outside looks impressive to me."

"You got that right. The head of children's work back then fought for it, to make it a place of beauty and imagination." She nodded emphatically.

We walked toward the adult section. There were computers, all in use, and a bookcase of trade manuals and prep books for licensing exams.

"That's the most popular section for adults. Like I said, folks are struggling here. Getting something like an MTA job or a taxi license is a step up. Otherwise, adults mostly take best sellers, urban paperbacks—you know, life on the wild side—and sports and music bios. We carry graphic novels, too. And…" she lowered her voice, "we have a reading skills workshop that meets here so we keep a bookcase of easy-to-read adult books. They circulate more than you might think."

She suggested I look around at will and then come back to her office. Savanna, the young girl at the desk, could show me the way and also take me upstairs.

"Upstairs, Mother Gaston used to give classes about African heritage. Savanna knows the story well because her mother was one of the students. Savanna isn't for the city in Georgia but for the African plains." She whispered to me, "It was her mother in her dashiki-wearing phase. Don't ask Savvie about it!"

Savanna was a slim, pretty teenager decked out in neat, elaborate cornrows and careful eye makeup. Savanna? Was she the girl that little gang had mentioned? The one they were waiting for?

She led me up a beautiful wooden staircase, now so worn parts of it were covered by ugly linoleum. And that was worn too.

The meeting room walls and bookcases were stripped bare, with piled up cartons in one corner.

"Mother Gaston was really a teacher. She gave free classes on African-American history and made it fun. Least, that's what my momma says. They had music and dancing and cooking. Everything here is already packed up. After the renovation, we're hoping to make a museum up here." She ducked her head shyly. "I mean, Miz Talbot hoping. Maybe I would help if I can, when I'm home summers from college."

"Are you starting college in the fall?"

"I am. I just learned, this week. I got a scholarship but I would have gone to Brooklyn College if I didn't. My mama said no chance I was not going. She's a scary, determined woman."

"Well, good for her."

"Yeah." She smiled again. "It's not cool for me to talk all the time about it, but yeah. I'm so happy she pushed me."

"Well, congratulations. Not that Brooklyn College isn't a huge gift itself. I went there and I was glad to have the chance. I'm in the City University graduate program now."

"Oh, no, I would never disrespect a public college. Some of my girls are going there and happy to be able to, just like you said. We have a gang, not a *gang* gang, just some homegirls. And we kind of all promised each other we would go. No babies, no jealous family, no boyfriends if they didn't encourage. Know what I mean?" She paused, assessing me, then said, "I'm going to Wellesley. That's where I got the scholarship."

That took me by surprise. I hoped it didn't show.

"I know you worked very hard for that! Your mom must be very proud."

"She so excited, she went right out and bought me a suitcase. Like I was about to start packing today. It means…" She looked away from me, her voice shaking, and whispered, "Sorry. It just happened this week, and she was all choked up and that gets me…."

"I know." I thoughtlessly patted her shoulder, mom instincts kicking in. She didn't seem to mind. "I have a daughter too. You girls mean a lot to us moms."

"I shouldn't go off like that to a stranger. You'll think we're all crazy around here." She squared her slim shoulders and gestured around the room. "Anyway, Mother Gaston did a lot of good things here. That's why she got called Mother. She not really a mother, she a maiden lady." She stopped and repeated carefully, "She was not really a mother. She was a maiden lady."

When we got back to the main floor, Ms. Talbot took me aside.

"We are having a little surprise celebration because Savanna has good news. Did she tell you? Would you care to join us? It's just a cake."

"It's very kind. Won't I be intruding?"

"It's a big cake!" She smiled. "I sent Wilson out to get one, and you know men. Twice as much is always better. And you are most welcome. Not many people from outside take an interest in what we do here. Feels like we are lost in the wilderness sometimes."

That's how I got to be adopted into the Stone Avenue staff. The cake was indeed enormous. The guard took a lot of kidding about it, and he kidded right back. Savanna took some kidding about an all-girls college, and she giggled and told us her momma thought that was a good thing.

"And what you thinking about it, girl?" Wilson asked. She only smiled back at him and said, "Not sayin'. You all know my momma too well."

I asked her what she did to get that scholarship, and they all laughed when she said, "Went to a really good high school and worked my butt off."

"I grew up right around here myself," Ms. Talbot said, "and I didn't go to the local school either. In my day, there was heroin-dealing out of the third-floor boys bathroom. Yes, there was! I went to Lincoln, but Savvie took that entrance exam and went off to Brooklyn Tech."

"That cute little thing can write computer code," Wilson said. "Scare off all the boys, I bet."

The other clerk said, "Oh, don't be so foolish, Wilson. Don't you know Tech has got twice as many boys as girls? They be lucky if she honors them with a smile. Am I right, girl?"

"I had to work so hard, I didn't have time for any of that foolishness," she responded with a straight face. Then she giggled.

Ms. Talbot raised her glass of apple juice and said, "To our own Ms. Savanna Lafayette, who is going places. We believe there will be a Senator Lafayette in years to come, or a Dr. Lafayette. And we can say we knew you when. We are mighty proud of you."

There was a round of applause and then they cut the remaining cake into tiny pieces to share with the library users all afternoon.

Savanna walked back out to the main room with me, asking if I'd ever been to Boston and what it was like. I explained I was a Brooklyn girl myself, like her, and just going out of the neighborhood for high school had seemed like a big step.

I thanked Ms. Talbot for all her help and Wilson asked if I wanted to be walked to my car. I said thanks but no; I'd be more alert this time. Damned if I was owning up to needing help, let alone wanting it.

I walked to my car, thinking about Savanna and hoping someone in her life would understand what a long leap it would be, from a Brownsville project to Wellesley. My daughter goes to private school, courtesy of a mountain of financial aid. I needed the extra child-care hours when I was a single parent back in school myself, but being part of that world has been a huge leap for me. And it was nothing compared to the one Savanna was about to take.

Chapter Three

I had spoken some brave words about being fine but my earlier encounter hit me after I got into the car. As soon as I was in a more familiar neighborhood, I pulled over and put my head down on the steering wheel. I shouldn't drive while I was still shaking.

When I was ready, I turned the radio to rock oldies, as loud as I could make it, and filled the car with sound. I sang along, slapping out the beat on the wheel, and by the time I got home, I was myself again, ready to be whirlwind mom.

The traffic home had been heavy. It was already getting late, already dinnertime.

"Hey, Chris," I shouted upstairs. "Let's go out tonight. I want some lights and noise, no dinner dishes. Half an hour?"

She came to the top of the stairs. "What's going on?"

"Nothing," I lied. "Just feel like a change."

"Okay. Where are we going?"

"How about the new burger place?"

She hesitated. "I'm trying out vegetarian…"

"What? Since when? Anyway, they have veggie burgers and fish, too."

She nodded. "Okay. Let's go now. There's always a wait."

The new place was noisy outside, with the waiting crowd, and noisy inside with the gluttonous crowd. I was happy to join them, and, torn between exotic elk or exotic venison, I gave up and settled for a beef burger with cheddar and a mountain of fries, the least healthy meal in a week. Sometimes a girl needs grease to absorb emotion. Chris tucked into her veggie burger, on moral grounds, but did not object to fries on health grounds.

It was far too noisy to talk and that suited both of us. It was brightly lit and decorated in primary colors. We waved to a family we knew. We gobbled up calories and enjoyed the antics of the many small children, pointing to catch each other's attention. The cheerful chaos was just what I needed.

There was a voice mail when we came home. A quavering but clear voice said, "I am trying to reach Ms. Erica Donato at this number. This is Ruby Cohen Boyle."

"Mom? This is for you. She sounds a hundred years old."

"Not quite. Only about ninety-one. She's a source for me, maybe."

"Oh. Your schoolwork." That was the limit of her curiosity. "I'm going back to mine. That insane Mrs. Grant thinks we only have Chemistry homework every night…" Her voice faded as she went upstairs.

Mrs. Boyle had called me. I was so surprised. Really, she was Professor Boyle. Or Dr. Boyle. She was Maurice Cohen's little sister, ten years younger, a retired Labor History professor.

I wasn't looking for people to interview. Using Maurice Cohen's book as a source, I needed some background on his life in order to understand it. I was astonished to learn about the little sister, never mentioned in his writing, and estranged for many years from her famous brother. I was more astonished when my research on him pulled up an article that quoted her. A recent article. It seemed she was still alive and capable, in fact, still very sharp.

When the professor gods hand you a gift, you don't ignore it. It would be interesting, and maybe helpful, to compare her memories to his. It wasn't that hard to track her down to her home in a vast and luxurious senior living complex. So I wrote to her. And here she was on my voice mail.

It wasn't too late to call back. I'd better gather my wits first. When I had my hello speech down to a few concise sentences, I made the call.

She listened to what I had to say and responded crisply, without a quaver. "You explained all that in your letter. Yes. I remember Brownsville very well. As one gets older, those early years oddly come back even more vividly. What would you like to do? I find long phone conversations somewhat tiring. Can you come to see me?"

"I would love to, at your convenience of course."

"Come the day after tomorrow. I am busy many days, but there is no activity that appeals to me that day. There is a pleasant café here. We can have tea. Do you know the way? It is tricky."

I know how to use a GPS. I'd find it. When I said yes, I was only embellishing the truth a little.

She ignored me anyway, and provided detailed directions from the highway to the complex and the building with the café.

Good thing I wasn't working at my part-time museum job tomorrow. I would have time to review what I knew and get ready with my questions. She had been described as formidable.

On a bright sunny day, I took the beautiful drive up Manhattan's west side along the Hudson River, under the massive George Washington Bridge and up the cliffs called the Palisades. A random piece of history trivia: an older name was *Tor*, Gaelic for a rocky cliff, and so it was. Not a bit like Brooklyn, most of which has a human scale. This was something else, sweeping and splendid. Palisades sounds like a western fort built of logs but tor evokes misty Scottish mountains.

The buildings were perched on top of one of the cliffs, with sweeping lawns looking west across the Hudson. I wondered what sunsets were like and if the inhabitants were still able to enjoy them. It looked like an unusually beautiful college campus and it was large enough that I had some trouble finding the right building. I was almost running when I finally got there, and pulled myself up short at the entrance, caught my breath, smoothed my hair, and made a calm entrance.

"Dr. Boyle? I am Erica Donato. Thank you for meeting me today." I put out my hand and she shook it slowly. Her old skin felt like tissue paper but understated makeup was in place and she wore an elegant mauve suit and pearls with her lace-up shoes.

"You are late. Not so easy to find after all, was it?"

The words were intimidating but there was a little twinkle in her eyes.

"I am so sorry. It was…"

"Oh, please. Just sit down. I've ordered tea and a plate of cookies, but you can have coffee if you prefer. Now. Let's begin. You tell me just what you are doing in your research. I've served on plenty of dissertation committees. We'll be talking the same language. Did you bring a tape recorder?"

I explained my work, a dissertation on how Brooklyn neighborhoods changed over time and the impact of different kinds of newcomers, and also that I worked part time in research at the Brooklyn History Museum.

"Do you love it there?"

"Most of the time, yes I do."

She smiled. "That's why they can pay you a pittance, as I am sure they do."

I admitted that was true, but I needed both the pittance and the flexible hours.

"Where do you live?"

I named the neighborhood, one that has gone from downhill to highly gentrified, helped by quaint brownstones ripe for renovation.

She looked at me shrewdly. "You didn't grow up there." It was not a question. How did she know?

So I told her about my deep Brooklyn childhood in the old neighborhood and my move to someplace completely different after my husband died.

"Interesting. I'm betting that was as big a move as going across the country. Am I right?"

I had to smile. She had nailed it.

"My generation, we children of uneducated, poor immigrants made an even bigger move just by going to college at all, to work with our brains instead of our hands. It seemed like the other side of the globe, that great bohemian world where we lived for ideas instead of for putting the food on the table."

She talked in complete paragraphs.

"We lived for ideas and we discovered sex, the first generation that ever did." She winked when she said that. "We ate, slept, and breathed Freud, Jung, Kafka. And the great political battles of the time, of course." She paused. "Some were great, but some were, after all, tempests in teapots. In Brownsville we grew up with heated politics all around us. We just argued with more sophistication. We were still poor but in a different way." She smiled, fondly, as if at a child, her own young self. "We were bohemians, you might say."

"You flew away, all the way to Manhattan?"

"Certainly. I went to graduate school at Columbia. It was quite the scandal for me to move into my own apartment. 'What would people think I wanted to do there?'" She flashed a mocking smile. "I did have my big brother as a role model, though.

"I worked hard and got on with my life. My parents had no clue about any of it, of course. They could barely explain to relatives that I was becoming a college professor, not a public school teacher." She smiled. "Working for the Board of Ed was about the highest aspiration for a girl that they understood. They did work 'my daughter at Columbia' into every conversation, though." She sighed. "And of course you've read my famous brother's books."

I nodded, afraid to say a word. If I admitted to how much I admired them, would that bring the conversation to a crashing stop? In Professor Boyle I had found a time machine; I wanted to listen for days.

She waved her hand dismissively. "In time, he turned into a foolish man. Maybe if he'd lived as long as I have, he would have acquired some wisdom. Or at least maturity. Good writer, mind you, but silly man. He feuded with everyone, and that included my very prominent second husband. They had a fight about politics and never made up. Politics really meant everything then."

She paused and sighed. "Or so we believed. He made me choose sides and of course I chose my husband. What did he expect? But he was on his third wife by then—maybe his fourth?—he didn't take marriage as seriously as I did. Still, I read everything he wrote and his book about Brownsville was a good one." She gave me another challenging look. "Did you find what was missing in it?"

"Girls' lives?"

"Ah, ha! I sensed you were a sharp one. He didn't have a word to say about what it was like for me or girls at all. It was different."

Then we talked about that, how they were encouraged to do well in school, but discouraged from big dreams. We talked about immigrant parents making rules for daughters who were growing up, it seemed, on a different planet.

"Of course that story is the same in every immigrant generation, is it not?"

We moved on to other memories. The desperate times when money was so short, boarders slept in the second bedroom and she slept on the sofa. The year her father and big brother shared one winter coat, going out at different times. The times her mother made her brother's clothes over to fit her.

"I was embarrassed, going to school in a skirt made from his outgrown suit pants, but you know? I wasn't the only one. We were all struggling. And when I started making a salary, I went right into Lord & Taylor and opened a charge account with a card that had my name on it." She laughed lightly. "I could only afford the sales, and barely that, but it was a long way from buying underwear at a Pitkin Avenue pushcart! I was so proud to have a slice of apple pie in their restaurant and say 'Charge it.'"

She talked about friendships that were forged in poverty, and that lasted a lifetime.

"I found an old friend right here! We ran into each other in the orchestra. We have an orchestra here, you know, and we are pretty damn good. It's mostly women, like everything at our age. Men are scarce. And they called us the weaker sex! Ha. Anyway, she plays the flute and I play violin. First violin, I might add. I invited her to join us later."

We looked at a street map of Brownsville and she pointed to one location after another and remembered them all: her favorite candy store; the dentist who took out a diseased tooth; the corner where a cousin had met an Italian boy, causing a huge family scandal.

"They were all sure he was a gangster."

I was about to say to that, "By the way, about crime in Brownsville..." when we were interrupted by another elderly lady, very thin and pale, using a walker, but brightly dressed in a hot pink velour running suit.

"Lil, my dear, meet young Erica Donato, PhD in training. Erica, this is my dear friend Lillian Kravitz. Now Lil, Erica wants to hear about Brownsville. I've been talking her ear off, but you can help with more details. I'm giving her the good times and the bad."

The other woman's pale face warmed into a big smile. She patted her old friend's hand. "We had friends, and we had fun, as girls will always find a way, but it was hard. We were so very poor. Remember when we made a little social club? You, me, and those girls from your building?"

"They were cousins. The Kaufman girls?"

"Yes! And we wanted matching club sweaters, but my parents couldn't afford that."

"That's right. So we all pitched in a few cents for you and you earned the rest. But how?"

"Working in a shop at holiday time. We worked and went to school, too. I don't know if we could have done it without our friends. Am I right, Lil?"

"Right as rain. We encouraged each other, again and again. Lots of support and no excuses." She shook her head. "Home was not so happy because our parents struggled so hard, there wasn't much energy left for anything else, even children."

"So we swore we would get to college and work hard and get out."

"Moved up and away, I would say. Right? We had better lives in time, and we earned them."

"What about the ones who didn't take that path?" I was trying to steer this wide-ranging conversation back to the subject of crime. "It's no secret that Brownsville was a hotbed of mob activity. Some of your classmates and neighbors became quite famous."

"For all the wrong reasons!"

"Did you know any? Your cousin's boyfriend you mentioned? What did you think of all that?"

"I never thought about it at all. Not one minute." Ruby gave me a hard look. "The boyfriend turned out to be a real sweetheart. Brownsville was made notorious because of the rotten few. Yes, there was crime, of course there was, like any poor neighborhood with desperate people. But you would think there were murdering gangsters on every block, carrying Tommy guns in plain sight."

"And there weren't?"

"No, of course not! We knew. We knew what those bums were. They were people to avoid. And you know what? We were the good, smart girls. We weren't looking for nightclubs and flashy jewelry, so those nogoodniks weren't looking for us." She added with a laugh "It's been many a decade since I used a word like 'nogoodnik.'"

Lil was looking away from her friend, as if her thoughts were somewhere else altogether.

Ruby went on. "I can say this: we could walk home from work, from the subways, late at night, even carrying money, and never be afraid. There were always people out and about who knew us and wouldn't let any harm come our way." She thought for a moment. "And the truth is that they did not bother upstanding, normal citizens. It was one gang against another. As I said, much-exaggerated."

Her friend was still staring off into space, and I wondered if we had lost her, when she turned back to us and said, "Ruby, you are full of crap."

Ruby gasped. Had we heard that right?

"Just full of it."

Chapter Four

Ruby turned pinker than her makeup.

"Lil, you are getting tired. I'm going to walk you up to your room." She turned to me, her self-control unaltered, but her voice now shaky. "Erica, it's been lovely. Call me if you have any questions. Now, Lil, let's get you up."

"I'm not going anywhere." She looked right at me, her face pale and her hands clenched. "Ruby's spinning you a nice story about the good old days. Old people like to do that, and she's old, we both are. Really old now. The only thing wrong is that it isn't true. I have a different story for you."

"You're calling me a liar?"

Lil shrugged. "You can hear liar, or you can hear losing your marbles, or you can hear telling a 'nice' story." She made air quotes with her fingers. "Your call. It doesn't matter to me anymore."

This had mysteriously turned into a conversation that didn't include me.

Ruby stood up, fumbling for her flower-painted cane. "I am very hurt by your attitude, Lillian. After all these years! Erica, thank you for coming here to see me. Come back any time."

She walked away, back straight, head high.

Lillian looked at me and smiled wearily. "She'll get over it. She'll decide I was affected by my meds. You can decide that for yourself after you hear my story."

Her tired blue eyes looked straight into mine, and I already knew what I thought.

"Do you have the time today? It's a long story, but I don't know if I myself will have the time to tell it again." She smiled, a little wry smile without much joy in it. "I am dying, you know." I said something that came out as in incoherent murmur.

"Oh, no, no, don't try to say something comforting. We are all dying, of course, but some of us have a more definite checkout date. Mine is coming up soon. I'm not sure I'll get to see those tulips I watched them plant last fall. Do you knit?"

I shook my head, surprised by the sudden change of subject.

"We all used to. A very useful skill. These days I'm thinking about dropped stitches. I want to pick up some of mine."

She shook her head as if to clear it. "If I tell you a true story about those days, will you do something for me?"

"Yes. Of course." I thought she meant, maybe, fetch her a coffee. Or do some outside shopping. Bring her a nice plant for her apartment.

"If you come across my brother's name in your research, tell me."

"I don't understand at all."

She held my hand and again, looked at me deeply. "You are researching Brownsville and you are interested in crime? Maybe you'll know how to look for this, for my lost brother. I always meant to do it myself, but then I ran out of time. The last time I saw him was dinner at home, July 16, 1936. He was twenty-two and I was ten."

She leaned back and closed her eyes, as if her story was finished.

I wanted to grab her and shout, "What are you talking about?" underlining each word. What I did say, softly, was "I think I need to know a little more. Like his name."

Her eyes flew open again. "Well, of course you do! What was I thinking? I should tell it from the beginning.

"People like Ruby say the crooks never affected us, their neighbors. It's a *shonda* they think, a shaming of the whole community. And there are people who even romanticize them.

Back when I still thought I could dig this up myself, I read a book that turned them into heroes, almost. Phooey on that. A lady doesn't spit in public or I would."

She was silent for so long, I thought she'd fallen asleep, but then she went on.

"Believe me, they were thugs, greedy, lazy lowlifes who would rather live off hardworking, honest people than do any work themselves. Some of them were smart, though, and they organized the thugs into a business. Assassins for hire, that's what they were. It was the papers that named them Murder Incorporated, when Dewey finally dragged them to trial. Now that was some brave man. The only time in my life I voted for a Republican was when Dewey ran for governor.

"They called it business, but you know, some of those hoods got into it because they liked it, liked hurting people. Them, I would call psychopaths. And I should know."

I gave her a puzzled look.

"Before I turned into a little old lady with failing body parts, I was a psychologist. Dr. and all. That was later, after the war." She smiled at my surprise. "Yes, I was. Some of us went to school and worked hard and got out the honest way."

"And your brother? How did he fit in?"

"Honest job. He was a butcher, a good job in those days, and he was a union man. Those guys. Besides the assassin business, they were in the protection racket, and the unions, too. They'd say 'Give us a job at the union—good pay, no work—and we'll protect you from those gangsters the bosses hired.' Of course they made the same offer to the bosses. Whoever had the most money got their so-called protection." She stopped and dabbed at her eyes.

"What happened?"

"He left the house for a union meeting and never showed up. End of story."

"No! Come on. No one looked for him?"

She nodded. "His friends, around the neighborhood. My pop. And some of his union pals, that same night. After a while word was passed around that they should stop looking. I learned all that much later, after I was all grown up."

"But I don't understand. Didn't your parents tell you anything? You must have been asking questions. And didn't they go to the police?"

She shook her head. "They sent me away, right after, to my uncle in south Jersey. He had a chicken farm, if you can believe that. I really did not want to go. I didn't understand until years later that they were protecting me. And of course I asked questions! Of course I did, but family life was different then. Grown-ups would say, 'Stop with the questions or you'll get such a smack!' And they meant it." She smiled again, sadly. "It's not an accident that I went into psychology, of course."

"But what happened when you came home?"

"They never mentioned his name. They had taken down his only picture and they never mentioned his name. Believe me, I got the message to keep quiet about it."

"I don't believe this. I don't mean I doubt you. It's just hard to accept that no one raised bloody hell about it. Pardon the expression."

"They were afraid. Everyone who knew those guys was afraid." She paused, considering. "This is how it worked—they ate in a diner and left big tips. Was the owner about to say no? They walked the streets like big shots. They'd ask a kid to watch the car or run an errand and give him generous money for it. Then, if the kid was eager, there would be other jobs."

"And the law?"

"Well, a lot of the cops were in on it too, so where could you turn for help? And everyone knew not to talk about them. You couldn't be called as a witness if you didn't see or hear or know anything. And if you were called, you'd better swear you didn't see or hear or know anything. Years later, when my parents were both gone—personally, I think they died of heartbreak—believe me, I asked everyone else and they were still afraid."

"And now?"

"I don't give a good goddamn. What can they do to me now that's worse than the cancer? They're all dead now anyway, and if there is an afterlife—which I doubt—they are most certainly not where my brother is."

She was quiet so long I thought she had drifted off but then she said, "Lately I feel like he's with me. Strange, isn't it, considering I'm an unbeliever? I feel like he wants me to know what happened, and I am ashamed I waited until now."

What could I say but yes? I tried to explain that my main responsibility was to my own work but she just hushed me.

"You'll be looking around in all those old records. Maybe you'll see something. Who knows? Maybe you'll run across someone who's an expert and might have answers? Or know where to look? Who knows? His name was Frank Kravitz. Write it down."

She tapped my arm, her polished nail surprisingly sharp. "Write it down. And come back if you see something." She smiled, a bitter raw smile. "Pretty soon it won't matter anymore." Her eyes closed, opened, closed again and this time stayed that way.

An aide with a wheelchair looked in, saying Mrs. Boyle had told her Ms. Kravitz was here. "I'll just take her back to her room. It's time for her pre-dinner meds."

She didn't need my help and I left, carefully finding my way through the complex of parkways.

Home and dinner. I had the television on, catching up on the news. When I heard the word Brownsville, I took a look. And then I couldn't move away.

A reporter on location, talking into a mike. "In the predawn hours a badly beaten young girl was found in this empty lot. She was spotted this morning by workers passing by on a sanitation truck, and police and EMS were called. She is now at Brookdale Hospital in critical condition and has not regained consciousness."

I could not tear my eyes from the screen.

"She has been identified as Savanna Lafayette, a resident of Van Dyke houses and an honors senior at elite Brooklyn Technical High School. Sources at her employer, the Stone Avenue branch of Brooklyn Public Library, reportedly told police that local gang members have harassed her recently."

And they introduced her mother on a film clip.

She spoke carefully, with tears in her eyes, and a wavering voice. "Someone knows the truth. Someone out there saw them, saw something, and knows what happened. Please, please step up and tell the truth." She looked at the reporter, who pointed, and then she looked right at the camera.

"I quote John 8:32, 'the truth shall set you free.' It would set all of us free, all of us who cannot have a moment of peace, not knowing what happened. All of us who know my daughter and all of us who have children we want to keep safe. And we are not the only ones who need the truth. All of you who know, really know, that you will not have peace unless you stand up for truth and justice, too. Please." Then she turned away, weeping, and was surrounded by a comforting crowd.

Ah, damn. I sat there for a few minutes, unable to move. That nice young woman. The girl who was going places. I remembered how Savanna talked about her mother with exasperation and respect. And I reached for the Kleenex.

Only a few years older than my Chris, who was at that moment safely on her bed, doing her homework. Or perhaps texting with her friends in spite of my social media blackout rule on school nights.

At that moment, I didn't care. She could be giving herself multiple piercings or painting her bedroom black, as long as she was safe at home.

In fact she was coming downstairs, looking for dinner. Then she saw my face and I had to tell her, as briefly as I could, while we ate.

She was horrified of course, and wanted to know everything I knew, which was next to nothing.

Her final words on the subject were, "Did they say they talked to her job? But that's just like grownups. They should talk to her friends! If there's something going on in her life, her friends would the ones to know."

It wasn't until later, when I watched the story again on late news, hoping for a positive update, that I realized what else was nagging me about the broadcast. I knew Zora Lafayette, Savanna's mother.

It was a long time ago. She was older now and her hair was different, neatly trimmed instead of braided into brightly dyed rows. She wore an ordinary grownup pantsuit not gangsta-style fashion. But I knew I had met her. Was it in a class? The first time I was in college, or the second?

Chapter Five

It came back to me slowly. I live in so many different worlds, I could see a face on the street and not always know if it was someone from my childhood, a class, Chris' life, or just a frequently seen face on the street.

But Savanna's mother? A large class on what? Sociology and family, something like that? She stood up and fearlessly challenged a guest speaker on his research about what working mothers need. Was that it? And said she was one herself, a student with a baby, and he should be asking people like her.

Leaving the classroom, I passed her and said, "Good for you. I know. I have a baby at home, too."

She wasn't impressed by my admiration but said something like, "These men! These expert men? Sometimes they just don't get it. Know what I'm saying?" And as she walked away, I saw on her pack a huge button with a photo on it. It was a smiling toddler, her hair tied in puffs with red ribbon.

I was pretty sure that was it, the memory I was trying to retrieve. Or something like it. Damn. That must have been Savanna.

What now? I didn't really know her, the mother, didn't think my contacting her would be anything but an intrusion. But I also didn't think I could forget any of this. It wasn't just another case of violence in a violent neighborhood. Not anymore. Not to me.

There was one thing I could do. Maybe helpful, maybe not, but better than doing nothing. I could call the number flashed on the screen, the one that said, "if you have information…"

and tell them about my encounter with those boys who had also been bothering Savanna. I didn't know if it would be helpful but it was something.

The number was gone from the TV screen, of course. I couldn't scroll back. My ancient TV does not have all the bells and whistles, as Chris has pointed out regularly. The words "stone age" come up on those occasions. It only took me minutes to find it online.

Call now? Or call tomorrow? Get it over with. What did I want to say? I wrote it down to keep focused. I called.

In just a minute, I was connected to a detective, Sergeant Asher. I told her about the incident, stumbling over my words.

"You say it was around three o'clock? At Dumont, just off Mother Gaston?"

"Yes, right around the corner from the library."

"But you did not see them with Miss Lafayette?"

"No, but I heard them talk about her."

"Any of their names that you heard?"

"No, but the guard at the library—Mr. Wilson, I think—saw them and he knew them. Like I said."

"Yes, ma'am. I'm double-checking to get the facts right. Did you see any identifying marks on any of them?"

"No, not really. Wait! Wait. The one who grabbed my arm? He had a tattoo." I closed my eyes. Visualize, I told myself. See it again. Ugh. "It was a snake, I think. Or something crawly. Crawling up his forearm."

"Ahh." That was a satisfied sound if I ever heard one.

"Is that helpful?"

"Remains to be seen." Those were the words, but the tone of voice was lighter. "Last question: could you identify them if you saw them again?"

I had to think about it. Could I see them now, in my mind? "Maybe two of them."

"Thank you, Ms. Donato. We appreciate your good citizenship."

"Was it even helpful?"

I thought I heard a smile in her voice. "Could be."

It turned out that making the call did not get it off my mind. Just the opposite. I had dreams all night, or so it seemed, about scary young men who turned into snakes. Or something like that. Mixed up with a little girl in red ribbons. The details evaporated by the time I was getting out of bed, but the ugly feelings remained.

And there was something else on my mind. Half awake, I went to a bookcase in the hall. Top shelves, overstuffed with old texts and notebooks from college and grad school, never looked at but I couldn't quite throw them away. The college stack. Sociology texts, family life. We did team projects. A folder with a syllabus and a class list. By the time I found it and pulled it out, I was covered with dust and papers were all over the floor, but at least no books had fallen on my head.

I keyed in the e-mail for a woman whose name was Zora Lafayette. It didn't make sense any more than it had earlier, but I couldn't not do it.

> We were classmates in sociology of the family at Brooklyn College. I saw you on TV last night. I met Savanna at the library that day and liked her. Can I help in any way at all? I have a teen daughter myself.

How to end it? Too emotional felt like intruding. We were barely acquaintances. Too matter-of-fact felt like ignoring her reality. Finally, I just told the truth:

> Sending best wishes.

In the morning, I told Chris not to talk to me until I had coffee. She took one look at my face and said, "Uh, fine. I'll get breakfast on the way to school." I knew that probably meant a doughnut and I didn't even care, that morning.

What was on my calendar for today? Not a day at my job. I knew that much. I hoped it would be a nice, quiet day of hiding in a library, doing my research, reading very old books in silence and taking notes. With many coffee breaks.

That's how it turned out and I was able not to speak to any human being except the librarian for three hours. My brain knew what to select from the research, my hands know how to type it into the laptop, and I didn't have to think very hard.

By the end of the day I would have all I needed to write this chapter and move on. That was my plan.

It was almost lunchtime, and I must have been feeling better, because a new name caught my eye. It not only caught my eye, it registered.

Frank Kravitz. I skimmed through my notes from the visit to the home on the Hudson. Was that Lil's brother, the one who disappeared? Though her story was interesting, I hadn't taken the request very seriously. I could not make it my project; I just had too much else to do. And what were the chances I would find it by accident?

Apparently pretty good. That was my first surprise.

I read the page again. He was only mentioned in passing, but not as a Brownsville hero. He's one of a list of "sometime associates of organized crime figures". That was my second surprise.

I flipped to the index. Was he mentioned anywhere else? No. I keyed his name into my computer screen? No. Dummy, I thought to myself. There I was sitting in the Brooklyn collection of the Brooklyn Public library system. And I did know the old *Brooklyn Eagle* newspaper was online. So, duh, as Chris would have said to me.

There it was, just a face in the crowd in a handful of photos with captions. One was a meat cutters union meeting where he spoke; another, Frank in the background, behind some very questionable characters. And just one final photo, with the boxer Bernie Rosenblatt, celebrating.

Who the heck was Frank Kravitz? Clearly he was not an important public figure. But was he the hero Lillian remembered? Certainly didn't look like it now. Where could I look further?

Courthouse archives? Maybe, if he was in fact hanging around with some of these notorious names. And then I had to think about where I'd have to go, and who I'd have to apply to, to get a look at them. I could not accept that he had entirely vanished. I could plow through a dozen other books, looking for traces.

Or I could take a little ride up to the other end of New York and speak with Lillian Kravitz again. My early morning, bad-dreams-induced lethargy was gone. I was ready for action.

I made copies of the photos I had found. They were not very good. Better, I bookmarked the *Brooklyn Eagle* site. I would show her those on my laptop.

I kept the radio on for the whole drive, wondering if I might hear anything more about Savanna, but no. I listened so hard I missed my exit and had to navigate through some back streets to find my way.

A desk attendant called her and she said she'd come down soon. It wasn't soon. When she finally got there, holding tight to her walker, she looked different. Makeup could not conceal the pallor of her skin, and the deeper shadows around her eyes. Today her track suit was canary yellow.

"I didn't expect you, my dear." A shadow seemed to cross those blue eyes. "Did we have a date?"

"Oh, no. I am sorry. I found some things, and had time… it was an impulse…" I felt like an idiot. "I should have called."

"No matter." She patted my hand. "I am a little unwell, fatigued, today and had no plans. Come. We will have lunch. I can order an extra plate for you."

So that is how I found myself choosing between vegetarian lasagna and tomato soup plus grilled cheese sandwich, in a room full of people old enough to be my grandparents. Even my great-grandparents.

She hesitated, looking around, until a worker came to say, "Would you like a private table? Is this one of your grandchildren?"

"Oh, no, she's…she's a friend. Yes, a private table. We want to talk. I guess.

"We have dairy at lunch, and meat at dinner," she explained to me. "Not that I care. I left all those kosher rules behind in my wild days." She sighed. "And we never have shrimp here. Or lobster. I miss it."

Her thoughts seemed elsewhere, perhaps on seafood, until I took out my pictures.

"Is this your brother?"

"That is very blurry. I have my magnifying glass in my bag." She handed it to me. "Here, you look for it."

When found, she stared for a while, as I pulled up the photos on the laptop. Her eyes filled with tears.

"Yes, it's Frank. My darling brother."

I showed her the *Eagle* photo. "Oh, yes, that's him. But who is he with? I can't read this."

I enlarged it and she read the caption out loud. "Alleged gangsters? Is that what it says? Then it can't be him. He never associated with that type of person." She stared at me. "Never heard of them in my life."

Lunch came just then, giving me a break to think about what I was going to do. She did certainly seem very tired, or ill. She certainly wasn't the outspoken firecracker of my earlier visit.

She concentrated on her food, occasionally stopping to say, "Now this is very good," and "I hope you are enjoying your meal. There might be ice cream for dessert, you know."

Lunch seemed to perk her up. She turned to me and said clearly, "Now what can I do for you, my dear? Let's move to the lounge where we can talk."

We moved, very slowly, and finally were settled on a sofa. "You asked me to keep my eyes open for any information about your brother?"

"Yes, of course I did. And did you find anything?"

I had showed her my findings not half an hour ago. I showed them again. "I don't know if you see the problem here." And I didn't know quite how to say it, either. I could not bring myself to say, Based on what is here, nothing you told me is true. "Do you recognize any of these names now?"

She looked at them again. A light seemed to go on. "Yes, that's my dear brother. Of course it is. And these men?" She stopped, thought. "They are crooks, aren't they? Gangsters?" She shook her head. "Impossible. This is impossible. They were not his kind of friend at all. I told you. He was a hero. Dig harder and you'll find out. I know you will."

I started to say something, but she held her hand up and went right on.

"He was a wonderful brother. He helped me with my homework and brought me little treats and even, sometimes, played tag in the street with me and my friends. He took me to the park. Whatever parenting I got, whatever affection, came from him. So don't tell me…don't tell me…. just find out what happened to him. That's all."

"What if I find things you don't want to know?" It was a hard question to ask when she looked so sad, yet hopeful, like a small child. "Should I just keep quiet about them?"

She turned to me with a fierce expression, much more like the Lillian I had first met. "What a shocking thing for a scholar to ask! We academics look the facts in the eye. I can take it." She smiled. "Besides, I know he was a hero and you will, too. So there!"

So there, indeed. That sounded a lot like marching orders to me.

A soft-voiced woman in a uniform came up to us. "Why, Ms. Kravitz, what are you doing here? It's time for your meds. Would you like ice cream to get them down?"

"Ah, my keeper is here." To her, Lil said, "Is there vanilla-fudge?"

"You know there is."

"Yes, if there's vanilla-fudge I will come." She winked at me. "Told you there might be ice cream. Come again if you can. I like having company."

Behind her back, the nurse whispered to me, "It's good for her. She hasn't been at all well."

Later that night, there was a phone call. A frail, sad voice with no name. She said, "I was just a little girl. What did I know about his life outside the house? Maybe I turned him into a hero myself."

Chapter Six

Two days later, there was still no additional news about Savanna. I was sure about that, because I was listening to the radio or TV all the time. I wanted to know those nasty young men were locked up, to hear that young Savanna was on the mend, to see her mother at another news conference talking about how relieved she was. None of that happened.

I already knew I would have to go back to Brownsville. My photos were only barely acceptable so I had borrowed a good camera. My ladies at the nursing home had given me some more locations I wanted to see and perhaps photograph. They were many years younger than Maurice Cohen and their hangouts were different. He wrote about meeting girls in the park in the thirties. They told me where they were when the war ended.

I had organized my cameras, notebooks, keys. I did not expect my dad to show up at my door.

Dad and I have a difficult relationship. It's getting better, partly due to Chris' desire to have him in our lives, but it's still touchy. I don't know what irritates me most, his desire to protect me and take care of me, long after I needed anything like that, or my lingering distrust, stemming from the woman who took over his life after Mom died. She dragged him off to Arizona when I really did need him, and then dumped him.

I didn't talk to him for a time, but Chris did. And then he came back home, to the little house in East Flatbush where I grew up. And then he tried to work his way back into my life. Sometimes I even let him.

There he was, ringing my doorbell.

"Dad? What's up? I was just on my way out."

"Off to school?"

"Ah, no. Um, off to another part of Brooklyn. It's, um, job research."

"How'd you like a driver? I've got no special chores today. Come on, I'll take you out to breakfast. Which way are you heading? I know how to find pancakes in any neighborhood."

He did, too. He'd worked as a cab driver until his retirement. He knew how to find anything, anywhere in the city. Sometimes it was eerie. And that healthy yogurt I'd eaten at seven a.m. seemed very long ago.

"Okay. But there's a deal."

"Oh?"

"If I tell you where I am going, no comments. None. Promise?"

"What exactly are you up to?"

I shook my head. "Promise."

"Deal. I'll drive. Just point me in the right direction."

"Out Eastern Parkway."

"Where are we going?"

When I told him, his expression changed.

"You promised, Dad. Not one word."

"What? What did I say? Nothing. But we'll stop for breakfast before we get there."

And so we did, at a diner he knew about. He always knows about a diner.

Over bacon and eggs I told him about my project, the chapter on crime for my dissertation, the photos, my visit to the nursing home. I left out my scary encounter. Not by accident either.

When he started to ask me why I had not asked him to go with me, I gave him a look, the one Chris gives me. "Because I am a grown woman? I don't need my dad to hold my hand?"

He didn't seem convinced, but he was smart enough not to say so. In the car, fully caffeinated and fed and then some, I gave him some specific locations courtesy of Ruby and Lillian. "This is how we'll do it. You stop and I'll hop out, take a few photos, and jump back in. Got it?"

He nodded without a word. After a few blocks on almost deserted streets, he stopped suddenly.

"I know this street."

I was flipping through my notebook, checking addresses, not listening. "Sure you do. You know every street, everywhere in Brooklyn."

"No, I mean I really know this street. I remember it."

The change in his voice finally caught my attention.

"Dad? Why are we stopping here? This is not one of my addresses."

"One of mine, I guess." He pointed. "Look over there."

"Where? What am I looking at?"

"My grandparents lived there, upstairs, above the store. It was a coffee shop then. Theirs, I think."

That was all news to me.

"Yeah, I just barely remember but my folks, your grandparents, had a photo that was taken outside. And you could see that building over there." He pointed to a large sign painted on the side of the building. Bricks showed through the ghostly, faded paint. "Abrams. Finest wedding clothes for rent. Brides and grooms." A second of surprise flitted across my brain and made a note. I didn't know you could rent bridal gowns.

He looked around. "Everything else is different. Or who knows? I'm not remembering it all anyways."

"Dad. How come you didn't say anything about this before? I'm working on this chapter and you never told me we had a family connection?"

"To tell the truth, I forgot. We moved away when I was real little. My grandpa died and grandma moved to Aunt Sally's building in Rockaway. I don't think I've been on this street even once since then."

"You know, you're useless when it comes to family history. Didn't your parents ever talk about it? Growing up here?"

"Not really. Not really at all. They were not at all interested in reminiscing about those so-called good old days. They weren't as good as the ones we were in then, I guess."

I knew it was true. Being very poor was being very poor, even in good times. I had Maurice Cohen to say it for me in print. And their early times were not good times for anyone. But the 1950s, that silent decade I had studied in a class? In the conforming suburbs of identical homes? Heck. For them, after the war, a brand new house of their very own, with a bit of lawn, was more than they had ever dreamed of. It was paradise. Not my idea of paradise, which is why I live in Park Slope, but then, I didn't grow up in Brownsville. Hmmm. Was this something I should write about? Or maybe a museum exhibit?

Not for the first time, I wished I had asked them more while I had the chance.

"Is it weird to think that your childhood is now part of history? Like, studied in class? Did your parents ever think about all the events they had lived through?"

"Naah, not really. It was just regular everyday life to us at the time. You know? Especially when I was a kid. I thought about stuff like, when would we get a TV? And how could the Dodgers leave Brooklyn?"

"Funny thing is…" Dad said as he started the car, interrupting my free-associating. "Wait. Where to next?"

I told him. "And you were saying funny thing is…."

"Funny thing about my grandmother and their past. I always had a feeling there was more to it. It wasn't just that she had no interest to talking about those days, she refused. Like, quick, change the subject and mutter a prayer. Or maybe it was a curse. Then she would bring out cake and that was that."

"Your grandmother? Not mine?"

"Yes. Ya know, later, I knew a few guys who lived in this end of Brooklyn, and Grandma did not like that at all either."

"Dad. What is this, dad's time machine day? You never told me any of this!"

He shrugged. "Never any reason to. I'm telling you now."

"No, you're not. You're just throwing me crumbs. Who did you know from around here? And what was it like then?"

"Like it is now, more or less. I guess. Sad. Angry. Rough. Lots of street fighting, even little kids. Most of those guys, their families moved away eventually. Really, I came to play pool. Somewhere around here. There was a place…yeah, it's kind of coming back to me." He made a sudden turn.

I looked around. "Dad, what are you doing?"

"Hold your horses, kiddo." We went a few blocks and stopped across from a long building with many tiny storefronts, many empty, at street level.

"See? At least I think it's here. The second floor was a pool hall. I did a certain amount of hanging out there in my misspent youth."

"A pool hall? Really? What would you have said if I…?"

"Another subject altogether. I'm giving you some information here. Want it or not?"

He sounded irritated. I responded with a polite "Yes, please."

"In my day, it was a pool hall. I was underage to even be there, but it's not like anyone ever asked. And I could get a drink, too. Betting, yeah, always, that's part of the game." He glanced at me. "And a place to find someone who sold weed, if that's what you wanted."

"Dad? You?" I was shocked. My dad was always a very by-the-book guy.

"It was a very, very long time ago. But you get what I'm saying? And the building was owned by a guy who was the Brooklyn Borough president for a while. If anyone asked about the pool hall, I guess he would have said he didn't know a thing about what his tenants did." Dad kind of snorted.

"Dad?"

"Okay, you want me to get to the point?"

"If you have one, which I am beginning to doubt, yes."

"There were old guys who hung out there. They always claimed this was the toughest neighborhood in the city and the pool hall used to be a through-and-through mob hangout back in the old days. I dunno. The storytellers were petty crooks, kind of gangster wannabes, I think. The gangsters were gone a long time by then."

We turned a corner, heading toward the library.

"Now this street looks a little familiar but I'm just not sure."

"They changed the name. It was Stone Avenue back then."

"Yeah, I know it now. I rented my prom tux along here somewhere. Powder blue."

"Please tell me you are kidding."

"Nope. Thought I was as spiffy as, I don't know, Frank Sinatra, maybe. Or The Four Tops. Yeah. This used to be the block where the wedding stores were.

"And here's something I forgot, speaking of weddings. When I started dating your mother, her mother cried and cried. She was sure I must be a gangster if my family came from Brownsville."

"Dad, you never told me any of this!"

He laughed at my indignant look. "It was such a long time ago. By then my folks lived in Levittown, the most ordinary place in the world, and I lived with them when I got out of the Army. But your grandmother, boy!" He shook his head in disbelief.

I thought hard. "But I remember visiting them when I was little, lots of hugging and kissing and me getting my cheeks pinched. It didn't seem like she disliked you."

He moved a hand off the steering wheel to make a dismissive gesture. "She got over it. I had too many cop friends, she decided, to be a crook. And I drove a cab every day for a living. That was proof to her. If I was a crook, I couldn't be a very successful one."

I had to laugh. "It sounds like Grandma's logic!"

We drove around slowly. I had a few more addresses to find, a few more old buildings to look for. I kept my eyes open for those boys, without saying anything to my father. Dad spotted a few blocks with new rowhouses, small and neat and bright. A sign of renewal, perhaps?

And it was Dad who muttered, "Now there's a sight you don't see around here much, I bet." He jerked his head toward the sidewalk without stopping. "White guy in the hood."

"Dad!" But he was right. And I thought I had seen him before. Blond beard, raggedy clothes. He turned into a building doorway. I gasped when I saw who stepped up to meet him. "That's…" And I stopped myself before I said, "the guy who threatened me." Instead I finished that sentence with a small, "…unusual. Yes, that's unusual."

"Drug buy," Dad said. "Or he's an undercover cop."

Late that night there was an e-mail message from Zora Lafayette.

> Were you that skinny little white girl who always looked worried? Yeah, I sort of remember you. My baby is doing badly, but we have a whole community of people praying for her. Yours would be appreciated too.

Ahh. My prayers couldn't be worth much but my good thoughts were hers, of course. I told her so, and to my surprise, I had an instant response.

> Good thoughts are kind if you are not a praying woman. Doctors at the hospital sent me home to get some sleep, but that's not happening. I don't want to take the pills they gave me, and I don't keep alcohol in my home, so for now it's just me and my buddy the iMac, working the midnight shift, trying real hard not to think. Can't cry anymore. All cried out.

Those words hit home. Without stopping to consider it, I typed:

> Been there. My Jeff died in an accident at 26, hit by a drunk driver. That's how I became a single mom. Even now, once in awhile I find myself wide awake in the dark, in this unreal place of silence.

And that's how we began. For the next hour, she wrote me about Savanna, her hopes and dreams for her only child, how she had kept her focused and safe in an unsupportive world; her rage at those lowlifes, whoever they are; her repeated belief that God would not take her. I wondered if she thought repeating that would make it true.

I offered understanding. That's all I could offer, really, but it seemed to be something, out there in the darkness of the early morning hours. You can't be warrior mom 24/7, but I was not in her real life. She did not have to be embarrassed by meeting me some time in daylight.

Finally, she wrote:

> Well, damn. It's 4 AM and my eyes are finally closing. Thank you, girl, for staying up on the late shift with me tonight. Good dreams to us both. And some advice. You wide wake before dawn? Go make your baby pancakes and bacon for breakfast and hug her tight. Hug her till she say to stop, and then hug her some more.

She signed off and I hit the cookbooks. And then I checked the kitchen for pancake ingredients and syrup.

When I woke up, late and foggy, there was already a message on my screen.

> Hey, y'all. Sorry about the impersonal but there are so many of you out there, asking about Savvie. No change, no change at all. Doctors say now we wait and see. Thanking everyone for your prayers and wishes.

> But looks like the cops did their job for once. Word out is they are holding these little wastes of oxygen that been bothering my girl. Everyone expects an arrest so there will be justice done. Personally I am hoping they spend the rest of their miserable lives in jail. And now we must pray for mercy for Savanna.

Ah, that sounded more like the somewhat scary Zora I remembered from class.

So half the story was over. Or at least, it was the beginning of the end chapter. One of the end chapters. Would it help Savanna? Not at all. Would it help provide some healing for Zora? Could you transform grief into the satisfaction of revenge? I thought back to the drunk driver who killed my husband and thought the answer was yes. Somewhat. Maybe. But it didn't change a thing.

Chapter Seven

I had a dinner date. Sort of. Chris would scoff at the use of the word. In fact she did, carefully explaining that a date only applies if there is potential for romance. Otherwise it is just "dinner plans."

I love being condescended to by my fifteen-year-old. Though she had a point. I was having dinner—which I would bring—with my friend Leary, who is older than my father and is overweight, grouchy, and ill. At least half of his many ailments are lifestyle related, a subject he chooses, vehemently, not to discuss. At his request, I would bring spaghetti and meatballs, garlic bread, and wine. I sneaked some broccoli onto the menu and some ground turkey into the meatballs. Good thing Chris likes broccoli, because I knew I'd be bringing it home.

Chris could come but she turned me down with homework as her excuse. She's met Leary and though she won't admit it, I think she finds him scary.

I had his number now, though. I first met him doing research. He covered Brooklyn as a reporter, way back when, and I needed to know what he knew about a long-ago notorious landlord. It took a while to get his cooperation. A long while, and several meals. Now I know the belligerence disguises loneliness, though he'd throw me out if I ever said so. I don't know if he was ever married, in love, had children. Most of his old friends seem to have moved away or died or forgotten him.

I went over to see him once in awhile, and when the weather was nice, I might take him out in his wheelchair. I tried to make the visits on Wednesday, when a housekeeping aide comes and his place is clean enough not to be a health hazard. Besides being grouchy, the man is a slob.

He also knows more about Brooklyn before my time than any human being has a right to. He lost a leg to diabetes so he can't get around easily, and he was never what you'd call a people person. To be honest, perhaps an anti-people person. I often wondered how he functioned as a reporter, asking questions, getting answers. Maybe he just scared people into telling him what he wanted to know.

He liked my visits, even if he would never say it.

His building is slowly deteriorating along with his neighborhood. The security door is often open, and often broken. I can get in easily.

"Leary!" I pounded on the door of his apartment. "Answer, dammit. I'm hauling heavy bags." I always worry if he doesn't respond quickly. Once I found him beaten up, and twice I've found him sick.

"Door's open."

I struggled in, and put my bags down. He rolled himself out in his wheelchair.

"I brought enough for two meals." I found clean dishes in the dish rack and set the table. When I moved the stack of mail and papers to another table, with more mail on it, I saw a flyer for the Espy exhibit.

"Would you be interested in seeing this?" Maybe I should think before I speak. I had no idea how I would manage that.

"I did see it. You think you're the only person I know with a car?"

"Drop the shoulder chip or I take the wine home."

"Tut, tut, where are my manners?" He paused and said in another tone, "Once in awhile, social services arranges for an outing. Ya know, through one of those do-gooder organizations."

"And? And?" I portioned out dinner.

"Okay, okay, it was a nice day out. Except for all the old ladies on the bus." He looked at his plate. "That's a bird-size serving."

"Here. I'll add garlic bread. '

"Ah, garlic, seasoning of the gods." He considered the small piece of butter-soaked Italian bread. "Worth the heartburn."

"Leary? Did you remember any of the Espy photos?"

"What? How old do you think I am? Sweet jaysus. But yeah, I have seen a lot of them before." He focused on his food, but I knew the smug gleam in his eyes.

"There's more. Spill it." I moved the garlic bread out of reach, just to emphasize my point.

"You got me. I knew him."

"Who?"

"Espy! What are we talking about? He was old by then, sick."

"Forgotten?"

"Not really. Never, really, but he hadn't chased a story in years. Naah, decades. He missed it. You never really lose that addiction, being an adrenaline junkie."

Like someone else I knew?

"I met him because we were doing a story about him, some anniversary thing. They got out a bunch of old pictures he took, and got one of him, himself, very rare. He always said he belonged behind the lens, not in front of it. He lived upstate then, all retired."

He reached for another piece of bread. "Really hated it. I mean, he could see cows out the window. This is a guy who lived across from a police station so he never missed out on a story."

'You're making that up."

"No, I am not and I didn't just hear it from him." He grinned at me. "Always have to have some corroboration and I did. I got the address and believe me, it was a real dump."

I looked around his living room without a word and he saw me do it.

"Worse. Way worse. One room, bathtub in the kitchen. But he could see the station out the one window, and could be out and on a cop call in two minutes. Like the man says, location, location, location."

There he was, Leary the living, breathing time machine. That's why I put up with him. And because I have become fond of him. Hard to explain but true.

"I have a book from the exhibit."

"Yeah? Learn anything?" He was now scraping tomato sauce out of the pasta bowl.

"Did you know he was a Brooklyn boy? He came from Brownsville."

Leary shrugged. "Don't know if I did, or not. It wasn't important. His whole career was shooting the dark side of Manhattan. And he started real young, like a kid. You could do that then. Ya know? No one cared about his roots."

"Well, I care. I'm looking at Brownsville now for my dissertation."

"When are you going to get that thing done?" He looked mischievous. He knows it's not a welcome question.

I shocked us both by tearing up.

"Hey, hey." It's probably the only time I've ever seen him with no words. He handed me a napkin. I mopped my eyes, took a gulp of wine and a deep breath. Two deep breaths.

"Sorry about that. I just feel like…some days…I'm stuck in the swamp. Forever."

He was silent, drinking. Finally he said, "Even been stuck in a real swamp?"

"What?"

"Your tears are clouding up your eyes, not your ears. You heard me. I said, 'real swamp.'"

I stopped crying. "I live in Brooklyn. New York. Not in, like, Louisiana."

"I thought so. No real swamps. Bet you've never even seen one?"

He seemed to be waiting for an answer. "True."

"You got no idea. I was in 'Nam. There are real swamps and then there are problems, okay? You have a problem. So fix it."

Strangely, his lack of sympathy helped. I took another deep breath, looked him in the eyes and said, "What do you know about old-time Brownsville?"

It turned out to be nothing. It was never his home or his beat, but he did have a few more stories about Espy. I couldn't figure out how I could use them in my work, but I wanted to.

Back home I left a note on my door for Chris, "Do not wake me," and staggered off to bed hoping to sleep a long time.

The call that woke me the next morning was the NYPD. They caught me just before I needed to leave for work. They wanted me for a lineup today, as soon as I could get there, to help identify some young men who had accosted me the other day.

Oh, crap, I thought. My days, my whole life, was tightly scheduled. There was no room for this.

I called the museum and told them I had an emergency. Then I e-mailed my actual boss with more details and headed out into the day.

A lineup would be a new experience for me. I told myself it might be interesting. I was trying not to think about the young girl in the hospital, in a coma, the real reason I was going to a police precinct first thing on a workday.

As I hurried into the station, the name of the detective contact in my hand, I walked right into a little crowd of an officer with Ms. Talbot and Mr. Wilson from the library. We shook hands politely, like the cordial strangers we were.

"You remember what I said?" Wilson said. "It's those guys, the ones at your car. They been following her…"

"Sir!" The officer snapped it out. "You remember what I said? We can't have any talk here. You come on with me now. Yes, you too, miss."

Into a small room, cement block, drab and crowded. A woman with a no-nonsense air came in and introduced herself as Sergeant Asher. She explained what we would be doing, reminded us this was an important case, and we were led off again, this time separately. I was glad I had work with me. I am never without it, because I am never caught up, let alone ahead.

I would make the most of my waiting time. And then I wouldn't have to think about where I was and why I was there.

A few pages into a scholarly source on Brownsville crime in the 1930s, when mob activities were a part of Brownsville life, I asked myself what in the world was I thinking?

I would have been better off at this moment with almost any other topic. A fashion magazine would have been good. Even a nice serious work on something far removed. Say, the Dutch in old New York. But not this subject, in this place. The building was from a later era, but I could imagine a few ghosts here, Kid Twist Reles and Pep Strauss and Tick Tock Tannenbaum, smiling at the cops, offering them a cigar and swearing to them they were on the other side of Brooklyn when the car was stolen and the body loaded into the backseat.

I shook my head and reminded myself I am a scholar, not a science fiction writer or a superstitious dimwit. There are no ghosts. I took out my laptop and started adding some scholarly notes to work I had already done. This fact. That date. Anecdotes, with the note, "Possible urban folklore." Apocryphal would have been even more scholarly, but it seemed ridiculously high flown in the context, which was Brooklyn tough guys who could not write a threatening note and get the spelling right.

Ten pages into my source material, twenty-three notes in my database, an officer came to get me. I was led to a dark room with a big internal window and they told me what to do.

Because four boys had threatened me, we would do this four times. I was calm and cold. I had seen a TV program about mistaken identification by witnesses but I knew I could identify two of them at least, the one who had grabbed my arm, and the one who talked most. The others maybe not.

So the first four were all the same size and age and color, muscular older teens, variants of a medium complexion. I had a minute of panic. What if I get it wrong? And then I closed my eyes, and thought of a voice saying, "Maybe we got to take her somewhere and search her." And his hand on my arm.

And there he was, a smile that only moved his lips. A nose that might have been broken.

I snapped my eyes open and saw him. "Number three."

"Sure?"

"I'm sure."

The second group was harder. It could have been any of them, none of them, all of them. I said so, apologetically, and the voice said, "Don't worry about it. Are you sure?"

"I'm sure."

The whole group walked off. Was one of them the one? I reminded myself that if I did not know I could not say.

The next one was easier. He was the one who did most of the talking, the one who called me "Little lady." It was not an endearment, not the way he said it. I had a very good look at him.

That day he wore a jacket with red leather sleeves and a wool cap with writing. Here the whole row was dressed in indoor clothes, plain long sleeved tees, hands hidden, but there he was. Short hair with a jagged cut hairline and a tattoo curling up the side of his neck.

"It's four. I'm sure."

The last was as impossible as the second. Someone came in to turn on the lights and tell me I was free to go. A thank you and a card for any further contact.

I was shaking.

The two library workers were in the hall.

"You came alone, so we thought we'd wait for you. It's stressful, isn't it? Are you doing okay?"

"Sure." And suddenly, I was a little better. "But how are you doing? I am just so stunned about Savanna."

"Stunned. Lord, yes. She 's been with us three years. We get attached to those kids. I know her aunt, so I spoke to her." She shook her head. "That family is devastated, of course. The aunt said nothing left to do but pray so we will do that."

I didn't know what to say. I'm not a great believer in the usefulness of prayer, but I did not want to be rude.

"Now I was raised up in the church too, but today, I'm thinking a couple of good friends with baseball bats would be more useful."

"Oh, Wilson, please! It won't help Savanna one bit."

"But it would make me feel better! After I became a grown man, I stopped beating on people, but right now..." He shook his head.

I won't lie. I kind of agreed with him.

"Did we all pick out the baby gangsta? One with the tattoos? He their so-called leader?"

We had and I was reassured. There were no mistakes on this and they knew the other two I had not been able to pick out.

And we had all chosen the same first boy.

"In my opinion, that one's a juicer. Got that muscled-up look, know what I mean? Because of boxing. Short temper, too."

"Around here a lot of boys box," Ms. Talbot explained. "They all think they could be the next Mike Tyson or Riddick Bowes. That's the only history some of them know."

I was surprised and Ms. Talbot snorted. "Oh, yes, they are both Brownsville boys. Lots of others too."

Wilson cut in. "Or some of these kids just want to look like they are boxers without doing the real work. They have short tempers and no sense. No hope, neither, but I am not feeling too sad for their poor little angry selves this day."

We had reached my car, and I offered to run them over to work. They invited me in to have lunch. It was the day the staff did a barbecue order.

The building would not be open to the public for a while, but a young girl was stacking books onto a cart.

"Deandra, come over here. No, nothing is wrong. I know you all been texting back and forth about Savanna. Is there any news? Have you seen her mama?"

Her eyes filled with tears. "No, Miz Talbot. I have not heard anything." Her voice was a whisper.

Mrs. Talbot looked at her with suspicion. "That includes gossip in your building lobby? And on the street?"

Cautiously, Deandra said, "Them boys who been bothering her? I hear they in for questioning. Lotta talk about it. Everyone afraid of them and think they did it."

Ms. Talbot turned back to me. "I heard some of that myself and I don't even live around here."

"I thought…"

"No, no, no. Not for years. Moved my family out to Long Island soon as I had the money. So maybe there is some progress. Some police around here don't care at all, lazy pigs, but some do. They were here and asked us for everything we know. And Zora? Savanna's mother? She is active hereabouts. She knows how to be heard, that's for sure."

"Turns out I knew her, just a bit, a long time ago in school."

"No! Small world, sometimes, isn't it, in this big city? Was she kind of outspoken back then?"

"Oh, yes."

Ms. Talbot nodded. "She was toning it down a bit in that news conference on TV. Did you see that? Of course she really is heartbroken. As we all are."

"If there was anything I could do…" I knew there wasn't. The words just fell out of my mouth. "You know, my teenage daughter was watching the news with me and she said, cops should be talking to all Savanna's friends. No adult really knows what's going on with a teen."

Behind us, Deandra dropped a pile of books, loudly, and scurried to retrieve them.

Chapter Eight

"Deandra! Child, what is the matter with you today?"

She was a tiny young girl, younger than Savanna, in tights and a giant sweater, and startling day-glo pink sneakers. She had a baby face under her makeup. She looked petrified.

"It's all right. It's all right." Mrs. Talbot softened her voice. "I know we are all upset. Just get that mess cleaned up."

We turned away, and then she turned back.

"Have the cops been doing their job, talking to all her friends?"

"Yes, ma'am. Lots of cops around."

I could see Mrs. Talbot looked skeptical.

"Home too? You live in the same building as Savvie. Talking to everyone?"

She nodded, looking like a mouse facing a cobra. Trapped.

"And you all telling them whatever you know, or is everyone too scared to speak up?"

"Well, some people. Well, lots of people, scared, I mean. I mean, everyone knows cops make you tell everything you ever did, and even things you ain't never did. Or other people's things they did. And then the other people would know you talked to them and be real, real pissed off." Deandra stopped, looking even more upset. "Sorry for the language." She went on, "And they be all up in your face about that. They won't be just talking neither."

Honestly, she looked like she was about to faint.

Ms. Talbot sighed. "Oh, lord, child. Just go back to work. But listen to me. If they get to you, you tell them anything that might help."

She shook her head as we walked toward the door. "That girl is no Savanna, sorry to say. Of course she isn't but fourteen but she is scared of her own shadow. She needs some survival skills."

I know I looked surprised at that. This was certainly a scary time for her and anyone who knew Savanna at all, let alone a real friend.

Ms. Talbot noticed my expression. "I know, I know. We are all hurting but she's like that all the time. A little mouse. Looks up to Savanna though and Savvie kind of big-sisters her. I've been hoping a little backbone would rub off."

It was time for me to go. I said my good-byes, was urged to stay in touch, and off I went. This time, I looked both ways, a long look up and down the block, before I even left the library steps for my car. And I had my car keys out, all ready for a quick entrance into my car. Or an impromptu weapon, as needed. No fumbling this time.

No sooner had I opened the car door than I heard gasping behind me. It was Deandra, running, no jacket on, and her neon bright shoes thumping the sidewalk.

She stopped short right in front of me, standing at my open car door.

"I had a thing to tell you." She was gasping for air and shaking.

I looked up the street again. No one was out. But still.

"Get in my car. Door's open."

Inside, doors locked, I offered her water from my bottle. Her gasping slowed down.

"There is a thing I know. Hardly nobody knows but me. Maybe one or two of her real close girls, but they not going to tell. What do I do?" She twisted her fingers. "I'm so scared, I'm not even sleeping nights."

My first impulse was to say tell the detectives who are asking the questions. Whoever hurt Savanna should not be walking the streets. My second, as I looked out my car to the bleak cityscape around me, was to remember that I am the white girl here. Grew up with cops. Friends with cops. Safe home in a safe neighborhood.

That was not Deandra's world.

"Is there anyone you can talk to?" I made my voice as soft as I could. "Your mom? Or maybe a pastor? Do you have one?" She looked horrified but nodded. "Even Ms. Talbot?"

She shook her head. "It Savanna secret and I swore not to tell. Not never to any of them. I can't rat out on that. My mom is…" She looked away. "Me and Savvie, we go to the same church, so same pastor. He an old man, kind of scary. Voice like God. I thought…you said you have a daughter…so maybe you would understand…even if you a white lady…." She spoke in a rush and then subsided to a whispered, "Dumb idea. I am so dumb."

"No, no. You are brave to even try." I gave her my best Chris,-I am-serious-pay-attention stare. Deep into her eyes. "Maybe if you tell me, I will know what to do with it. And I'll never tell where I got it."

She looked up then, not with trust, not even close, but a flicker of something. Maybe hope? She sighed deeply, all the way from her pink shoes.

"Savanna have a boyfriend. Big secret. Her mama would put her in forever lockdown if she knew. And his people would not like it, either, I guess. She say that to me. His people." She came to a sudden complete stop and then pulled frantically on the door lock. "I got to bounce. Got to go back to work. I sneaked out."

She was gone, running, before I could even say, "Tell me more." But yes, she had told me something and I had the whole drive home to figure out what to do with it.

I had a lot more to figure out when I was home and keeping an ear on the evening news while I threw together a meal of leftovers. Lots of them. Could we have meat loaf and lo mein and egg salad in the same meal? I hoped Chris' growing-teen appetite would distract her from noticing what a poor excuse for a supper it was. My mother, queen of the grapefruit starter, meat-and-two-sides dinner, must be turning over in her grave.

I thought, "Sorry, Mom, but this is my life for now."

I heard Savanna's name on TV, dropped the forks on the table and went to watch. "Four boys have been brought in for questioning for the brutal attack on a teenage girl. Two names, two withheld as juveniles. Detectives describe this as an important breakthrough." There was video of them being escorted, cuffed, in to the station. Though their hoods somewhat hid their faces, I knew instantly who they were.

Now what should I do with Deandra's secret? Was there any point in calling it in if I could not give them a source? So I called Mike the cop. I hadn't heard from him lately and I thought our not quite romance was probably over. No hard feelings and he could be useful.

As soon as I said I had a cop question, he chuckled and said, "I'll be downtown at court tomorrow. Good day to have lunch?"

"Better than good. I'll be downtown too, working at the museum."

For now, immediately, the clear plus was that those boys could not hurt anyone else. I assumed there was more evidence than today's line-up. I would go to bed somewhat relieved. I hoped Zora was feeling the same way. Just a little, anyway.

Chris and I plowed through supper, each preoccupied with our own thoughts. My quantity without quality strategy worked; I don't think she even noticed what she put in her mouth as she read her chemistry book.

"Chris!"

"Huh?" She did not look up.

"Put the book away. You need a break."

"Um, okay." She looked up, eyes unfocused. "Anything special going on?"

"No. Tell me about your day."

"Nothing to tell. School. Homework. Chem test tomorrow. I hate chemistry with the heat of a thousand suns. You know?'

I did know, but it would have been counterproductive to agree completely.

"I admit, Mrs. Grant is tough, but every teacher there can't be a hand holder." I remembered my own overworked public high school teachers. Some of them were dedicated, but some hated the job and hated us. Some barely knew our names.

"Mom! That is very unfair. Believe me, the high school teachers are not holding our hands. Unless they are trying to put more work into them."

"Okay. Sorry. So I'll tell you about my day."

I did, and thanked her for her off-hand comment about asking Savanna's friends for information. She seemed impressed for five seconds. Then she put her dishes in the dishwasher, heaped up a bowl of ice cream and headed back upstairs, chemistry book in hand. I thought I should get up early tomorrow and make her a real breakfast before the exam.

Next day, Mike and I met at a fish restaurant. One of the things I did like about Mike was he made me eat like a grown up, sitting down and having a proper meal.

I gently led into the subject. "I saw the news last night about that poor girl, Savanna Lafayette. I was out there in the neighborhood." No way was I telling him more than that about my experiences.

"Why in the world?" I ignored that.

"So. I know a little something. Maybe it matters and maybe not, and with a probable arrest, I am having trouble seeing what I should do with it."

"You need to stop playing detective." He pointed his fork at me for emphasis.

"What? Do you think I am playing?"

He just gave me one of those get real expressions.

"Listen." I said it calmly. "I was in Brownsville originally for research. And then I met people and I heard things."

"Mmm-hmm." Was that a skeptical sound or a convinced sound? "So, tell me what you learned and I'll see if I can give you any advice." Now he was in cop mode.

I took a deep breath. "There are those four boys. So

theoretically, anyway, the process moves on. Do I have that right? But they're not arrested yet?"

He nodded. "Bet they found a bunch of reasons to hold them for awhile. Substances, guns, old issues."

"Does that mean anything further I learned is irrelevant now?"

"Depends. How about telling me what it is, instead of tiptoeing around it?"

"A friend of Savanna told me she has a boyfriend. And it is a big, a huge secret. She seemed petrified to be telling me, and was too petrified to tell anyone in her world."

He nodded. "Scared it might get out that she told? I get it. The code is to never tell anything to anyone in authority. Never. She didn't tell you anything more?"

"Only that Savanna's mother would be furious - 'total lockdown' was what she said and also, that the boy's people would not like it either."

"What did she meant by that?"

"No idea."

"I don't suppose you'd like to tell me who told you all this?"

"You're kidding, right?"

He smiled. "It was worth a shot." He thought for a moment. "It looks like they think they've cleared the case but I know who's on it. I could pass the word. Just in case. Would you talk to them?"

"Sure. Of course."

"Okay, Nancy Drew. Enough work talk. I believe there is a piece of Key lime pie with my name on it. Two forks?"

We moved on to other topics, talked about a movie we had both seen but not together, talked about other news of the day. It was a pleasant break in my routine. Nothing more.

Whew. Done. Back to work. Back to juggling work, dissertation, parenting. Daughtering. That was more than enough to make me crazy, without adding in a relationship that really was not that meaningful.

I wasn't planning to tell Chris, though. I needed to keep a zone of privacy. Plus, I did not want to hear whatever she had to say.

A quiet day at my part-time museum job, doing research for a new exhibit about children's lives in Brooklyn over the decades. I had to look over files and files of snapshots, filtering for the curator who would make the final selection. Some distant day, when the funds were available, they would all be digitized. It would make the selection easier, but any historian would say there is value in handling the originals. At least, that's what I thought they would all say. What I would say.

When I had a day like this, the doubts about my choices fell away. I was fascinated by everything—the stickball games; potsy, a New York sidewalks form of hopscotch; the complicated jump rope combinations. The little Catholic girls, decked out like brides for First Communion. When I was little, that seemed as exotic as a grass skirt. The old-time eighth grade graduations, with girls in white dresses they had made in home economics class. No one taught home ec anymore, I thought. And here was one from Espy himself, children lined up like sardines on a fire escape, sleeping outdoors on a suffocating summer night. A rare Espy photo with no death or violence.

It occurred to me that I had a living source of information for this topic. Ruby Boyle and Lillian Kravitz had plenty of stories about growing up in Brownsville. An interview recorded or on wall posters would be an effective addition to the exhibit. They would be actual voices from the past. And we should capture them while they were still around.

I sat back, thought about it, and typed a memo for the curator. Ruby and Lillian could talk about Brownsville childhoods. Who else? Where would we find some other elderly, talkative folks from other neighborhoods, who still had good memories?

I stopped myself. If I suggested it, I would own it. Right? And I would be crazy to volunteer. I did not have room for one more responsibility on my plate.

Oh, heck. I was excited about this idea. My fingers flew over the keys as I described it for the curator.

I hit Send emphatically. And then looked at my calendar to

see what would be a good day to go back for another visit. Or if there were no good days, what would be a possible day.

And then, mindful of Lillian's request, I shot off a note to my friend Jennifer who worked at the Municipal Archives. I was pretty sure the official papers from the Murder Inc investigation and trials had ended up there. Maybe, who knows, if I ever found the time to look, or to beg or bribe my friend to look for me, maybe I would find something. Not likely, but at least I could tell Lillian I was trying.

Before I left the museum, there was a response from the new exhibit curator. She'd be happy to have me look into recorded memories as part of the exhibit. She loved it. She sent me names of some oral history organizations that might be helpful resources.

I had certainly gotten myself into that one but I went home happy with my day's work, a plan for dinner, an evening to catch up on schoolwork. Chris was in a good mood, thinking she'd done well on her chemistry test so we celebrated with hot chocolate. I dug the marshmallows out from way back in a cabinet.

On the evening local news, half watching, I glimpsed the Brownsville police station again and the four young men, sweatshirt hoods shielding their faces, but—wait a minute. They were walking out, not in. What? This looked all wrong.

It was not a replay from last night. An African-American man in a sharp suit was declaring at a near shout, "Justice is here today. My clients are not guilty of this tragic crime and their release confirms that. If NYPD had done their work, they would have known these boys have alibis for that night. We all offer our sympathy to Savanna's family and we hope with them to have the right perpetrators—I say, the *right* ones!—held responsible soon."

What? How was this possible? I pushed the button to replay. That only showed me I had heard it right the first time. "Well, damn!" A lot of people in Brooklyn were saying that, but I wouldn't hear it, live, until later.

Later, when I was deep into work, my phone made the funny noise that said I had a text. Phone? Where was it? Hidden under a pile of notes? The sender was already gone but the message said, Kin we talk more???? and was signed D. D. Who was that? Was this even real, not spam?

Then I realized it might be Deandra. I tapped in: Call me and my phone was ringing in just about a minute.

Chapter Nine

"Miz Donato?" She sounded breathless. "It's me, Deandra?"

"I thought so. What can I do for you?"

She took a deep breath. Then words tumbled out. "I thought some more, and I want to tell you what I know. I got to tell someone or just bust open." Then she gasped.

"Oh, crap. I thought I was alone here."

There was a long silence which ended with me frantically shouting, "Deandra, are you all right? Are you still there?"

Finally, she whispered, "I'm all right, I'm all right, but I can't talk to you now. Not now. Someone too curious hanging around here. I'll call again if that is okay?"

"Yes, of course. But are you safe for now? Is there anything…"

"Safe enough." Then she was gone.

I didn't even try to go back to my work after this disturbing call. Had my advice somehow gotten her into trouble? She said she was all right. I didn't know what to do, but thought I would call her tomorrow if she did not call me. Or maybe go find her at the library. I wasn't planning to go back to the neighborhood but it looked like that was going to change.

The news the next morning droned on and on about budget hearings, Albany, some idiotic Hollywood starlet. There was nothing more about the only subject that interested me. But there was a text from Deandra. "Sorry. I okay. Will call."

I grumped to myself the whole time I showered and dressed like a lady, to the extent my wardrobe allowed. I was making another visit to Ruby Boyle. In fact, I was taking her out to lunch. She wouldn't appreciate blue jeans.

She had responded with pleasure to my late evening call. There was a diner nearby, she told me, with an eight-page menu that would accommodate any special food need and any special craving, too. She had a bacon-lettuce-tomato sandwich in mind, something never available at a home accommodating an observant Jewish population. "Of which," she added emphatically, "I am not one."

There she was, right on time, standing in front of the reception desk, spine straight as a ruler, in a smart tweed suit with a silk scarf. Perhaps the style was a few decades out of date—I wouldn't really know—but it was definitely an ensemble. I couldn't apply that word to anything I owned. I was glad I had ditched my jeans.

However stylish she looked, she did not look happy. I helped her into my car, not that she really needed it.

"We are not going to lunch," she announced. "We need to go see Lillian. She is in the hospital."

"What? What happened?"

"Silly woman got up in the night and fell. No walker. Of course at our age a fall like that means broken bones."

"When did this happen? Do you know how she is doing?"

"Last night sometime. At least she did have her emergency button on. An ambulance came. She can have visitors now so let's get going."

She looked around my car as if surprised to see we still hadn't moved. I pointed out she had not told me the hospital name or location.

"You see how upset I am? Montefiore, and it's close. I can direct you."

With some confusion, we finally succeeded in finding the hospital, the parking lot entrance, the signs pointing to visitor reception. Ruby moved along briskly as we negotiated the long walk, using her colorful cane only where the sidewalk was uneven. I trotted along, keeping an eye on her balance.

At reception she announced, "We are here to see Lillian Kravitz. I phoned and was told she could have visitors today."

"Just give me a moment." The young woman tapped a few keys and looked up. "Are you Lillian's family? There is no other visiting until later."

"Young lady. I am ninety-one. I can't wait around until then. And Miss Kravitz," she added some emphasis, "is also ninety-one. She has no family left at all. Please make the necessary arrangements for my companion and me. This is Erica Donato and I am Dr. Ruby Cohen Boyle."

Behind Ruby's back, I tried to look apologetic to the girl at the desk.

"Let me see what I can do." A few more taps on the keyboard. "Well, why didn't you say so? You are listed right here as her primary contact. Off you go." She wrote the room number on a card. "Just follow the green line on the floor."

There was Lillian, looking older than when I had last seen her. Older, smaller and frail. Her eyes were closed, but Ruby put a hand on her hand and she came instantly awake.

"How do you like this? I am dying of cancer, but a stupid fall is what gets me into the hospital!"

"Stop the cancer talk, you vain, silly woman. You were trying to get around without your walker, weren't you? And now you have a broken pelvis."

Lillian looked sheepish. "I wake up and I forget. In my dreams I am young. Twenty and ready to jitterbug all night."

"Just as I thought. When they let you come back, you are going to behave yourself, right?"

"Of course. I'll do whatever they say." I noted that the expression on her face did not match her compliant words.

Ruby exclaimed, "Oh, where are my manners? Look who I brought to see you."

"My dear, thank you for coming. It's good to see a young face." Did she remember me? My guess was that she was on substantial pain meds and did not.

"Now, dear, how are you eating? Is that your lunch over there?" Ruby leaned across to see the tray.

"See for yourself."

She uncovered bowls of soup, Jell-O, and some kind of cereal.

"What is this mess? Do they call this a meal?"

"They seem to think I need to be on a soft diet. Told them I broke my pelvis not my jaw. I haven't forgotten how to chew and swallow."

"We'll see about that! I'll be right back. I'm going to have a discussion with the nurse in charge!"

Off she went, before I even had a chance to say, "Do you want me to walk with you?"

Lillian gave me a slow, sly grin. "Now we have a few private minutes to talk."

"Did you know she would react that way?"

"It was a good hunch, wasn't it? Now tell me quickly, have you learned anything?"

So she did remember me. I reported what I had done, which sadly wasn't very much. She looked at me with a calm, unemotional, expression.

"I'll recover from this current stupidity, or so they tell me, but I am running out of time. If I were in better shape—and of course twenty years younger—I'd do it all myself."

"Why didn't you, back then?" I hastily added, "I'm just wondering. Not criticizing or anything." Though perhaps I was.

"Good question. That would be another whole story." She smiled and closed her eyes, drugs kicking in.

"Lil, darling. Listen to me." Ruby was back. Lillian opened her eyes slowly, with effort, at the sound of her voice. "The nurse apologized and said you will have a real dinner tonight. *And* young Erica and I can go to the cafeteria and bring something up for you. What would you like? I'm thinking of a BLT for myself."

"Mmm. Pasta. Something pasta would hit the spot. And chocolate cake." She drifted again.

"Off we go, Erica."

It was a long walk, a very long walk, to the cafeteria on the other side of the connected buildings, but when we got there, we found lasagna, chocolate cake, and a BLT for Ruby. Plus a chicken wrap for me.

Ruby talked and ate, and I listened. No, she was far too upset about Lillian to be bothered with making a recording now. Yes, she would love to do it another time. Childhood memories? Of course. She was already making notes.

"You know, dear, my memory, good as it is, really is not what it once was. Fortunately for your request, the old memories are more vivid and accessible than the newer ones. I remember the number of my first telephone."

I tried to look impressed. No, I was kind of impressed.

"She's dying, you know." Ruby looked past me, toward the other side of the cafeteria, but I knew she was seeing something else.

"It's been a joy to have her here with me. We were so close, back when. I only had my big brother, who was horrid to me, and she had one big brother and baby sisters. So we became like each other's sister. Then we lost track. She went to Douglass College in New Jersey and I was in New York and..." She shrugged. "Things happen and you lose people along the way." She blinked hard, rapidly, for a minute. "And now I will lose her again, and soon."

It was on the tip of my tongue to ask her about Lillian's brother, if she could add or expand that story, or even tell me it was true. The words were right there, but I stopped myself just in time. It was Lillian's story and her choice to talk to Ruby about it. Or not.

Instead, I cautiously asked, "Did you never connect after you went to college?"

"Of course we did. Weddings, reunions, all that. But it was never the same, and then over the years, there are husbands and children and moves. My second husband was a professor at Yale and Lil never married at all. She liked men, though. And they really liked her. She had a very, very good time in those days.

I know she thought I disapproved. Perhaps I did." She saw my face and said, with an edge, "Are you shocked? Did you think your generation invented sex? And now…and now…"

She looked around, not seeing, and then stood up. "Let's get back to her room. Can you carry the tray?"

Lillian was awake, just barely, and Ruby just barely got her to eat a few bites. She drifted off again, and we knew it was time to go. Determined, talky Ruby had not one word to say in the car. That was fine with me. I was having a flashback to my mother's last weeks in the hospital. She had been ill, on and off, for a long time, but we all thought she'd make it to enjoy some of my dad's retirement. She didn't.

It was a lonely ride back to Brooklyn, with too many thoughts in the car. I played the classic rock station, full volume, but it only helped a little.

Home with a massive headache. I had to park many blocks away from my own house. The weather was sharply chilly for spring. In the planters in front of my house, a few buds were coming up, daffodils that had survived from last year. I didn't plant bulbs this fall. I was too busy and Chris was now too grown up to think it was fun. I remembered when she was little, so excited to see the bulb plants peeking up, sometimes through the last of the snow. It seemed like a miracle.

A beer from the refrigerator did not raise my spirits. The smart, mature thing would have been to do something productive. Instead, I took a nap, curled up under a frayed, stained comforter that was a long-ago wedding present. At some point I must have come to. I heard voices and laughter, but fell asleep again.

The next time I woke up the house seemed deeply dark and quiet. No sounds from anywhere, not even the street. I got up and looked out the bedroom door. No light peeking out from under Chris' door or glimmering dimly from downstairs. What time was it? Three a.m.

Back in my room, eyes more open, I found a note Chris had left on my bed.

You were out cold so I left you alone. Joe came by to see you
and stayed to cook eggs for us both for dinner. He called me
an abandoned child. Just kidding! I called him Uncle Joe
and he laughed. Said to tell you he was here. Sleep tight.

That was thoughtful. It seemed there was hope for her as an
adult human being. Except for the sarcasm of course

Now I was up and awake for real. I raided the refrigerator,
watched re-runs of a television show I had never even liked in
real time. It seemed better in the dark of night. I did not feel
awake but knew I would not get back to sleep. Another night
on the dawn patrol. Damn

I thought I'd do some work but I was sidetracked by a middle
of the night message on Facebook. It was Zora and it wasn't
personal.

> Y'all heard what happened? Those nasty little
> creeps who hurt my girl? Now they're out walk-
> ing while she is in the hospital tied up to every
> machine. And that SOB lawyer. Oh, I know him.
> He's only interested in making his big name. Did
> you see him on TV? All up in the microphones
> about justice? Alibis, pul-leeze! We know what
> we know.

> And he's going to get his ass bit over it, too. We
> are planning a demonstration, right over there at
> the cop shop where he had his news conference.
> Two days. Details up tomorrow AM. Sometimes
> you just got to holler. Know what I mean? Pushing
> those fool cops to do their job and get the right
> ones off our streets.

> Information attached. Y'all come and make some
> noise

There was a ping from my mail. Something else from Zora
and this time it was personal.

You come too. See it in person. It will be big. It's going up on Facebook and we got posters up all over the hood and beyond. We got to make something happen. Ya know? Not just for my child but other people's children too, I'm going to send you a flyer. Be good for you to be making some noise.

Chapter Ten

Zora was not exaggerating. All the local Brooklyn neighborhood listservs and bulletin boards—and there are plenty—had a blizzard of notices. I belong to one though I seldom have time to participate. When I saw the activity on it, I started exploring. Crime in Brownsville? Work, right?

I emerged a few hours later, having gone down the social media rabbit hole. The one thing I knew for sure was that many people were writing about Savanna, and the caught-and-released boys, and how to make a noise. Or if it was worthwhile to try.

Even Chris had picked up a reference to it, a flyer from somewhere in downtown Brooklyn.

"This is the girl you told me about, isn't it? So I was wondering…?"

"No," I said immediately. "Not a chance. It is a school day and you are not going. It could get ugly."

Deep sigh. "I figured."

I didn't tell her I was going. Maybe I should have, but I was not up to having an argument about it.

In the next day, there wasn't a word on the news media that I could find. Not television, not radio, not the newspapers. Then, the night before, finally, there was a small reference to it on the local evening news, with a brief video showing some of the posters up around the neighborhood and a photo of the police station. The officer in charge said, "We protect everyone's right to assemble and speak up and at the same time, we are preparing to make sure a peaceful assembly doesn't become a riot. That will not happen here." I wondered where he got his public relations training.

I looked at my calendar for the last of many times. I knew what I should be doing tomorrow, and I knew what I would be doing. Yes, sometimes you have to make some noise.

That didn't mean I wasn't nervous. Even without a public demonstration, it was a neighborhood where feelings ran high, tempers were short, and guns were common in spite of our activist mayor's efforts to stop the gun trade.

Nevertheless, I was on the subway the next morning, I'd be crazy to take a car today. My wallet and phone were easily zipped in an inner pocket of my light jacket. Clothes were my usual student-sloppy style. I wasn't representing anyone today, not a job, not looking like a serious scholar, not a mother. I was not responsible to anyone today. Only myself. And besides, the clothes would make me a little invisible, I thought. I hoped.

I found the precinct without any trouble, and there it was, a full setup, with a platform for speakers, some news cameras and microphones, lots of cops standing in the back, a block closed to traffic I wondered how Zora pulled that off, or if it was someone else.

I found a spot next to a building, a little sheltered, where I thought I could see and observe as the closed off street slowly filled up with people.

Most of them were dressed in shabby clothes or the flashy styles sold in cheap local stores. Neighbors, I guessed. But there were others, too. The tall, gray-haired man in the dignified suit was the long-time congressman. I wondered how Zora had gotten him to come out for this. A matronly woman in a smart spring coat and churchgoing hat was the city councilwoman. And there was the lawyer representing those boys.

Was he invited? After what Zora had said about him? How was that possible? I was keeping my eyes on him, waiting to see what happened as the others began to take their places on the platform. An older man in a circle collar and a younger woman in clerical robes with stylish high heels peeking out underneath. A white man in a suit, very busy on his phone. I was betting he was the mayor's rep. A black man in police dress uniform with a lot of gold on his cap.

People continued to stream in from all directions, some in groups carrying signs. One group, all ages and sexes and colors, had signs that said "For Savanna. Brooklyn Tech Teachers and Students." The adult faces were grim; the teens were teary. Another was a group with a big sign from the municipal workers union. A group from a semi-socialist fringe political party that has never gotten any traction that I knew.

As the street of people turned into a crowd, I saw that most of them looked grim and solemn, but some—and they were not just the teen-agers—were acting as if it was a social event. High fives, loud scolding of children, teens jostling and joking around.

The crowd grew and I was glad I had found my little spot early.

The platform seats were full, the mics were being tested with the usual shrill noises, and the man who was clergy was standing with Zora at the podium.

"Dear friends…" he began. That got nobody's attention and the crowd's buzz only grew louder. He dropped his voice to a lower register and moved closer to the mic. "Friends! All you all here! Listen up. Let us begin."

That time it worked and the buzz subsided, as all attention was turned to the platform.

"Let us begin with a prayer asking our Lord's help in making our voices heard in the highest offices."

Most of the crowd grew silent and many heads were lowered. He kept it brief and to the point, and the final "Amen" was joined in by almost everyone. Even me.

He introduced Zora. She stood up tall and very straight, dressed in a bright green dress with a leafy pattern.

"I do not wear black today," she began. "I do not wear mourning. My precious child is with us still, though her life is hanging by a thread. She is a fighter and in tribute to her, I am wearing her favorite of my clothes. She pushed me to buy this. She said, 'Mama, you are still young. You need to have something pretty and bright sometimes.' Honey, this is for you!" Her voice caught in her throat; then she went on.

"She is not in the hospital due to an accident. She is not lying in the hospital, fighting for her life, due to an illness. She is there because of strictly human evil. And the cops got the wrong guys. Give them credit—they got someone! Later, we'll have some people up here to talk about why that doesn't happen more often. And they had good reasons to suspect them, but, my, my, those boys had better alibis. Who would have thought that was possible? Let me hear you. Who expected that?"

There were some shouts. She said again, "Let me hear you again about those so handy alibis." This time there was a much louder response.

"I hear you saying you don't trust police and I am with you on that. I know. I know. We all have our experiences. But today isn't about that. It is about knowing who did this to my child. And see that they get what's coming to them. Someone knows. You, or your friend who left town or your neighbor with a hangover? I am asking you to man up, whatever sex you might be, and see that these animals are not still out there. Going after your child next."

She separated each word in that last sentence and emphasized them like sticks hitting a drum skin.

"I thank you all for coming out and showing love for my little girl. Please keep her in your prayers. Now I'm going to turn the mic over to the Honorable T. Darrel Thomason, our own congressman. He has kindly offered to speak himself and introduce everyone. Please put your hands together for him. We can make some useful noise along with our protesting, right? Because this is not a funeral, and Lord, we are praying it won't become one."

A young man near me stage-whispered to his companion, "Who that be in the suit? I couldn't hear good."

His friends looked back at him in disbelief. "You fool! That be T. Tommy. A big man around here."

An older woman snickered and they turned to her in a split second. She looked at them through hooded eyes. "Don't you be giving me that look. It was funny how she say 'He kindly consented.' He's a politician. He likes to get his face on TV. Kindly! And for all his work you boys don't even know him." She snickered again.

I knew that in a neighborhood where only the really interested are organized and motivated enough to get out and vote, he'd been sent back to DC for ten straight terms, usually unopposed. He was doing something right.

I didn't feel the need to join their conversation. And I assumed I would not be welcome. Today I was an observer, a witness to an event as it unfolded.

The congressman kept it mercifully brief. He outlined his efforts to get more money for the district, hoping to use it for a new recreation facility. "We all know," he said—and I heard a loud buzz of agreement around me—"our young people have too much time on their hands and too few productive activities They are young, active, bored. No wonder they get in trouble, whether making it or—" he turned toward Zora—"being on the receiving end."

He acknowledged no one knew, yet, what had happened to Savanna. Or, he said carefully, very carefully, no one knows enough to make it stick in court. Ha, I thought. So he too thinks they had the right guys.

I was not the only one who took that meaning from his carefully worded phrase. There was a buzz around me and then the boys' attorney stood up in the audience and shouted, "You are libeling my clients. I cannot and will not allow that to happen."

"Now why would you think I was doing something like that?" By his smooth response, I could guess the congressman had been heckled before. "I mention no names." Now his glance swept across the audience. "Come on, you all. Did you hear me mention names or accuse anyone? Can I get some support on that?" This time the buzz was loud, with a few louder shout outs. "No you did not." Then from the other side, "Isn't like we don't know they did it though." And louder. "Yeah, been bad apples all this long time and the cops did nothing."

The Congressman said, "Let's not use this solemn occasion for shouting insults. You hear me? That's not respectful." He nodded to Zora and then turned his gaze back to the attorney. "Sir, I am not sure why you are here today, but perhaps you'd like to confer later?"

"I'll be waiting," he responded and then moved to the sidelines, and stationed himself where the persons on the podium would have to pass him. Was I only imagining that two men in suits, tall, fit, one black, one white, moved quietly to have him in their sights?

The Congressman was speaking again, "Now I want you to give a welcome to Lieutenant Leo, who will talk about police efforts and try to put the rumors to rest. My friend, Lieutenant Leo." He enunciated it very clearly.

Applause was scattered and spotty, certainly reluctant. It takes more than that to faze an NYPD career officer. Cops lined up along the building seemed to tense and move in a little, as if preparing for something. For anything.

"I'm giving it to you straight. The young men we thought responsible had stellar alibis. Come on! You don't want us to hassle young local men before they do something? But you want us to hold some of them when we can't charge them? So if you know something different, come on and say it out loud. There's a number. We've got it on flyers in the back. No one, and I mean that, I swear to that, will know who you are if you call in. And if you know something else, not about them but about Savanna, call it in. Here's where we're at on this: it's no secret there is a great big gang problem hereabouts." He looked over the audience. "You know about that?"

The group of boys standing near me tried to hunch down into the hats and hoods when he said that but the adults were nodding in vigorous agreement.

"Yeah, well, this attack doesn't look a bit like a gang issue. Might have been a robbery that went all wrong but you know she's a girl from the projects. She wasn't carrying much. What animals beat a girl almost to death for nothing? You hearing me?

"We are canvassing all around where she was found, her building, her school. Any of you out there her girlfriends and know something we maybe don't? You want to see these snakes, whoever they turn out to be, put away? You know what you need to do.

"We are going to get him or them or whatever. That is a promise." This time, the applause was a little more robust.

Congressman Thomason was back. "We have time for some questions and then the choir from Savanna's family church has kindly offered to close this event with a hymn or two. We have people with mics so get your hands up."

"I got a question for big man attorney over there?" It was an angry looking man in coveralls.

"I'm sorry, he was not part of the program, and that's…" Zora whispered to him and then he said, "If he wants to come up and answer a question, he can."

And he did.

The questioner continued, "How you squaring it with your own slick self, defending boys you must know are guilty? And if not for this, then for something else? They a menace to us all and you don't look good, standing up for them."

The attorney leaned in to the mic. "And, dear sir, what would you say if it was your own son arrested?"

The people around him laughed, and poked each other and I heard quite clearly, "He got you there."

The questioner became flustered and distracted, smacked away a woman's hand, and finally said, "My son ain't the issue today. Don't you be changing the subject. You getting fame and money defending them, and they getting out, and what we getting except more trouble?" He nodded decisively. "How do you sleep at night?"

"Just fine, thank you. And if this line of questioning continues, about my clients who—let me remind all of you!—" His voice was rising with every word. "Were released for lack of evidence—lack of evidence means there is nothing to say they are guilty!—you all got that? What are you saying, the cops always get the right person? We all know better!" Lots of muttering and loud agreement on that. "If this discussion about my clients continues, I'll be taking legal action." He strode off the stage, indignant. Holding the crowd's eyes.

I could see his face from where I stood. He was perfectly calm as he shook hands with a few people. In fact he looked happy. I thought his performance was just that and wondered what his goal was, but I didn't get to think about it for long. Near me a woman was talking in a heated whisper with her friends. I could hear her saying, "What is so special about this girl? She not the only one ever got hurt around here."

"I believe her mama organizes…"

"What the hell do I care? Every week some child in trouble threatened, hurt, dead, ODed. But oh, every fool person love *this* child! I only came 'cause you all was coming."

Someone else, not from her group, turned and said, "If that's how you feel, why you ain't getting up and saying it out loud?"

"I wasn't talking to you." At that moment, I was glad I was not the questioner. "But I believe I will, no thanks to people who mind other people's business."

She looked all around before turning to the podium.

"What I want to know is where the hell you all been all this time? You think this Savanna so special? Maybe she is, no disrespect intended, but every child is special to someone, and we losing children all the time around here. Why all you big shots not coming around with promises sooner? Why we don't have better policing, with police who see the difference between them gang boys and our good sons?" She gestured to the stage. "Why you not showing concern about my little nephew who was shot by accident when two gang fools had a beef?" She looked around at the crowd. "Why you all not marching about those girls who had a beat down about some stupid boy and one died? About the gangs in their nasty hanging-down-to-the-knees pants, threatening our younger kids?"

She started to breathe hard, as people around her were clapping. She turned to a knot of teenagers near her. "Yes, I'm talking about you. Don't you be looking at me with those eyes. You know who you are and what you done."

Three of them started shoving through the crowd, moving toward her, when a big man stepped in their path and the scene exploded. Punches were thrown. Yelling and cursing. People nearby were moving away as fast as they could, except for the ones who were piling on.

And I watched with shock at how fast it happened. And fascination. It happened so fast, I didn't even have time to be scared.

In the melee I spotted a familiar face. Deandra. She was moving backwards, away from the fight, toward another girl I couldn't see well. I tried to go talk to her but I couldn't push through. Then the fight shifted, the crowd moved and she was gone.

It was over as fast as it began. People pulled the fighters apart and dragged them away but not before the angry woman walked up to one of the original boys and threw a punch of her own.

Does it make me a bad person to say I admired it?

Friends led her away but I could hear her response. "I showed them. I showed them. I did it."

The friend who was pulling on her arm snapped, "I suppose you didn't see the gun one of them had in his hand? You one crazy-ass woman."

Up and away from the confusion, Zora was still at the mic, looking shaken. The police officer was shouting to everyone to calm down while his uniformed colleagues were rapidly positioning themselves to be ready for more.

"Dear neighbors. Dear neighbors." Zora's clergyman was trying to be heard, and after the third try, the turmoil started to subside. "No one could argue that our neighborhood is permeated with violence and our own children are the victims even when they are also the perpetrators. Maybe today will make a difference. Maybe some of our children are hearing what we say and will find another road. Maybe some of our politicians will hear us and see they have to do better. You see we have news cameras here? So let them hear us saying we want change."

"Change! Change!"

The congressman said, "This is how it works." He made a sweeping gesture, including all the assembled crowd. "You got to make some noise. You got to show up. You got to keep asking. No, demanding. And you got to vote. I hear from the people on this platform that this is just the beginning. Maybe next we take the message right over there across the river to City Hall. Who's in?"

The response approached a roar and I wondered what would happen next. The reverend gave a benediction, praying for Savanna and all the children, and the choir sang them out with Savanna's favorite hymn, "Precious Lord, Take My Hand."

They put their full choir voices into it, and I have to admit, when they hit, "Through the storm, through the night, lead me on to the light," I was singing along.

As people began to disperse along the side streets, I saw the lines of cops spreading out too. Keeping an eye on whatever would happen next? It was a lot of people, some of them short-fused, and some armed, and most of them worked up.

I stayed put, waiting for the crowds to thin out and I could head for the subway without fighting through.

"Miz Donato!"

It was Mr. Wilson from the library, along with Ms. Talbot and a few other people I recognized by sight. Mr. Wilson carried a sign.

"You came all the way out here to stand up for Savanna? Well, welcome." Ms. Talbot shook my hand. "As you see we all decided to come together, representing. These crowds make me a little nervous. Of course our pages went with their friends. Some of these kids here seem to think this is an outing." She shook her head. "I've seen groups talking and laughing. And drinking. At this hour! But our library workers are pretty shaken up."

"I saw Deandra! She was backing away from the fight and didn't see me. And I couldn't get to her."

'You saw Deandra? Are you sure? Really sure it was her?"

"Well, yes." I thought about it. "Yes, it was her. I saw her face, and also those crazy hot-pink sneakers. What's surprising about that? She was a friend of Savanna, right? So she came out today."

"Deandra been missing these three days."

Chapter Eleven

"I don't understand."

"She hasn't been to work, not since the day you was there, and the other kids don't seem to know one thing about where she at." Wilson was frowning. "Her mama is off in la-la land most of the time and didn't even know she wasn't around."

Ms. Talbot nodded. "It's not like Deandra, either. She's one of the more responsible kids we've ever had, too scared not to toe the line, I think. But I was all set to chew her up after she missed one day. And then she missed more."

But she called me. I almost said it and then thought it might still be her secret.

"We called her number and her mother seemed like she never even noticed. Couldn't even say when she last saw her."

"How you just misplace a child? You know what I'm saying? I lived here my whole life, and my momma before, but some of these fools…"

I would never have said it, but I kind of agreed. Just how do you misplace a child? And when did I need to tell someone I had heard from her? Was she in trouble, or actually hiding safely?

Ms. Talbot said, "Her mom came by one time and Deandra seemed embarrassed. Anyway, she seemed to be saying Deandra was old enough to do her own thing. When she most certainly was not."

"You want to come meet Savanna's mother?" Wilson pointed to the little group near the platform, talking away. "We going over to say hello, pay…hell, no. I don't want to be saying 'pay respects.' Sounds too much like…you know. And don't want to be saying that either."

"Wilson, maybe you just want to not talk for a minute. We are all so upset. Anyway, do you want to come see her with us? You'd be welcome."

I did want to go with them. Zora had said I should come say hello. And I didn't want to talk about Deandra any more, until I could figure out what to do. I worried that my advice got her into some kind of trouble. I knew there were dozens of other ways to get into trouble around there, but still.

So we walked through the thinning crowd and waited, a little off to the side, until Zora broke off her intense conversation. Up close, she didn't look like the firebrand on the stage. She looked exhausted but her face lit up when she saw our little group.

"Why, it's the library right here!" There were hugs all around. She stopped when she saw me. She looked me over and took her time about it. "Well, damn, if it isn't the little white girl from that bogus sociology class! Isn't it? Live and in person. You haven't changed much."

She turned back to the rest of the group. "Thank you all for coming. We must believe that everyone's voice matters, we must, or we just lose the way altogether. And wouldn't my Savvie be mad at me if that happened?"

"Well, you know we are all praying for her. Every day. Now we got to get back to open up the library. Ms. Donato, would you like to walk with us and we'll take you over to the train station?"

"Erica." Zora turned back to me. "I'm tied up here with all these people." She smiled at me. "Men in suits. After all these years, they're still with us." I smiled back. "We'll be talking."

There were many knots of people, talking and arguing, even though the street was now open to traffic. They were excited, revved up, rallying, with loud, excited talk and flamboyant, excited gestures. Out of the buzz of conversation, voices rose. Sometimes a louder single voice could be heard.

"I say we be demonstrating every day AT City Hall until they pay attention. There other ways to send a message than just talking." Then all his friends started talking at once and I had no idea what came next.

A couple of teenagers walked near me. "You ever been to City Hall?"

"Aw, hell no."

"City jail more like it than City Hall."

The first boy hand wrestled the second. "You know it. I don't even know how to get to City Hall, don't know where it's at."

Someone screamed out, "My purse! She got my purse!" She was an old lady but she moved fast in pursuit. One of the many cops moved faster and soon had a young woman collared in one hand and the purse in the other. She continued to shout, "They always be picking on me. Think I'm too old to fight back. What am I?" she shouted to the struggling young woman. "Do I look like an ATM to you? Now do I? Your mama know what you been up to?"

The cops spoke quietly and she answered, "Hell, yes, I want to press charges. This is the third time this month."

Who would snatch a purse right in front of a precinct, with cops all over the block? I remembered Mike telling me that most everyday criminals are really quite stupid.

It seemed as if the whole place, where the crowd should have been dispersing, was on the boil. I wondered what would happen next. Was there a next? I was glad to be walking in company.

We passed a small, dark, unpromising lunch counter and both Ms. Talbot and Wilson said they'd like to stop to pick up a sandwich. "No other place between here and work. Even a McDonald's would be an improvement."

Counter stools and the few tables were filled with neighborhood men. Rough clothes. Rough language. One man with his head on a table sleeping off a hangover or a long night on the night shift somewhere. Ms. Talbot and I were the only women in the place, and I was the only white person. Some of the men at the counter stared hard and cold at me, but most were deeply absorbed in their coffee and eggs.

I stood there pretending to be at ease. While I did, I overheard two men, one behind the counter working, and one on a stool. The one behind the counter was big, wearing a grease-stained white tee-shirt. His friend was skinny, snaky, in a black leather jacket. They were discussing a fight.

An overflow of something from the demonstration? Some gang activity? Gangs came and went here; this was a time they were coming back strongly. I was curious, fascinated, a little sickened by the discussion of more violence. And trying hard not to stare.

Finally the big guy behind the counter said, "Wait till Friday night. I'm gonna whip his ass because he don't know nothing about playing chess."

I didn't smile. I didn't want them to know I had been eavesdropping. Not that I had a choice, the place was so small. But I was smiling inside.

Sandwiches bought, we went back out, crossing the street that had been filled with a crowd earlier.

"I know a shortcut," Wilson said, "right through this project. You'll be all right with me."

We ate as we walked and then I stepped over to a row of trash cans to drop my bag of scraps and waxed paper.

I moved the cover while I was talking and scarcely looked to toss in my bag. Then I gagged and dropped the cover with a crash. I doubled up on the ground.

"Ms. Donato! Are you all right? Do you need an ambulance?"

I didn't lift my head from my knees. "Too late for that. Too late."

"Now you stop this. You are scaring me." Ms. Talbot handed me her soda. "Sip a little."

"I'm okay. Just shocked. Call 911. And don't go near that trash can."

So of course they did. Mr. Wilson promptly turned as pale as a dark-skinned man can. Deandra's neon sneakers were sticking out over the top of the can.

"Oh, lord. Oh, lord. Oh, lord!" Ms. Talbot voice shook. "To see this…."

"I saw her. I mean, I just saw her, not fifteen minutes ago." My mind refused to take in what my eyes were seeing. I had seen her when I lifted the trash can lid. She was crumpled, her small body lying upside down on the pile of trash bags. Eyes closed. Hands folded. Legs sticking out, as if someone didn't quite finish the job of hiding her. Blood all over her pink jacket.

I knew I would never forget that sight. I could scrub my brain with bleach and I would not forget it.

"It isn't decent, us staring like this." She slammed the cover down and called 911. Before we stepped away, she said, "Be at peace, little girl."

We were a half-block from the precinct, and a team was there in seconds. They asked us questions, separately and together. Others lifted the body. Deandra's body, I thought to myself. Not THE body. HER body. Someone's child. Someone's friend.

They were very interested in my earlier glimpse of her and wanted to know exactly where that was and what I could tell them about the person she was walking toward. Which was precisely nothing.

They wanted to know who she was with, and I was clear that she was alone. They wanted to know what she was doing, and I could not tell them a thing that was helpful. "She was sort of pushing through the crowd, toward the outside of the demo."

"Did she seem scared? Was she being followed?"

"I don't know. I didn't see that, it was too crowded. She seemed, well, purposeful. Like she was trying to get somewhere."

"Meeting someone? That's what you said?"

"Could be but I can't say I know for sure."

"Anyway," Ms. Talbot chimed in from a few feet away. "Anyway, she always looked scared. She was a very timid child."

Finally they were done and let us go. We looked at each other, at a loss for what should come next.

Finally, Ms. Talbot said, "We go back to the library and I have to call admin on this. And we call you a car, missy. No subway this afternoon."

"And then we close down the library out of respect."

"No we don't! She was not killed there—I can't believe I am even saying these words—and our users need us to be open. But I have another idea."

That is how I found myself helping to make a big poster in Ms. Talbot's office. It said, "We are in mourning for our library assistant, Deandra Phillips, who was killed this morning in/near the demonstration. If you know anything about this, call this number. Do it now."

It went right on the door.

Ms. Talbot had told the rest of the staff first thing. They cried. She said, "Stop crying. You need to think about Deandra. Anything she might have said, any time you saw her in these days she disappeared. Cops will be here doing their job, asking—at least I hope so!—so you all need to dig into your brain. Wilson, call Ms. Donato a car, will you?"

"Already done. Got a friend driving for First Class Cabs."

"Ha. It won't be first class, I promise, and it won't be a licensed cab either, but it will get you home. Probably not just what you're used to."

Who did they think I was? "What I'm used to is the subway. I never take car service, legal or otherwise, because I can't afford it."

"Today you can."

I normally reacted to being bossed around with an immediate desire to do the opposite, no matter what, but a car seemed so appealing just then. And Ms. Talbot's take charge behavior felt like being mothered.

Wilson walked me to the car, helped me in and said to the driver, "Take care of her. She's good people."

He nodded and said, "Have her home in fifteen if the traffic ain't too bad." Those were the only words he uttered the whole drive and that was fine with me. I could not have responded to a chatty driver just then. I could not even have been polite.

I barely saw anything on the drive home. I could not have said what route he took, if there was traffic, was I seeing a different part of the neighborhood. Some silly part of my brain thought about how disappointed in me my dad would be, not to notice what a cab driver was doing.

The main part of my mind was thinking about Deandra. I looked around for my purse, where I always have a small notebook, and had a moment of panic before I remembered I had not brought it. So I thought and thought and didn't write.

How could her mother have lost track of her for several days?

She was killed by a gunshot. I heard the cops talking, but I had also seen the blood. They thought it was probably the cheap pistol always available on the streets. It was either murder or she was caught in the cross fire of someone else's life. A gang beef, a drug deal gone wrong, a romantic rivalry. Not at all impossible. But how could she be shot in a crowd and no one noticed?

Or, it was related to Savanna. The two girls were somewhat friends, allowing for the gap in age and personality. Say, friendly. And Deandra knew something secret about Savanna. I had told the cops and they seemed interested in that connection to Savanna.

Of course they were. Savanna's beating was an unsolved crime that was becoming very high profile. I wondered how they would pursue it. With Deandra dead, did anyone else know Savanna's secrets?

Well, someone must. Another, closer friend of Savanna. Or one of Deandra's friends. Girls talk. They can keep secrets when they need to, but normally they tell each other everything. I thought about Chris and her friends. I was betting someone in Savanna's life knew all about the secrets she held. Deandra could not have been the only one.

Unless she had been caught in random crossfire after all. I was back to that. I was glad it was not my problem to solve, though I knew I would not stop thinking about it. How could I? I had never seen a victim of violence before. I'd seen my husband when I identified him after the accident. My mother in her hospital bed. But this was the first time with deliberate death, blood and gore, a child. I closed my eyes there in the decrepit cab and all I could see were those sneakers.

At home, I hugged my daughter so fiercely she struggled out.

"Mom, what's wrong?" And before I could get "Nothing" out, she added, "And don't you dare say nothing. You're *radiating* stress." So I told the truth while she held my hand. When I was done, she hugged me. I did not struggle out.

"Poor Mom! You need a cup of cocoa. Or a drink? There's some Scotch in the cabinet. You sit right here."

The cocoa was grainy with undissolved powder and not hot enough, but it seemed perfect to me. And it didn't hit me until much later that I should have questioned her knowledge about the Scotch. Perhaps it was time for a better hiding place? But not now.

I sipped while Chris moved around the kitchen. Soon there was a peanut butter sandwich in front of me, crusts off, cut into triangles.

That's when I started to cry. That was Chris' comfort food meal when she was small. And now she was babying me.

Plus my whole day had been about girls and violence. Girls who were lost. Mothers who were grieving in pain far beyond mine.

"You're kind of scaring me. Should I call grandpa?"

I almost said yes. Almost. But I did not want to hear his scolding. Though I'd learned over the years that a full-out shouting fight with him can be a great way to let out some stress, no, not this time. It would just create more. I know that now because I am a grown-up now.

"Darcy?"

I shook my head. "On a business trip."

"Uh, Mom? There are cell phones now. They've been around for a long time. You could talk to her."

She took my phone from my purse, texted a message, put it back.

"I asked her to call when she could. Are you doing better? Peanut butter helps; I learned that from you."

"You did? How funny is that." I gave her a smile even I knew was pathetic. "Yes, I'm better. Thank you. It was just, you know—it was a reaction to all…to all…to all this."

I had run out of words.

"So now I need to eat something too and get back to work, okay?"

"I could make something…"

"No, you could not! Drink your cocoa and rest. I'll forage in the refrigerator."

"Where did you learn to be so bossy?"

She gave me that teenager exasperated look. She might as well have said, "Duh!" She left me in the kitchen with another sandwich and warmed up cocoa while she made a plate piled with miscellaneous edible—I hoped edible—items. I spotted a hot dog and a pile of leafy stuff. She went upstairs and I tried to think about what I should do now.

Put on my historian hat and make notes about this day? Maybe it would all drain away, the public anger and pressure. But maybe it wouldn't and this was the beginning of something? Today I was right there, inside history as it was being made. I always told the children visiting the museum, "History is happening every day, all around us." This day, it was all around me.

Should I see what the TV news crews had caught? Or maybe just record tonight's news, and watch it all tomorrow. Not now.

The real question was, how could I blot the sight of Deandra's pitiful body being lifted out of the trash container? And the answer was, I couldn't. Not tonight. Probably not for a long time.

I recorded the local news, and then I thought about what might be on the webs. Chris laughs at me, says I'm a historian stuck in an earlier time, only interested in old documents on old-school paper. Which is completely untrue. Okay, maybe it's a little true. I know about the world of instant communication, I just do not find it very useful in my crowded life.

Even with Deandra's last name, there were other Deandras. It was not as unusual as I thought. And there was no news about this Deandra.

I tried Brownsville and killing. There was, tragically, plenty from that search, but nothing about Deandra. Too soon for anything official? But we had seen her body taken away from a trash bin in a project that housed thousands and there were other bystanders. It was all surrounded by tall apartment buildings with lots of windows. No one had seen anything? And was already emoting about it on Facebook? Or somewhere? Maybe they were all just texting with their own friends?

The headache right between my eyes was growing. Just as I was thinking about whether I needed ibuprofen or caffeine, the doorbell rang. What? At this hour? I glanced at the clock. Not actually so late. It only seemed like the middle of the night to me.

It was Joe. My friend. We'd met years ago, when I first moved into my very shabby house, and an old friend had asked her cousin Joe, a contractor, to do a little basic work for me. We became buddies. We bike together, hang out when we both have a free evening. When I finally scraped together enough money to put a twentieth-century kitchen into my house, with a refrigerator that worked and appliances that were not antiques, Joe had built it, overseeing the crews and employing Chris for the summer.

Now he and Chris are firm friends, too. He is the pretend uncle, somewhat taking the place of her lost father, I guess. I know she tells him things she doesn't tell me. That is when, I also guessed, she came up with the ridiculous idea that there was romantic potential. She is fifteen. What does she know?

But I was so glad to see his friendly face that night. And she wasn't wrong about how attractive he was, big and fit and capable, graying streaks in dark hair. Of course he also teases me.

"Thought you might like some company." In one hand, he had a large coffee from the most expensive coffee bar in the neighborhood. In the other, a pint of ice cream. The real deal, no frozen yogurt nonsense. "Choose your poison."

"Come on in." I hastily ran my hand through my hair and discarded the napkin tucked in to my waist. "How did you know?"

"Call it a hunch." He went into my kitchen, which he knew better than I did, put the ice cream on the table and pulled out two spoons. "Dig in."

My favorite, vanilla chip. There was a container of still warm hot fudge sauce, too. So we dug in, silently for a while, and after ingesting enough sugar and chocolate, my brain seemed to turn back on.

"No, really. What brought you over tonight? Because something happened today…"

"Heard it on the grapevine." He was concentrating on the ice cream and not looking at me. "But do you want to tell me all about it?" Now he was looking at me.

So I told him, and it was a relief to say it all right out loud. I didn't have to protect him as I did Chris. I didn't have to be defensive, as I did with my dad. I could just tell him everything that was on my mind and know that he was listening completely.

"How did you get so deep into this?"

"Oh, I don't know. I met people, we talked, I asked questions. And then, these are kids. And someone I knew a long time ago. And it started out being about my work, but now?" I closed my eyes, not wanting to think about my next appointment with my advisor.

"Stand up."

"Huh?"

"Stand up. We're going for a walk."

"No, we are not. It's late, it's…nine o'clock? That's all?"

He was already pulling a light jacket off the coat tree near the door.

"Nice spring night, crisp, not cold."

I was standing, being led to the door. He still had keys to my house. He shouted to Chris, "Taking your mom for a walk. Be good."

There was an incoherent response, just enough to let us know she was alive.

Chapter Twelve

"I thought some fresh air would be therapeutic."

"You always think that. Exercise heals everything." I stopped and thought it over. "Sometimes you're right."

He smiled. "So you up for a ride? 5-K in the park?"

"Are you out of your mind?"

"It was a joke."

"Are we going anyplace in particular?'

'Yes."

"Are you telling me?"

"No."

"Joe, I don't have time for this. I have piles of work…"

"You weren't working when I got there, and you wouldn't be if you were there now. Tell me I'm wrong."

I didn't want to agree and I didn't want to lie, so I said nothing. The idea that I would do anything productive tonight was certainly my own fantasy.

We were heading away from the great park and going down the gentle slope that gave Park Slope its name. We were pointed to Fifth Avenue. Stopping for a drink at a stylish bar? Did he think a little time feeling young and trendy would be the cure?

Fifth Avenue has completely transformed from small, dingy grocery stores and hardware stores, sad during the day and a dangerous hangout for dangerous people at night. It has become the hot strip for trendy restaurants and bars.

But no, we crossed it and went on.

"Joe?"

"Surprise. Don't worry."

We crossed Fourth Avenue, a major road that takes six lanes of traffic from one side of Brooklyn all the way to the other. It had been known for auto repair shops, tire shops, taxi garages. If you needed an auto repair at midnight you could find it. The chop shops were open, tiny businesses in garages working on stolen cars late at night. If you wanted a girl friend for an hour, you could find that too.

Recently though, shiny new apartment buildings have sprung up and some weird transformation was occurring. As an urban historian, I found it fascinating. As a regular person, I was dumbfounded that people were paying high costs to live in an apartment with a terrace that had a view of six lanes of traffic.

And then we were going into one of the buildings. It was still a work in progress, with building permits on the windows and "Caution" signs all over.

Joe opened the street level door with a set of keys.

"Come on. I'm doing some work here, not housebreaking, if that's what you are thinking."

"No, no, not at all." The thought had crossed my mind, though. He's definitely not a criminal, but he has many oddball skills. And I have seen him pick a lock.

The dark lobby was filled with construction material but the building seemed finished. Here were walls, a floor, and windows. And an elevator, which is where Joe pointed me.

"Is this safe?"

"Don't be silly. The crews use it every day to get up and down. The construction is done. We're working on making it pretty now."

Up to the top floor, silent and smooth. Into an apartment, to which Joe also had keys. It was empty, with an odd chill. There were glass doors facing us and a terrace. And this one did not overlook six lanes of New York traffic.

Joe opened the doors and we were gazing right out over Brooklyn roofs to the harbor. Right and left, Brooklyn Bridge.

Manhattan Bridge. Verrazano Bridge. They were outlined in lights against the darkness, massive tons of metal and stone looking like fairy tale creations. Across, there was the Manhattan skyline, dark patches against the darker sky making a zigzag pattern decorated with bands of light. They went off on one floor and then on again on another. Off. On. Twinkling. And there was a cruise ship at the new Brooklyn Terminal. I wondered what the vacationers thought about docking at, well, the Brooklyn docks. Not a lot of New York glamour there, but the ship looked splendid, all lit up in the night.

I took a few deep breaths. Joe, having seen it all before, was standing against the wall with his arms folded.

"A little respite? Feeling better?"

"I am. And there is no rational reason for it, is there?"

He smiled. "We're the city dwellers. No mountains handy to refresh ourselves, but we can do this."

"Joe, I didn't know you are a philosopher.'

"You don't know everything, in spite of your advanced education." He wasn't smiling now and he was standing closer. "One of the things you don't seem to know is that you can count on me. You could have called me tonight. Or any night."

"But…"

He put his hand on my mouth. "Shh. Shh." He patted his shoulder. "You need to remember this is yours when you need it."

I shocked myself by kind of falling against him then, my head right on that shoulder, my face buried in his shirt. While tears ran down my face, his arms went around me, first comforting, and then tighter and something more than comfort. When I was done crying, he patted my face with his big man's hankie, but one arm still held me. And I liked it. What would I do if he kissed me then?

Instead, he said, "Time to go home."

Walking back up the slope of the neighborhood, he kept my hand held tightly in his big, calloused one. It felt fine. It felt like just what I needed.

Now I could think a little. "Did Chris call you tonight?" I interrupted whatever offhand remark he was making.

"Why would you ask that?"

I grabbed his arms and stopped him in mid-stride.

"Look me in the eyes and say she didn't."

He tried but then he started laughing. "She did, she did. She was worried. Be glad you have such a thoughtful, smart child."

"Oh, I am. But…ah. Actually, no buts. I'm glad she did."

We were home by then.

"Joe, thank you." This felt as awkward as a first date.

He gave my hair a brotherly rumpling. "Take care. Don't do anything stupid about all this mess you're caught up in. Okay? Promise?"

"Yes, dad. I promise to be good." I said it with a grateful smile.

"Dad? Oh, yeah?" And then he did kiss me. Not fatherly. Comprehensively. And walked away before I had my breath back.…Well…I had something new to think about.

Chris was already asleep so I could not ask the questions on my mind. It did disturb me that she was meddling in my life. Meddling is *my* mom job. But it didn't matter right now. The couple of hours with Joe were what I needed at the end of this strange, heartbreaking day. Tomorrow everything could come flooding back in. Tonight maybe I could sleep without dreams.

And then Darcy called. From India. What time was it there? I guessed wearily that it was not the middle of the night.

She is my best friend, an unlikely one to be sure. We met at a school bake sale, all those years ago, and instantly clicked over the chocolate cupcakes. She is older and has four grown kids to my one teen. I'm a Brooklyn girl and she's a Darien girl, and she has an MBA from Wharton and I started out as a kindergarten teacher. I don't know how we turned out to be the friend we each didn't know we needed.

I don't have a lot of friends. My parenting responsibilities keep me from hanging out with grad students; my academic life took me away from most of my old neighborhood friends. Darcy just takes me as I am.

"What's wrong?" She'd seen Chris' text.

I spilled it all, my adventures in Brownsville, my exhaustion with my dissertation, Deandra. Savanna. I didn't tell her about my moment with Joe, though.

"Are you having any kind of life?"

"You sound just like Chris!"

"So? You raised a smart kid. Big surprise. Are you?"

"Ah…"

"You need a vacation."

"That's ridiculous, I can't…" Sometimes she forgets that she is rich and I am struggling all the time.

"Hear me out. I have more airline miles than I will ever use up in this lifetime. And I have a few days in London on my way from Mumbai. I'll give you some miles and you can meet me there. Big room's already paid for."

"But Chris…"

"Has no friends who would take her in? Come on! Write down these dates and go to bed." I wrote them down. We said good-bye. Suddenly I was collapsing onto my bed, eyes already closing. I didn't know if I would do this, but maybe the idea would reset my dreams tonight.

It did. I couldn't remember the good dreams in the morning. I thought there had been some redcoats on horses. And a cathedral? A park? As a bonus I had a calm ordinary day, too. I worked at my museum job, made dinner for Chris and me. I even did some housecleaning. I was tidying up my own nest, the one place in a messy world where I had that power. I watched the news, but there was no mention of Deandra.

My friend Jennifer, who worked at the Municipal Archives, returned my call from a few days ago. After the usual catching up, she said, "Those trial archives? We have them, sure, and we keep them in offsite storage. There is a lot of paper. Thirty-five running feet."

"And what's that in English?"

"Sorry. It's about twenty medium boxes."

It would be a chunk of time I did not have, to look at every-thing. Other people had covered these topics. Couldn't I just use secondary sources?

Then I gave myself a mental smack. I was a scholar. Sort of. In the making. I needed to use the sources or leave it out. Hmm. Leave it out? No, no.

"Yikes. It's a lot of paper."

"Try moving those boxes! Which I did personally, just a few days ago. Here's the strange part."

Stranger than a government archive that held not only paper but also the bullets that killed a gangster? Rope used to strangle an informant? Maps showing get-away routes?

"Someone asked about those very same boxes this very same week. So how strange is that?"

"Could there be two of us writing about the same subject?"

"Sure, it happens. Suddenly, for some mysterious reason, an old piece of history becomes the topic du jour."

"Maybe I should talk to that person. Maybe we could be useful to each other." I was thinking that if someone was cov-ering this for, say, a long New Yorker-type article, I could be useful. And if a more serious scholar were doing the research, that person could be useful to me. "You have a name?"

"I do, but I can't give it out. Seriously against the rules." She paused. "You know, Erica, it's a mountain of paper. I mean, they were lawyers! They're a wordy bunch and they love their documents. So, if you were to come in when I was here, who knows? Maybe some sign-out information would be carelessly left out, mixed in with all that material."

"Do you mean…?"

She laughed and didn't answer. We made a date and I went back to work.

An e-mail from the curator I was working for, asking how the recorded memories project was coming along. Oh, crap. In the midst of everything else, I had completely forgotten about it. So I wrote her, "Fine. Just fine. I'm waiting to get some appointments confirmed." And then I got busy to make sure it would be the truth.

I called Ruby. She put me on hold while she consulted her calendar, and then told me, graciously, that she could give me a few hours tomorrow. It made me laugh, though I held it in until we had stopped talking. Lillian was home from the hospital, but was staying in the rehab building, having physical therapy and extra care. She would arrange for us to visit her but warned, "She tires easily, even lying in bed talking. You won't be able to get much from her. And come early. After breakfast seems to be her alert time."

I had my marching orders for tomorrow. A note to the boss, to have it in writing that I had updated her, and then I could not resist trying to find out what news, if any, there was about Savanna.

Nothing on the Web news sources today, but what was this? A Facebook page? Someone had started a Facebook page? I was surprised, even if I shouldn't have been. Mostly I ignore social media. I don't have the free time to play that way, but even I know in theory about Facebook pages being a central source of information and updates. I would not have thought of this. Maybe Chris is right and I do live in the past. So what? That's my job.

Here was a place for pictures of smiling Savanna with girl friends and family. Deandra was in one. And there was a place for some essays she wrote. And a place for information about the progress of a solution to the crime. I looked. Nothing I didn't know. There had been no updates. And a place for her story, with information about her medical status, too. I looked, holding my breath.

She had been moved from the original hospital to one with more advanced specialized facilities. And it was near me, an ever-growing hospital center right in the neighborhood.

I did what any mom of a teen would do in this situation. Some experiences make you sisters under the skin.

In a Personal Message I wrote, "Zora, the new hospital is a short walk from my house. Any way I can help? Check in on her

when you can't be there? Offer you a meal or a place to sleep if
you are there late? It would be living room couch, but you are
welcome to it."

Then I went back to searching for information about
Deandra. Nothing. I for sure had no official or even legitimate
reason for asking questions, but I wanted to know. Wanted to
know someone was working on this. Wanted to know someone
remembered her.

I gave myself a shake and changed my screen back to work. I
needed to make a list of questions for Ruby and Lil. I did hope
we would be able to include Lil. I liked her acerbic honesty
and thought it would be a good contrast to Ruby's somewhat
nostalgic story telling.

Dinner was done, and I was doing the last bit of kitchen cleanup,
when my laptop pinged with a message.

"Thx for offer. Appreciated. Care to drop by tonight? No
family could make it. Z"

That was a surprise. And I could.

"Will do. Need anything?"

"Serious coffee would be lifesaving. Sweet and creamy."

And a walk in the spring night would be good for me.

I called up to Chris, "Going out for a bit. I'll be home soon."

"Okay." She appeared at top of stairs. "Before you go? Battle
of Lexington before or after Bunker Hill?"

I paused.

"Yes, I know I could look it up, but I am in a hurry to get
this assignment done. Please just share your infinite knowledge?
Please?"

"Before. Be good while I'm gone."

She was already back in her room.

It was a nice night. It had been a cold spring but as I walked
along I passed tiny front gardens where the crocuses and miniature irises were poking their heads up at last. Almost every house
has a garden and they are all different. Some were carpeted with
ground cover like ivy. Some had clipped evergreen shrubs and

some had small trees, a miniature red maple here, a graceful dogwood there.

My own garden space had been paved over by some previous owner. A bonehead move for sure, cheap and ugly. I tried to compensate with big potted plants but I didn't have the time or the green thumb to take good care of them. One day, if we ever had some money, I would remove the concrete entirely and put the garden back. For now, I had to appreciate my neighbors'.

The hospital is a maze, as hospitals always are. I got lost a couple of times but finally found the right unit. I steeled myself before I knocked on the door. I didn't know what I would see.

I knocked again.

"Zora?"

"Here. Come on in."

The room was darkened, with a circle of light at the guest chair. The curtain was closed and there was a low hospital hum and a slight disinfectant smell. I was more nervous by the moment. Maybe it was not a good idea.

She stood up. "Why, it's little white girl!" She saw my face. "Okay, I'll stop. You're no one's little girl anymore." I handed her the giant coffee cup. "And thank you and not just for the coffee."

"How are you doing?"

She gave me a look that said it all. Not good.

"Hoping and praying." A tiny smile. "And harassing the doctors of course."

I smiled back. "Goes without saying."

"So come on in. Do you want to see my Savanna?"

"I don't know. Do I?" But the look in her eyes told me I did. Because she needed another live person tonight, sharing.

Savanna was motionless under her cover and hooked up to machines, bandaged around her head and one arm. Her pretty face was swollen and bruised in an array of colors.

"It was worse." She said it calmly. "The bruises are fading a bit now. I tell myself that means she is getting better." She shrugged. "Hoping it is true and afraid to hope, both. Know what I mean?"

I nodded.

"You can say hi to her. They tell me, the docs and mostly, the nurses, that people hear even when they are like…like this. Or a stroke or whatnot. Or maybe they do. So it's good to keep talking. Let them know they are not alone and keep their brains working. I been telling her every story I could think of but I'm running out."

She smiled sheepishly. "I've taken to reading her celebrity magazine stories. Yes, I have! I never would let her have them in the house. What is a smart girl doing with that nonsense?" Her eyes filled with tears. "If she can ever read again, I'm subscribing to every one for her. You don't want to know the latest on Beyonce, do you?"

I almost laughed at that.

"No, I am not kidding! I know it all. But please don't tell anyone."

I swallowed hard. "Hey, Savanna. It's Erica Donato. We met at the library and you were super helpful." I turned to Zora. "Should I tell her about what I'm working on?"

"Why not?"

So I went on for awhile, a monologue in a soft voice, in a scary setting. I talked about work. I talked about my daughter. I talked about college, not that I really knew much about going away to school. There was no response but the occasional flicker of her eyelids. They did not open.

Zora stood on the other side of the bed, holding her daughter's hand, and sometimes responding to what I said.

When I couldn't talk anymore I turned to Zora. "Now I need coffee. Can I get some for you too?"

"The coffee from the machine is nasty stuff. I've already learned that." She rubbed the space between her eyes. "I don't think I had supper. Let's go to the cafeteria."

A cup of coffee and a stale muffin for me, a cup of coffee and steam-table mac and cheese for her. She only ate a few bites before she put her fork down. "Bad choice. I'm too stressed to eat this gooey stuff."

"Can I get you some fruit?"

I came back with a banana and an apple. She ate them both, barely noticing what she had, but after, she looked less drained.

I was somewhat uncomfortable. No, strike that. Very uncomfortable. I didn't know her that well. I barely knew her at all. What was appropriate for me to say? Or helpful? So I went for direct and blunt.

"What are the doctors saying?"

"They have some hopes here. Special machines. Special therapy even now." She shrugged. "Who the hell really knows?"

Okay. What now?

"How did the demonstration seem to you? Was it at all useful?"

"It gave me something to do. Focus on. Know what I mean? And there was plenty of anger around the neighborhood, like always, and this gave a focus for that too. Will it do anything? Who knows? Some folks are planning another demonstration at City Hall." She looked at me with a mocking smile. "Want to come?"

"What are they demonstrating for? Or against?"

"Better policing, seems like, or less policing, or both. They haven't quite worked it out. When you live in Brownsville, believe it, you've got your choice of police issues." She shook her head. "I'm not involved in that. I was really just trying to see if it rooted out anyone who knows what happened to Savanna. Just trying to make a noise." She smiled for real. "I happen to be good at that."

"You sure are. You've got that, I don't know? Presence? Plus a voice."

"Yeah, I can go loud if need be. It all comes in handy in a lecture hall. I'm teaching college now. I never need a mic in the classroom and none of those kids give me any attitude."

"What? Wait—you're teaching?"

"Yeah. Lecturing at Kingsboro and Medgar Evers, both." She smiled at me. "Sociology. Yeah, true. After that bad class we took together I felt challenged to do it right." She stared off as if going a long way back. "Me and Savvie used to sit around the kitchen table, doing our homework together. She was such a bright candle in my life. Is. She IS a bright candle. One more year of teaching. That's all it would take, one more, and I would have enough saved to move us out of the projects for good. My little Wellesley girl could come back to a clean new home on a safe, clean street." Her eyes filled with tears. She angrily wiped them away with a napkin and stood up quickly. "Time for me to go back. I don't like to leave her alone too much."

"Are you staying the night?"

"Chair makes up into a bed. Not really comfortable for a tall woman like me, but she's only been here a couple of days. It seems like a pretty good place but I want to be around."

As we approached Savanna's room, we saw a skinny young man step out, pull up his sweatshirt hood, look both ways and turn down the hall.

"What the hell?"

Chapter Thirteen

He heard Zora's shout and began to run. She shouted again, calling for security, and then gasped and ran into Savanna's room. I was right behind.

Savanna was just as we left her, under the covers, hooked to all the machines, breathing lightly, unharmed.

Zora was breathing hard, almost to a panic attack. "I got so scared. So scared. What if...what if..." By then a nurse was in the room, checking everything and I stepped out, out of the way.

A security guard was walking toward the room, wanting to talk to Zora, and—when he realized I was right there—to me.

But what could I tell him? What happened? There wasn't much to say. Someone had been in Savanna's room without anyone's permission. Could I describe him? It was a boy. Probably. But could have been a girl, and even, maybe, a small adult. Race? I hadn't really seen his face but I had seen his hands as he ran. Dark? Height? Short. Clothes? Dark pants, dark hoodie. Build? Thin.

The guard looked disappointed, edging into disgusted, and I couldn't blame him. Zora had nothing to add, and no, she had no idea who it was.

"I didn't even get a good look at his face, but he didn't look familiar from the back. All I know is he was here in my baby's room, alone, with no permission from anyone. How in hell did that happen when a girl was beaten half to death? Anyone could come by to finish the job. She is not supposed to have visitors at all except me and who I bring."

Her shaken, whispery voice got louder. "What kind of security do you have here, anyway? Did you catch him?"

"No, ma'am. He was real fast and I was at the other end of the corridor. By the time I heard the shouting he'd jumped into an elevator and was gone."

The guard was big and uniformed, but she clearly had him cowed. He was apologizing all over the place and promised his boss would come talk to her in the morning.

Zora accepted that, not graciously, and then collapsed onto the chair, fanning herself. "Goodness, I was scared. But all's well that ends well, I suppose." She chuckled, faintly. "That kid in uniform sure got an earful from me. And I'll be having a conversation tomorrow with his boss, you can bet on that."

She looked over at me, almost as if she'd forgotten I was there. "You can go home now. I am going to put on my night things and catch some sleep." She shook her head. "Sorry if that sounds rude. I'm running on empty about now."

"I got it. Go sleep."

I walked out through the lobby, and then walked back in. I had seen something. Maybe. Maybe I had seen something, a kid, sitting on a bench, facing the elevator. Hood up, face down in a magazine. He was not turning the pages.

There were lots of people coming and going. I was sure he had not noticed me noticing him. I wanted to keep it that way so I moved away from his line of vision while keeping him in mine, and approached a guard. I whispered the story of the intruder running from Savanna's room, and he nodded and silently sent a text. "Calling upstairs, where you were. I'll get someone down to look at him."

While we waited, the boy never moved. Was he asleep?

The elevator doors opened to disclose another guard, and also Zora. The two men motioned her to stand back, with me as they approached the box. Then they very quietly moved to stand near the boy. He never noticed when one of them dropped into the seat next to him, but he jumped when a large hand grasped his arm.

"I need you to come with me, son."

The hood was down and we saw him at last, a skinny kid with frightened eyes. They darted this way and that, looking for a way to get out, but he soon saw there was no chance with a guard on either side.

They motioned to Zora and me to follow them and we went to an office off the lobby.

"Ma'am, could you identify him as the boy you saw leaving your daughter's room? Or Ms....?"

"Donato. And I would say maybe. We never saw his face, so it's hard to say, but the build is right, and clothes are the same. Of course any kid could be wearing a black hoodie and black pants."

"He looked familiar to me," Zora said. "What she said about tonight. I kind of remember his shoes, every kid is obsessed with having the right shoes, but there's something else." She was staring intently at him. "I seen him somewhere. Check his ID and I bet you find him in Brownsville." He started at that.

"Yeah, I got you, don't I? Right out of the hood. Kind of a long way from home, ain't you?"

He shut his mouth in a grim line but his hands were shaking.

"Now I want to know what you doing in my little girl's room." While her speech became more ghetto as she talked, her voice grew louder. In the small room, she was approaching gospel preaching volume. "If you know something about her, you best get ready to start talking. And if you don't, what in hell you doing there?"

The guards were looking very concerned, and double teamed her, to get her calm and seated.

Good thing, too. She looked ready to blow up. The guards looked determined and the kid looked terrified. I don't know how I looked, but certainly I was motivated by curiosity. What in the world would happen next?

A guard sat up close, looking right into his face. "You are going to be talking to cops because they will be very interested in how you know Ms. Lafayette's daughter."

"Aren't you cops?"

"No, you moron. You can think of us as cops here in the hospital but we are private security officers. Our job right now is to figure out what this has to do with keeping the hospital safe. If you help us out here, it might go better for you when cops show up."

"Nothin'." He mumbled.

"What you say?"

"Nothin'. I'm not saying nothin'."

Zora stepped over to him and peered into his face.

"You stupid little kid. You think you're a man, hanging tough? You think wearing your pants down to your knees and a gang tattoo—oh, yeah, I see it—you think that makes you a man? Someone beat up my girl and if you know anything at all, you better speak up. You know what jail is like?"

He shook his head, terrified.

"You being tough now? You have no idea how fast you gonna crumble like a cookie."

"I wasn't doing anything." He whispered it. "I went to see how she doing, that's all. I know her a little bit, but my..." He stopped himself and shut his mouth in a tight line.

I was keeping close to the corner of the room, hoping no one would remember I was still there. Probably I shouldn't have been.

One guard turned to me while the other kept a wary eye on both the boy and Zora.

"You the person who saw him first?"

"Yes."

"And who are you in this?"

"I was keeping Zora—Ms. Lafayette—company in her daughter's hospital room."

"Okay, you stick around. Cops on their way, they might send you straight home or want to talk to you some more."

Cops were there almost before he finished, and the small room suddenly became even more crowded.

The officer seemed to be acquainted with the guards who filled him in.

"I need to figure out if we are moving this to the precinct or a private room here—you got one for us?—or arrest this kid. You!"

The kid looked up, fearful but determined.

"You ready to tell us a story?"

He shook his head. "Didn't do nothin'."

"That would be a matter of opinion. Mostly mine. Being up in Savanna's room, you were trespassing at least. You ever heard of something called a material witness?"

He shook his head.

"Hand over some ID and quit wasting my time. I really don't like that at all. And you really don't want me to be angry at you so soon." His voice was calm but his expression said no more fooling around.

I doubted this kid was in danger of being arrested, but thought the threat was having some effect.

The boy reached into his pocket and came out with a school ID.

"Jackie Isiahson. That you?"

He nodded.

"Quite a mouthful, that name. Where do you live?"

Mumble, mumble.

"That's right next to us. Another project. I knew I'd seen you around, you little..."

One of the guards put his hand on Zora's arm and she shook it off, angrily, but did not move closer.

"You hang out with that gang mostly taking over the play-ground at night." She was angry, breathing hard, but turned to the detective and said, "I can give you names of a couple of his dumbass friends. On the record. I bet he's already known to cops out there."

He nodded. "So kid, what are you doing here? Long way from home?"

Young Jackie stared back and the detective looked irritated. Before he made his next move, one of the guards blurted out, "Isiahson? You must be related to Tyler Isiahson!"

"No!" He looked up sharply and turned a few colors. "Am not, never heard of him."

The cop turned to the guard, impatient and annoyed.

"Apologies. I shouldn't have said nothing. I got carried away. That Tyler's the hottest boxer coming up out of Brownsville since Tyson."

The officer turned back to the kid. "No? Unrelated? You saying there are lots of folks in the same neighborhood with that unusual name? Ms. Lafayette, does any of this ring a bell to you?"

"I have more useful things to do than follow boxing. Boxing! And he still hasn't said what he was doing being anywhere near my baby."

"Don't think I overlooked that. So we've got good statements from these two ladies? Ladies, you can go and we are moving this to the precinct. Stand up, kid." In an instant he was being marched out the door. "We are going for a ride."

Zora stood up. "I'm coming too. I want an answer. And my friend is coming with me." She stood tall and straight, a woman who was not taking no for an answer, but her eyes were begging me to agree with her.

"No, you're not. And Ms. Donato, you're not either." He sounded deeply irritated and not a little surprised. "You can't be in the interview room. Even this kid has some rights. Besides, you'd only be in the way."

She took a deep breath. "But there is something I can do. I have Savanna's friends in my phone now. I can text them all, asking if they know him." She made a dismissive gesture. "Don't tell me that wouldn't be useful."

"You can wait in the lobby." He looked exasperated. "But you get there on your own dime, not in a patrol car."

We could walk it. Zora walked fast; I could hardly keep up. She wasn't talking. I wasn't sure why I was coming along, but I was swept up in the moment.

Finally she said, "Sorry, I've been lost in thought. I really, really don't like that he was in her room. Who the hell is he, to be visiting her like that? And lurking after? You saw him in the waiting area. He was lurking, wasn't it?"

"Yes, I'd say so. He was watching the elevator."

"To see when I came down? So he could go back?" Her voice started to crack. "Who could possibly hate my baby so much? And why him? I don't believe she even knew him, that pitiful excuse for a man."

And then I wondered what other secrets Savanna might have. Did this connect with what Deandra had told me? Could this twerp be the confident Savanna's secret boyfriend? Not a chance.

I took a deep breath. "Do you believe you knew everything about her life?"

She stopped dead in the middle of the sidewalk. "Mostly, I do. I mean, she's at school and it's a magnet school, too, so her friends are from all over Brooklyn. I wanted her to know there's a world outside of her 'hood, you know? So I'm not there following her every day. But I know where she went and with whom and what time she was coming home. She knew not to mess with a curfew. And all her school activities too. Everything I can be sure about, I did."

I was not so sure and I could see that now she was not either.

She gave a decisive nod. "We go to the precinct—lord, I hate being there but I want to hear anything they learn right away. And I have a phone picture of that Jackie. Off it goes to her best friends."

"What if they know but won't tell?"

"Next step is I go and beat on their doors. They will be more scared of me than whatever else is stopping them." She smiled. "There are some good things about being a tall woman. Intimidation does come naturally."

I remembered her in class, all those years ago. She was telling the truth about that.

We sat in the uncomfortable chairs in the waiting area. She worked her phone, and I watched for the emergence of the detective, took notes, read the book I carried, sent a note to Chris.

I wondered how I could tell this hard-working, desperately worried woman that her daughter had a few secrets? To be honest, that conversation was a scary thought.

"Did she ever mention a friend called Deandra?"

"Mmm." She was still busy texting. "Mm, no. Not that I…" She finally looked up. "From the library?"

"Yes. Younger? A nervous kid?"

Zora shrugged and went back to her phone. "She kind of adopted her. Not much of a home life there, I heard."

I took the plunge. "She told me something about Savanna you might not know."

"*What* did you say?" She wasn't looking at her phone now.

"After Savanna…I was there at the library and she had something on her mind. She was anxious to just tell someone and she chose me."

"You? Why was that?" She did not look friendly.

"I was safe, I guess. She thought I wouldn't tell anyone in her world."

"Give it up or I go scare it out of her myself."

I looked right at her for a minute, not saying anything, and she started to crumble.

"Deandra? Oh, no. Oh, hell. Is she that little girl they found…? I heard about it. Oh, no. Poor baby. I did meet her a time or two." She straightened up. "Now. Are you going to tell me what she said?"

So I did.

"I don't believe that. I would know. She must have got it wrong somehow." I had the sense to keep quiet. In a more subdued voice, she said, "Was that all? She didn't say anything else?"

"No, not a thing. Just that it was a secret, that you would not like it." She made a sound of annoyance. "And that he had people who would not like it either. I don't know what that meant."

She put her face down in her hands and didn't move. When she looked up, her first words were, "It couldn't be that kid could it, that Jackie?" She looked at me and suddenly started laughing. We both did.

"That kid with Savanna? That's not possible, is it? Nooo!" For a minute, we were helpless with laughter. Then we stopped as suddenly as we had started.

"I have to think about this. I always thought…and I hoped… but girls will be girls." She smiled wryly. "How do you think I got Savanna?"

"And I want to tell that cop." She stood up. "I wonder how we contact him on the other side of that door?" She began a discussion with the desk sergeant and I thought about calling it a night.

The cop emerged. He didn't seem too excited by my information but agreed it might pry something out of young Jackie.

"We probably can't hold him, you know." He sounded apologetic. "He didn't really do anything."

"You think he was in Savanna's room to bring her flowers? Come on! You let him go and he'll most likely try again, whatever he was up to."

"Then next time we'll catch him at it. We'll be watching."

"Oh, hell no. I'm staying right here until I know something."

I went home though, luckily hopping a bus to take me from one end of the neighborhood to the other. Chris was already asleep and I collapsed on my bed.

Sometime in the night my phone pinged, but I didn't get up. No one was calling me. Just a text. I went back to sleep. Maybe I even dreamed it.

In the morning I knew it was no dream. I had a photo on my phone. I couldn't tell who sent it. It was a handle that didn't look like a name, and that I didn't recognize. But I knew the location. It was where we had found Deandra. There were some modest flowers wrapped in paper, or single blossoms, obviously from a corner deli; a teddy bear; balloons. It was an impromptu memorial for an unexpected death.

Chapter Fourteen

I had a date. Nothing as exciting as breakfast out, let alone any more intensive form of fun. I was expected at the Municipal Archives at ten sharp. Many subways converge there in downtown Manhattan. Parking is really not possible during the day unless I was prepared to pay a garage the equivalent of a week's groceries and perhaps including my right arm. I was on the way to the subway stop in good time, properly loaded with laptop and the no-tech backup, a notebook and pens.

I hurtled down the station steps to the sound of an incoming train, slid in a second before the doors closed, and twenty crowded minutes later, I was getting off at my stop, a few blocks from my destination. It's a non-descript part of the city, north of the interesting tip of Manhattan, filled with drugstores, bank branches, sandwich shops, cheap clothing, all services for the army of office workers from nearby towers. With no temptation to explore, I arrived ten minutes early. That could be a first in my over-scheduled life.

I think my mouth dropped open when I went in. I expected a plain, cheap, mass-produced office building. What I found was a vast lobby, with marble pillars and a riot of carving painted in pastels. The soaring staircases criss-crossed each other in an elaborate pattern. What in the world had this been originally? I would have to find out, but not today.

Today I went through a metal detector and down a hall into the modest space of the Department of Records library.

Labeled archival boxes were out on a sturdy wooden table, ready for my attack. And here was a copied page from a request-tracking sheet. Well, well, well. With a name and the information for these very boxes. James Nathan. The name still meant nothing to me, but I would look further. The page disappeared into my backpack for safekeeping.

And I dug in. It was a true scholarly effort. I had questions I wanted to ask these pages. These criminals' own testimony about their activities would tell me a lot about them and how they saw their worlds and their careers. At least I hoped so. Personal memories about the time and place often conflicted, and were shaded by emotion. Here was the testimony, on the record.

Of course I had to consider that criminals, even under oath, probably lied with every word, claiming innocence when they were guilty, ignorance when they were right there, and importance that existed only in their own minds.

Besides answers to my prepared questions, there is this in searching in any collection of documents: you never know what you might find. That's part of the fun. Of course, sometimes those discoveries derailed lots of work, too. That situation was key in a famous mystery novel I had read many years ago.

I sat at the table, looking at the boxes and thinking, "This could be an entire thesis, right here. And it's just a chapter of mine. What have I done? I don't even know how to get started. And where can I get more coffee?"

And then I did get started, because I did know how, once I got past my panic. There were finding aides, which meant a guide to the boxes, and one for each folder within, all very methodical. Each folder listing had a name, a date, and a few phrases to indicate what was held. I started at the end, hoping to find the summaries of the trial, and then I looked for some of the Brownsville names I had—the notorious Gurrah Shapiro; Lepke Buchalter; Kid Twist Reles, the guy who betrayed everyone; Pep Strauss, also known as Pittsburgh Phil and a few other names; Louis Capone, not related to the more famous Capone but in the same line of work. They were mentioned in many places but I wanted their own testimony, their own words, to give me some idea about what created them.

And their own words would liven up that chapter. Who says a dissertation has to be boring?

I looked up after three hours, my eyes bleary and fingers itching from the unavoidable dust. My biggest conclusion was that these were very boring human beings. I should have guessed that. You can't be a person who kills for a living and have a lot of imagination.

And most of these guys, however vicious their actions, were not even as high as middle management in "the organization." The old mob leaders like Luciano, Siegel, Lansky, Anastasia, the ones at the top? Were they really smart and innovative "businessmen?" Perhaps. For sure, that was how they wanted to be seen in their lifetime and after. But these hometown Brooklyn gangsters? They were privates in this army.

They had trouble spelling the words in a threatening note. They used a grandfather's funeral as an alibi. They used a dying mother as a way to avoid an assigned job they did not want to do. They said talking about having a conscience was too deep for them. One of them, at least, did not commit crimes on the Sabbath. They methodically mapped out escape routes while planning a job. That job was often murdering someone, and sometimes the someone was a close friend. It didn't bother them. They compared their first killing to a DA giving his first speech in court; you're nervous at first but you get used to it. They followed orders.

Sometimes they sounded like lovable Damon Runyon characters. Until they started describing what they did with a rope and an ice pick.

I wasn't sure whether I had struck gold or pyrites. I was writing a PhD dissertation, not a blockbuster novel. This all might be too exciting. I had pages and pages of notes in my laptop now, right from the source. I would have to run all this by my adviser.

I tidied up the cluttered table, but as directed, left the files for the staff to return to order. I could not work anymore, but on a whim, I did some web surfing on James Nathan, the mysterious researcher of old Brooklyn crime. Nothing. I had an inspiration and wrote it in as Nathan James. Still nothing. There were lots of hits for the name, as it's not uncommon, but none that were useful to me.

So he was not famous in any way. Never been in the news. Had never written anything that was published, whether in a national magazine or a scholarly journal or probably even a college newspaper. Evidently Mystery Man was neither a journalist nor a historian after all. Maybe he was merely a nut with an organized crime fixation.

One last whim. With Lillian's voice in my mind, I skimmed through all the notes to the material, every description for every box and every file, just to see if her brother's name came up anywhere. No, it didn't. That didn't prove he was not in the gang, of course. Maybe he was so obscure he was never mentioned in the testimony. Maybe he was there but not important enough to be listed in the index.

One overpriced deli sandwich later, I was ready to think about the rest of the day. With my mind filled with gangster names and stories of old Brownsville, I would hop on the train, spend the long trip organizing what I'd learned today, and go look at some of the real places I'd been reading about. And not beat myself up about why I had not had all this completely organized the first time I went there to look around. It's a process, period. Sometimes you need a second look. That's what I said.

I had the exact location of the Moonlight Min Candy Store, the corner of Livonia and Saratoga. The back room there had been the Murder Inc. headquarters. They certainly weren't putting any of their profits into a luxury workspace. And I wondered how Min felt about it all? I'd been intrigued to learn today that there was a real Min and she was a criminally inclined tough old broad herself, nobody's moll. Not a kept woman in any sense, but a female who fit right in with the big boys. She deserved a sidebar all her own. Or maybe she was a potential article subject. Not exactly a feminist example, not even a little, but women who defied, or ignored, the norms for their gender are always interesting.

My mind was speeding ahead with the speeding train, and I jotted it all down.

One more look around and then maybe I was done with Brownsville. I could write this chapter and move on.

The candy shop was easy to find. It's right next to the station stairs. That was one of its desirable qualities in the old days, good transportation and on a busy corner. What it was then—and I knew because I'd seen old pictures—was the kind of all-purpose candy/stationery/soda fountain shop that was already disappearing from most of New York when I was a kid. You could get a birthday card for your mom, a box of candy for the wife on Valentine's Day, the afternoon paper, take your girl for a malted, use the pay phones.

At Min's, in the back room, you could also place a bet with a bookie or pick up a game of pinochle, if you were so inclined and if Min let you. And order up a mob hit along with your sundae.

Now it was a mini-mart. No soda fountain, but you could buy bottled soda and beer and a quart of milk, plus a box of diapers or condoms or cigarettes. *The Daily News.* Hit the ATM for cash and buy a legal state lottery ticket.

The hatch in the sidewalk, allowing deliveries to be slid right into the basement, was still there and looked old enough to be original, but the front of the building had different windows, mostly covered with signs listing all the food stamp programs that were accepted. It was shabby and sad, and probably always was, but the old pictures did have a bit of the quaintness time brings.

Then I gave myself a mental slap. Was I a scholar or a nostalgic tourist? Old-fashioned Coca Cola sign above the door notwithstanding, this was never quaint.

I took some photos with my phone from the safety of the other side of the street, safe enough with people coming and going to the train and other stores. Finally I went across and looked in the windows. A shabby but legitimate business. I went in boldly and bought a soda to justify my presence. People went in and out, making the small purchases that keep this kind of business alive. Barely. Another reason to wonder if there wasn't still some action in the back, perhaps drugs for sale.

No one that I saw went into the back room. Cartons from a beverage distributor blocked the entrance.

The woman behind the counter was ethnically unplaceable, with tan skin, long black hair, T-shirt decorated with a picture of a singer. Latina? South Asian? Arab? When I tried to ask about the back room she didn't seem to understand, and responded, "No, no. Back? No!" I couldn't place her accent. Not Spanish. In Spanish I might have muddled through. I didn't believe she didn't understand me.

I didn't believe it even more when I was hidden at the back, browsing, and heard a customer ask what kind of diapers were on sale. She said clearly, "We got that no-name brand, and Huggies are also reduced this week."

I went out and looked around. There was a kind of alley along the back. Probably where they kept trashcans, I thought.

And then I did a stupid thing. I walked around the corner and into the alley. Maybe I could see through a window into the back room.

The only window was covered with a metal security screen and too high for me to see in. There was a door, metal, no windows, no doorknob, no way to get in from the outside short of a blowtorch. I was not learning a thing here. Time to go.

I turned and almost bumped into someone right behind me. Way too close behind me.

It was that derelict-looking white guy I had spotted before. Scary clothes, smelling of alcohol, a large open bottle of Colt .45 in one hand. A knife in the other.

"You." He seemed to have trouble focusing. With visible effort, he tried again. "You. Go away. My place. Mine." And he waved the knife at me.

Even in my fog of fright, I could see it was a jackknife. Really? I thought in one tiny corner of my mind. You want to be a menace in the hood, and you're using a jackknife. A jackknife?

On the other hand, I did not want to find out if it was still sharp enough to do damage.

I held up both hands so he could see I was unarmed. I took one tiny step away from him.

"I didn't mean to trespass." A blatant lie. Of course I was trespassing. "Not on your space. I didn't know. And I'm very sorry. I'll go now."

"You could have stolen my things. I have important things here." Stubborn. "I keep them hidden." But his eyes shifted slightly and I saw the clean plastic garbage can with a chain around it and two enormous padlocks.

"Well, do you see any place I could have hidden anything?" I turned slightly, just enough to show him my backpack. I sure didn't want to turn my back on him. "See?"

He stared and stared, and then he lowered the knife and stepped aside. A wave of his knife hand pointed me to the entrance of the alley. I left as quickly as I could. I didn't break into a run until I was out of his sight. His parting words, shouted behind me, were "Don't come back. Or I'll get you good!"

My brain said he was in no shape to harm me. My adrenaline said, "Even if he's a strung-out junky, he could be vicious. And unpredictable. Move!"

I didn't stop until I was around the corner, under the elevated train tracks. There were stores nearby and some foot traffic. I felt safe there, though that might have been a fantasy. In one of the highest crime rate neighborhoods in the city, would anyone come to my aid if he did follow me? There was not a cop in sight.

When I could breathe again, and stopped shaking, I reached for the soda I had bought, and realized I must have dropped it in the alley. Damn.

I looked around the intersection. A boarded-up pharmacy. An old freestanding news dealer kiosk, also boarded up. A couple of bars not boarded up. And there was another tiny market where I could replace my soda before going home. I hoped the sugar would calm my inner shaking; on the outside, I put on my street face, the one that says, "Don't mess with me."

Soda in my hand, leaning against the wall outside the shop, nobody gave me a second look. I guessed I was not the only one on the street with shaking hands, gulping down a drink.

I had one more thing to do before I left the neighborhood. I wanted to go see for myself the improvised memorial to Deandra. I knew where it was. Right there where I had found her. Under all my busy, ordinary activities, that picture never fully left my mind.

I walked carefully this time, alert to any activity near me. It wasn't hard to find. Even though all the buildings in a project look the same, I remembered where we were going that day. I stood there, silent, for a long time. There were more balloons but the flowers were starting to look frayed. I wished I had brought some.

No one was there but me, and then I sensed someone standing behind me.

A cracked, old lady voice. "What you here for? You the white lady who was here that day?"

I turned. She looked grandmother age, wrapped in a heavy sweater over her shabby dress, misshapen canvas sneakers on her feet, scarf over her gray hair. Squinting eyes.

"Well? I asked you."

"Yes. Yes, I am."

"You knew her? Dee?"

"I met her once. Nice girl."

"She was that. I knowed her all her life. I be her aunt." She stopped. "Kind of like her aunt. Long story. That child needed some mothering." She looked away from me. "I stepped up."

I had no words. All I could find was "I'm so sorry."

"Young people get in trouble. Or trouble finds them." She shook her head. "Poor baby."

I was so uncomfortable, I said the first thing that came to my mind. "How is her mother doing?"

"How you think? She sobbing and wailing. Begging for money to pay for a funeral that she not making any plans for." She made a face. "She easing the pain just like always. Lots of people give her what she want, for a price. You know?"

I nodded. I understood.

"I need to go now." I fell back on what I'd said before. "I'm so sorry."

After I turned away, the old lady spoke out loud. To me? To herself? To the air around us? "Baby girl had secrets worrying her."

I turned back. "What did you say?"

"Secrets." She stepped back from me. "She had secrets."

"She told me one, but not enough. Did you know what was on her mind? It might help police solve this."

"Police? Po-leece??? They don't care. They ain't gonna make a move and they ain't talking to me." She stopped and thought it over. "They came around but didn't find me. And I ain't talking to them either."

What if I argued with her, made her see it my way?

As if reading my mind, she said, "Ain't gonna bring her back." She walked away, just like that.

It blew my earlier scary incident right out of my mind. I did turn back to the train then, saddened by the old lady, more saddened by what she'd said about Deandra's mother. I was trying hard not to judge what I did not know enough about, not fully succeeding, and wishing Deandra had told me a little bit more that day she felt like confiding.

They came out of nowhere. I was walking along and there they were in front of me, two of the boys who'd accosted me at the library. And the weird guy I'd met earlier.

They stood across the sidewalk. I had no way to keep moving. Could I go the other way, and outrun them? Not bloody likely.

"Don't even think it." I hadn't said it out loud, or moved, but the leader must have read my mind. He stepped closer, right into my space. "Let's take a walk."

"I'm not going anywhere with you."

He didn't say a word, just smiled.

His friend was there now, holding my arm.

"We walk there, behind the building."

I was too scared to move my feet, but somehow we ended

up there, in a sheltered corner. Even if anyone came along, it was doubtful if they would see us. Or think about it if they did. "Street face!" I told myself silently. "Street face." And I tried to straighten up.

"We not intending to hurt you," he said. In all this time, the others had not said a word. "Not now. But me and my man, Jimmy N. here—" he hooked an arm about the blond man's neck—"me and my man have plans for that building. So you stay away, hear?"

I squeaked it out. "You mean the store on the corner?"

"Well, duh. Where you were today? Yeah. Stay the fuck away. We need to never see you there again."

"I was only buying a soda."

"You were snooping in my place." So he could still talk, that blond guy. He sounded indignant. "You have no reason to be there. Stay away."

"Don't matter even if she do have some b.s. reason. We gave a real solid reason not to. Our place now."

I nodded, afraid I couldn't get any words out.

"You got that?" He let his jacket open a little so I could see the gun in his belt. "You not interfering with what we doing no more?"

I nodded again.

He jerked his head toward the end of the building.

"Now bounce. Don't look back."

And bounce I did, walking as fast as I could, around the corner of one building and then another, till I could be sure I was not in their sight. Unless they followed me. I peeked around. No one.

It wasn't until a long time later, safe at home, that it hit me. They'd called him Jimmy N. James Nathan?

That was ridiculous, I told myself sternly. I was way over-reaching. There was something not right about that guy. And why was he hanging around this very unsavory neighborhood? That alone was off base. Unless he was buying drugs every day.

It was impossible to imagine him having focus enough to get on the subway, get himself to a city building, get admitted in his filthy clothes. Do research. Focus enough to read for hours.

So my thought was ridiculous. And anyway, it didn't matter. I was done with my Brownsville research.

But still.

The next day, it still seemed absurd and it still bothered me. I called Jennifer at the Archives and asked her straight out, "Did you see the person, this James Nathan, who wanted to see the same records I did?"

"I did, for a minute when he signed in. Why? What is going on?"

I sighed. "Probably nothing. It's just that, well, maybe he and I could be helpful to each other? If we're working in the same subject area? You know? And I am trying to track him down. He doesn't show up anywhere. But maybe I met him somewhere? Sometime?" Not altogether the truth, but close. "What's he like?"

"He was polite, very soft voice. He didn't sound like a professor but he wasn't even as weird as some of the other people who come in here. Trust me on that."

"Wearing normal clothes?"

"Oh, sure. Nothing stands out so he must have been."

"Anything about his hair? Beard?"

"Erica! What is this? Did you find hidden treasure or something in those files?"

"I'm sorry. I'm still thinking he might be someone I already know, that's all."

"Oh, sure. Sure he might." I didn't miss the sarcasm. "If I tell you, will you tell me what you're really doing?"

"Yes. Over dinner next week one night?"

"Nothing I noticed about his hair. Clean shaven. Blondish. You want his weight, height and age too?"

"You don't have his shoe size?"

"I was kidding."

"I knew that." I sighed. "Me too."

"He was maybe fortyish? Five eight or so. Totally non-descript. Average everything. Dinner next Wednesday? I'm partial to sushi."

"You're on."

Right size. Right coloring. Right age. Exactly like a million or so men in New York. And everything else was wrong.

Chapter Fifteen

Late at night. I couldn't sleep. There was too much information, too many questions, too much sadness running around in my brain and I was failing completely at turning it off.

I finally decided the cure was getting some work done. It was a good plan but I sabotaged it by looking at Facebook first.

On Savanna's page I spent some time scrolling through the long list of comments. They poured out sympathy and support. Most mentioned prayer. Some offered interesting anecdotes and memories about Savanna. After a little while it began to feel uncomfortably like a memorial page. And there was no real news. Zora's last update merely said she was stable.

And just before I was ready to admit this was pointless I was caught by one more comment. "Savanna not the lil angel y'all think. She getting up to plenty and taking what don't belong to her." It was signed StarrGurl.

I was genuinely shocked by the cruelty. Not that I did not know some people love to spew out hate, especially on social media where you always feel anonymous. I'd have to be a deaf moron not to know the modern meaning of the word troll.

I sent a note off to Mike asking if he thought the detective team was looking at this page and would pick up that name. And could they trace it? He wrote right back, asking me what I was doing on e-mail at three AM and adding of course they are and would and can.

And then, because what happens at three AM is not real life, it is dreamtime, I read all the other comments StarrGurl had put up. When I was done, I wished I hadn't.

She sounded like a teenager. After I got past the slang and the profanity, the abbreviations and the emoticons, I could see that every word she wrote was steeped in resentment. I didn't have to be a teenager to know this was not about a missing sweater.

As I was looking at the screen, moving around, jumping here and there, trying not to lose track, one more post from StarrGurl popped up right in front of me. "Oh, ha! They picked up Jackie Eye, that baby wanna be, trying to see skanky thief. What he up to? And got let out cause he not a N who hollers. Maybe he trying to give a message?"

This made a little sense. Maybe. Honestly, I wanted to smack this anonymous twit.

I was starting to feel sleepy at last, but I made a quick click over to Zora's page. She was in despair.

My baby not much better. Not much worse. Tonight her fingers move and I get all excited. They say it don't mean a thing, only a kind of reflex. They say, all these medical people that she is doing ok, but I don't see it. I don't see it. My whole world now is this hospital room. And nothing new on finding who did this, either. Cops had those boys been bothering her, then let them go. Than they had a kid who CAME TO HER ROOM. No reason for him to be there a-tall. And they let him go. I need to tell my Savvie no one will hurt her again. When can I do that?"

There were some responses from other night owls. I didn't know there were so many of us.

Now my eyes really were closing. I barely made it back to bed. And then my phone was ringing. I squinted at the number. It was Joe.

"I'm working on your block today. Do you want breakfast? I'm going to get some for myself."

"Just woke up," I mumbled. "What time is it?" I squinted at my clock, unable to focus.

"It's nine-thirty, young lady. I've been at work for two hours already. Were you out late on a spree last night?"

"Uh, no. Not at all." I tried to focus. "Bring breakfast here? When?"

"Soon. Fifteen minutes?"

I agreed and stumbled off to splash water in my face, brush my teeth, replace my pajamas that looked like workout clothes with actual workout clothes.

I found a note from Chris, stuck on the bathroom mirror. "You seemed so tired, I didn't wake you. Left for school."

When Joe rang my bell, my eyes were open and my hair was brushed. It was a fair imitation of being awake. I could smell the coffee and bacon-and-egg-sandwiches right through the wrappings. I was glad to see him. I thought I was. Perhaps I was not awake enough to know how I felt.

"Here." He handed me my coffee. "Drink. Eat. Don't try to talk until you are fueled." I suspected he was laughing at me. I didn't care, because he was the guy who came bringing coffee. It was still hot.

I sank into my kitchen chair, drinking and unwrapping my sandwich. Joe, restless, wandered around my kitchen that he had built.

"How's the garbage disposer working? All right since I fixed it?"

"Mmm-hm." I sucked down my coffee.

"Cabinets look good." Doors were opened and closed.

"Dishwasher holding up okay?"

Slurping sounds. And chewing. I ate the sandwich right from the waxed paper wrapping. Joe helped himself to a mug, a plate and a knife and fork for his. He was a better host than I was.

Finally I was able to smile at him. "What have you been up to?

"Same old. I'm about done with that building I showed you.

We have a walkthrough later today, get the punch list and send some of my guys over."

"How nice that you have 'my guys.' To send hither and yon." Now it was me laughing at him. "Is that like 'my people talk to your people'?"

He raised an eyebrow. "Did you get that from a TV show? But yes, it is exactly like that."

We chatted, but he seemed quieter than usual and I was not entirely awake. Finally fed and caffeinated my brain switched to on. "Joe, you are a sports fan, right?"

"I follow a few teams, sure. Why?"

"A few teams? Giants, Knicks. Yankees? And Tour de France still?"

"Don't forget tennis. Yeah, you got me. It's more than a few." He looked at me quizzically. "Since when are you interested? You barely know one from the other."

"Unfair. I knew them when I was a kid!" I left out the part about wasting time. "But you are getting me sidetracked."

He looked amused, but I plowed on.

"Boxing." I took another gulp of my coffee. A big one. "I want to ask if you know anything about boxing."

"Some. I might watch it if I have nothing else to do. Why?"

"I need to know something."

"Of course you do."

"Ha. Very funny." I stopped, concentrating on breakfast. "And?"

"There's supposedly a local boxer who is terrific, a real up-and-comer. Name of Isiahson. Do you know anything about him?"

"There's buzz. It's been a long time since there was a real American boxer that good. Why?"

I looked away, not answering. If I told him the whole story, one, we'd be there all morning, and two, he would disapprove.

"You could find out a whole lot by typing his name in a Web search bar." He smiled. "Aren't you supposed to be good at this?"

"I *am* good at it. I just happened to think of it while you are here. And I shouldn't be investing a lot of time into it, either.

So I'm doing it the old-fashioned way and asking a live person. My source for guy stuff."

"Am I? Should I be flattered?" Now he was definitely laughing at me.

"Of course! Just like Leary is my source for Brooklyn unwritten history. And Darcy for finding whoever is needed to get a job done."

"Your dad?"

"Uh, let me think. Yes, yes! Best route for getting anyplace by car. And knowing about a diner wherever that place is."

He did laugh then but also handed me his cutting edge phone and there was a story about Isiahson. He was straight out of a Brownsville project. An old tradition.

Something clicked into place. The part of my brain that had real academic work to do just shook hands with the part that wanted to know more just because. Because it was now. Because real people I knew were involved and damaged. Because two of them were young girls.

I hadn't looked into boxing in the twenties and thirties as a third way out for Brownsville boys. I should have.

"Anyway, I have a friend who is a serious fan. He could tell you what you need."

"Is he a friend from your misspent youth?"

"Not at all. I renovated his house a few years back. Big time lawyer. And he's the kind of guy who likes to always have the inside story on things. Tell him Joe sent you."

"Now you are being silly. If you would..." But he already had his phone out again.

"Archie, it's Joe." "Yeah, too long." "Hell, no, no one is suing me. It's all good." Finally, "I have a young lady here, name of Erica, who has some questions about boxing and of course I thought of you." Listening. "Yeah, sure. Ever been to a Cyclones game? It's not the Yankees but a lot of fun."

He handed me the phone. "Meet Archie."

"Hello?"

"Good morning, Erica. I'm getting ready to head to the office. What would you like to know? In two minutes?"

When I explained, he said, "Oh, hell, yes. The kid is a phenomenon."

"Does he have any family? Any education?"

"Background? I don't exactly know but I could find out. I'm thinking there is a large family. Anything else?

I took the leap. "I don't understand boxing very well. Is it still kind of a sleazy business?"

A long silence, followed by a more thoughtful voice. "There were some sleazy people in it, yes. You know anything about early rock and roll? It's like that. Slick operators and ambitious, naïve, very poor kids are always going to be a bad combination. But overall? It's cleaned itself up a lot. Look, I got to run, but I can find about Isiahson's family. Call me at this number seven sharp tonight."

"Thank you. This is so helpful!"

"Your boyfriend is a buddy. Happy to help out."

He hung up before I had time to correct him about Joe. Maybe I didn't want to.

"You have been a life-saver this morning." I waved my hand over the now littered table.

"I'm thinking of ordering a new business card." His eyes lit up. "It could say Home Renovation. Manly Information. Life Saving. Good idea?"

He was joking but. There was definitely a 'but' in his expression. He was not moving. He was not laughing. He was just waiting, completely calm and completely focused on me. I was thoroughly unnerved.

"Joe, the other night?" I stopped because I had no idea what I wanted to say. "I'm not..." I felt myself turning pink, but he didn't move. "I don't..."

He finally smiled at me. "You're an idiot but you're cute. One day you'll figure it all out. Don't take too long." He stood up. "Duty calls, before a hysterical home owner harasses my guys."

He hugged me at the door and it was not at all brotherly. Which, it seemed, was fine with me. More than fine. Then he was gone and I threw myself back into work. I refused to think about that hug right now. I was sure I did not have the time or energy for a real relationship. And I was sure you cannot go back to being friends if it doesn't work out. And I wasn't even sure if I believed any of that.

The solution was to bury the questions under a blizzard of work.

First, I hit the 'Net for a search on Jackie Isiahson and that up and coming boxer who was, perhaps, his relative. Nothing about Jackie but lots about Tyler. Lots of comparisons to Mike Tyson, not the only boxer out of a Brownsville project but the most famous. One jackpot of an article discussed the history of Brownsville boxers going all the way back to my time. The time I had begun to think of as mine.

So boxing in Brooklyn did have a long history as a road up and out for poor, badly educated young boys. And also, then and now, there was a constant need to defend yourself, defend your friends, or perhaps become the one who threatened. So every day provided lots of fighting practice.

All that was easy to pick up but what I really wanted to know was whether slippery young Jackie was a relative. Now I knew almost everything but that.

Some of the boxing stories, though, sent me back in a productive direction. I would need to add something about boxing to my chapter. The whole topic of the chapter was the choice of crime as a way to grab part of the American dream, in contrast to the way Maurice Cohen and Ruby and Lil and an army of others did it, through education. But apparently boxing was yet a third way. Or perhaps just a slippery false promise, an oasis of fame and fortune, shimmering out there.

And I did have a secret weapon when it came to all things about Brooklyn and its less glamorous walks of life. I went to buy Leary a good meal.

His response to my first question was, "Do I look like an athlete?"

"Hell no. But you do look like someone who liked boozing and smoking cigars at late night events in questionable venues. That might include boxing bouts?"

"You got me there." He was slurping down lo mein using the included chopsticks with surprising dexterity.

"Did you know I wrote a series about boxing gyms?" He put the chopsticks down. "Try drawer seven for the clips. About half way back in the files."

Leary might be a complete slob in every other way, but the second bedroom, his workspace, was immaculate and uncluttered. If he said drawer seven, halfway back, that is where I would find it. Not for the first time, I thought about how revealing this was of what mattered most to Leary.

Right there, files neatly labeled Boxing, Background, and Boxing, Clips, 1955- 1970. I flipped through the articles on great mid-century bouts, Louis and Graziano and LaMotta. And finally, a set of articles from the *Brooklyn Eagle*, bylined J. Leary. about neighborhood boxing gyms. I only recognized one name, Brennan's. It was still around and located in some part of Brooklyn even I could not find.

Leary had fallen asleep after lunch so I got to work. It only took me a minute to fall down the rabbit hole, getting lost in the research, going way beyond what I needed, about a subject in which I had no interest. A whole strange world opened up to me. Time disappeared.

I tackled the background folder. This would cover the period I really needed, the twenties and thirties. So yes, there were many Jewish boxers coming out of Brownsville, including a number of champions. I couldn't help wondering what their poor, immigrant parents thought of this. Were they grateful for the money that put food on the table? Or horrified that their sons chose this violent, foreign road?

And then, as other opportunities opened up after World War II, those young men lost interest in boxing, replaced by a new group of tough, ambitious immigrants from the Deep South.

And now there were newer immigrants, from Asia, the Caribbean and the former Soviet Socialist Republics.

Leary kept up with it, long after he retired. Here was an article from a neighborhood paper about Brennan's moving to Williamsburg, a place I could and would find, and another about young Isiahson. He was big and handsome, all of twenty years old. A stepfather had taken him to his first gym. His mom hated his boxing, he said, but was getting used to it. Yes, he said it; the money was a big help to her.

I turned back to the oldest items, making sure I had not missed anything useful. And it turned out that I had.

There it was, an informal photo of the famous Brownsville boxer, Bernie Rosenblatt. He was dead at thirty-five but he looked like a teenager here. There he was, surrounded by a group of neighborhood friends. They all looked like kids. And one of them looked like Lil's brother.

I said, to Leary, "Wake up, old man. I have questions and then I have to go. Come on, you lazy old thing." But my hand on his shoulder was gentle.

"What?"

"Can I borrow the folders? I'll make copies and bring them right back."

He nodded, still half asleep.

"Come on! I need you to look at some photos. Do you need something? Orange juice? Water? Pills?"

He denied knowing anything at all about most of the photos, but when I showed him the one of Rosenblatt and friends he nodded.

"That's Barach Rosenblatt. They called him Bernie."

"Yes. It says so right there. What about the others?"

"I'm getting there!" He planted a stubby finger on the photo. "Maybe I know who this one was but it's a bad photo. What do you want?" He shrugged. "It was a tabloid newspaper, meant for a quick read on the subway going home after a long day at work, and then used to wrap up the garbage."

He waved his hand over the papers on the table. "You can take the folders, but I want it all back. And soon."

I promised to get his folders back, I thanked him and then I had to go home. Before I opened the door I looked back at Leary. He looked off, too tired for midday, and breathing noisily.

"Are you all right? Is there anything you need me to do for you?"

"Oh, hell no. No more hovering. I won't put up with it. And say hello to Tommy Brennan for me, if he's still kicking around his gym." He winked at me. He knows me too well. In fact I had already called Brennan's gym and I asked if I could talk to someone.

I worried about Leary as I drove away, but then a clueless driver with Florida plates stopped short in front of me, taking his time to figure out where he was. I had to brake, zip around him, then aggressively reclaim my place in heavy traffic. All other thoughts flew away while I had to concentrate. Later, my only thought was "How did my dad do this day in and day out?" I could ask him sometime. I could do that. In the meantime, I was on the way to meet Tommy Brennan.

When I called, I got the man himself and he said, yes, sure, come on over, he wasn't busy. When I mentioned Leary he said, "He that old reporter with the missing leg? Didn't even know he was still around. Yeah, he was pretty smart. And hell raising? Woo. I kept him away from the boys. He was a bad influence."

So off I went, to Williamsburg, the formerly old, rough, industrial community right on the edge of the East River. The abandoned factory buildings, with huge windows and huge space, attracted poor artists, which led to hipster coffeehouses and restaurants, which led to real estate development which led to artists being priced out altogether. A real New York story. Maybe *the* New York story.

Brennan had moved his gym there when no one wanted the derelict buildings and got a whole warehouse building for less than the cost of a new studio apartment now. Did I know this before? Of course not. I learned it from Brennan himself.

He's an old man now and he's turned the gym over to his sons to run. They teach young kids to box and fund the ones who are promising. He told me emphatically they still train professional boxers too. I saw the photos covering one long wall, very young, very muscled men, trying to look fierce and sometimes succeeding. One was labeled Tyler Isiahson.

Brennan said he didn't do a thing now except sit and watch and tell stories but in the hour I was there, he was up five times to correct a boxer or take a teacher aside for a conference.

In between he talked to me.

"So you're interested in boxing? I've been around it my whole life. What do you want to know? I don't remember just what you said on the phone. Are you a reporter?"

"No, not at all. I'm writing a history dissertation about Brownsville in the old days and I've just realized I need to include something about boxing because..."

"Dissertation? Well, well. I can't even spell that word, but you want to talk to me?"

"I do."

"Well, hell, yeah, boxing and Brownsville go together. We've got a different kind of operation now, but if I set up in Brownsville tomorrow I'd have kids pouring in the same day, begging for training."

"That sounds like it's still a poor kid's sport?" I looked around at his gleaming, spotless gym.

"Always was, always will be. Don't need a team to play on, don't need a school, don't need much equipment. And they make good fighters because they are hungry. They all got big dreams."

"How does that work out for most of them? Those dreams?"

"You're kidding, right? Mostly, they don't get far, but a few? They got talent and drive. Plus luck."

"Like Mike Tyson, going back a generation? Bernie Rosenblatt in the old days?"

"You been doing your homework. Yeah, that's it. There were lots more, too." He looked smug when he added, "Now we also get these hotshot Wall Street types, cause they live in this neighborhood. Plus we run a place now that has working show-ers and doesn't smell like sweat, so it's not so much slumming.

"Kind of funny, isn't it?" He shook his head. "We charge them a bundle for the privilege. They're paying for the free kids classes." He winked at me. "Income redistribution.

"How far back you going? I knew some of those great old Brownsville guys back in the day."

"You did? What day was that?"

"When I was a kid gym rat, trying to find a way in to the pros, and they were the geezers. Now that's me."

He told me some stories then. Highly entertaining, some-times scandalous, and none of them useful for my work, but I had at least an idea now about how it all worked back then. And I'd spent more than an hour here, watching young men work out, and get yelled at and work harder. None of them yelled back, tough as they were. Interesting. But I had to wind this up now. A few more questions.

"So exactly how does it all work? Just an example, I've been hearing of this new Brownsville kid, Tyler Isiahson."

"Yeah? He's one of mine."

"So he comes all the way here? How'd you hook up with him?"

"Cause we're always scouting, visiting the other gyms, going to the little bouts to see who might be a comer. Like, Ty started out in a neighborhood place, and they gave him a good start but we knew we could take him further."

"Did you steal him?"

He was amused. "Time was, we would have. All in the game. But that gym owner scouts for me. So we made a deal, money changed hands, and there's no hard feelings."

"Money changed hands? You bought him?"

He looked offended. "We didn't buy *him*. That would be illegal. We bought his contract. And Ty was plenty happy about it. He knew he was going some big steps up the ladder."

"So the first step is basic skills, and the next one is getting a top trainer? And then?"

"Small fights when they're ready. Then bigger ones. And we train, train, train. Keep them working hard. Get them off their turf and maybe even out of town to train. Watch out they don't get caught up in anything that will damage their health. No drinking, no dope, no steroids, or I cut them loose." He stopped. "Nothing we can do about the girls and trust me, they are a distraction."

"So there was money to buy his contract?" I was feeling my way here. "And you don't come cheap either. Who pays for it all?"

He pulled back, annoyed for the first time. "Why do you need to know that? You said you are some kind of student? You really from IRS?"

"What? No! Of course not! I am really just what I said, trying to put different pieces together. That's what I do. It's my own detective work."

"And I'm a piece?"

"Exactly."

"Well, tough. I'm not telling you who's investing in Tyler. None of your business."

"Really? Why is it a secret?"

"Now that's what I don't ask cause it is none of my business. They put up the dough and want to be behind the scenes, who am I to question? Maybe the wife don't want him investing that way. Maybe he's, uh, hiding some money." He shrugged. "You know, it happens, whatever the law says. Don't know, don't care."

He thought it over. "It's like this, it's like show business You put up some money to support a new show, hoping it's a hit and you'll make a fortune."

"Really?" I could hardly believe anyone did something so risky with their money. "Do most investors even make it back, investing in boxing? Do any??"

"What do you think?"

"They lose it all?"

He nodded slowly.

"And they do it because…? Why? Why in the world?"

"They love and support the sport? Or show? Or they're star f…Ahh, pardon my language." He took a breath. "They like meeting stars. Hanging out with the champ, taking in a Knicks game, going for a beer. Pick one or all. And then sometimes the kid turns out to be Mike Tyson, or the show is *Cats* and runs forever. Which, by the way, I was dragged to by the grandkids and thought was the dumbest thing I ever saw. But Iron Mike? Him I would have spotted right away and got a piece of the action."

I was scribbling notes as fast as I could. He had objected to recording.

"Ya know, the only way to really understand boxing is to put on the gloves yourself." His smile was half way between teasing and vicious. "You up for it?"

"Me? Are you kidding?"

"Most people pay real money to do that here. Some of those Wall Street types are women and a couple are pretty good. Downright vicious, those dames are."

I know a challenge when I hear one. Someone, that Brooklyn kid I used to be, was not about to be inferior to a Wall Street woman. At least that's how I explained it to myself later.

I was quickly laced into a pair of child size gloves and introduced to the punching bag. I hit it. It didn't move. I hit it again, harder, and felt the impact all the way to my shoulder. It still didn't move.

He put his hands on my shoulders and arms. "You need to relax here. And here. And you're pushing the bag, when you want to snap at it. Try again."

I did. And nothing moved, again, but it felt different. It shivered slightly. Maybe I could move it if I kept working at it, but not now. Or ever. I held my clumsy hands out to Brennan.

"Good try," he said. 'You could do it if you worked hard."

As he took off the gloves he found some knuckles turning purple.

"Ah, you put more into that than I realized. Go on in my office and sit down." He pointed. "I'll get some ice and be right there."

He returned with a cup of ice and gently stuck my fingers in it while he talked on the phone.

"Told you it wasn't going to work. Told you." "Yeah, yeah, I'll get him on track." I wasn't listening, he had turned away, and I was dumping out the clattery ice, but I thought he said, "Jackie's a bozo" then a little more clearly, "Yah, I'll come outside and meet you. Yeah."

"Do you know Jackie? Jackie Isiahson?."

"Why do you want to know?"

"I ran across him and I've been trying to find out who he really is. Thought I heard you say the name."

"There's a lot more than one Jackie in this world, but yeah, I know that one. He's connected to Tyler, some kind of relation. Comes around sometime, claims to be tight with him." He shrugged. "Family's a typical hot mess. Mom and an ever-changing cast of characters." He shook his head. "Just a distraction from the work."

I finally left with my useful new knowledge, but actually thinking more about Jackie, still wondering what the hell he had been up to at the hospital.

It was spring, still light outside with the low sun setting the East River on fire. It was a perfect Williamsburg scene, with gritty industrial buildings in front and a glittering glass apartment tower rising behind them, and the Manhattan skyline across the river making a dramatic background. An entire history in one image.

I felt an impulse to take a picture with my phone, not an easy job with my bruised knuckles. Clumsy as I was, I couldn't resist.

In one corner of the parking lot, Tommy Brennan was talking to some well-dressed men in front of a very large shiny car. I had to maneuver to keep them out of the photo.

Chapter Sixteen

Home at last. Park the car. Head to a local copy place to have the entire contents of the folders copied. They promised to have it for me first thing in the morning.

I'd thought ahead when I bought Leary's lunch, and Chris and I had a Chinese take-out meal all ready for a quick feed. In an attempt to set some standards, I put it out on plates. She came to the table with her history text, so I opened the paper. We wolfed down our dinners.

She stood up. "Chemistry calls. And English."

"And friend texting. And what else? Facebook? Instagram?"

"We younger generation can do several things at once, you know."

She took a cookie and disappeared. I needed to do the same.

Much later, she came to my little office and said, "I wonder if you should see this." She had her phone in her hand, the fanciest model, a birthday gift from my dad.

"Look here. Or I can get it on your computer screen if you prefer."

It was some new form of social media. I guess. I was not even sure which one, but maybe it didn't matter. Someone had posted: << Yo, Brownsville homies. I did it. Put hurt + fear on bitch messing w/ my man's head. Me! She still in hospital. No shouting gonna fix that. Who the man NOW? >> It was followed by some idiotic comments from readers. And then one more from the original: <<Naw, not me to Pink Sneaks. Haha.>>

"What? What the hell?"

"That's what I thought too." She was messing with my computer. "See? Look here?"

It was the same message, now easier to read. And it came from someone calling himself YoungfistB. But there was a photo, and even with a Knicks cap hiding some of his face it looked an awful lot like Jackie.

It took a minute before my mind was hit by the question that should have come first. "Why is he sending anything to you? Do you know him?"

"Mom!" She drew it out to three syllables. "It's way too complicated to explain how this works. Uh, long story short, I have a friend who knows Savanna cause she, my friend, she has friends at Tech. You know. And we were talking about what happened. So we get connected from one person to the next. Lots of degrees of separation, way more than six."

"You don't know him or any of his friends, then?" All kinds of alarms were going off in my head.

"No. Aren't you listening? And I won't, not ever. I don't even know the person who knows the person who knows him. But focus here. It's not about me."

In my own world, it's always about her, but she was right.

"I'm kind of flabbergasted. Can I send this to someone else?" She nodded. "I fixed it so you can. Holler if you need help."

I shuffled through accumulated piles on my desk. Here it was, the direct line to Sergeant Asher, the lead on Savanna's case. I tried to write a brief explanation and hit Send.

Then I sat there, unable to work, unable to get up and go to bed, unable to stop my mind from whirling. Is this about Savanna? Looks like it. Could Jackie be stupid enough to post something so informative? Astonishing but yes. I knew the cyber-world is full of people that stupid. Should I send it to Zora? Would it help her? Or make things worse?

I had no answer for that one.

Sergeant Asher responded. "Thanks, but we're already on the way to pick him up. We have some young cops who follow this social stuff. And as my first sergeant used to say, we can't rely on criminals to be stupid, but it's convenient when they are."

I went to bed. Next day I was busy at the museum until lunchtime. While I munched on a sandwich from home, I caught up with news online, trying to stick to the more reputable sources. And then, after I admitted to myself I did not care about the next primary election, I typed Deandra's name into the search bar again.

All I found was a tiny news item saying investigation was ongoing, they knew how she died but had nothing further to report. It was noted that a connection to the demonstration was still not established, though the body was found in the vicinity.

As if. As if it could be completely separate, happening in the same place, same time.

They had a picture, looking even younger than when I met her. It was blurry, an enlargement from an elementary school class photo. Did her mother not have any more recent photos? That tiny question broke my heart.

It stuck with me as I went on with my working day. Finally, I gave in and took a long break, searching thoroughly to see if there was anything else out there. No. Not one thing.

Then I went to Zora's page. Perhaps she had good news about Savanna. Perhaps she knew something about Deandra who was, after all, Savanna's friend. Sort of her friend. Perhaps I was grasping at straws, wanting to know something. Almost anything would do.

There was the same photo of Deandra and a note:

> My Savanna isn't the only child hurt recently. Pray
> for Deandra's soul, her life here on earth cut short
> before she had barely lived.

Well. This wasn't helping. Back to work. I spent some useful time organizing my notes from the Municipal Archives. I went over the list of files. Some of them included personal names, in "People vs. X" or in lists of material witnesses. I noted which names I recognized and added a few words to find them quickly. "So and so's gang" or "car thief and driver" or "convicted." And made a new list of names I did not recognize at all.

That's when I finally caught the name Feivel Krawitz. Could that be Lil's brother? The archives own notes said watch out for variant spelling. Damn. I'd never thought to ask what his original name was. He surely did not come from Poland as Frank.

Damn again. Because now I would have to figure out a time I could get back to the archives and look for information under this other name. If it was really him. That I could find out, maybe.

Census records, 1920, all written out in the original neat script of the census taker. And then 1930. And it was all online. Another cup of coffee and dig in. And here it was. Feivel Krawitz, aged ten, living in Brownsville with his parents and younger siblings including a baby sister named Lillian. In 1930 he was still there, and now he had a job, working at a butcher shop, and Lillian was a fifth grade student. I wondered, in passing, what her original name was. Perhaps, being the first one born in America, she started out with an American name.

I called Lillian. We spent some time on politeness, her health and my research and she laughed with me about something Ruby had done. Finally I was able to ask, "Was your brother ever called Feivel?"

"Sure he was. It means 'shining one,' you know. Named for one of our dead grandfathers. He became Frank when he started school but he was Feivel at home. I called him Five when I was small." There was a moment's pause. "But I am wandering. Why do you ask?" There was a longer, fraught pause. "Don't tell me you found something?"

I bit back what I wanted to say, about how much time I had wasted due to her not sharing this critical information with me. Instead, I said, "Maybe. I have to go take another look."

"Come see me, dear, when you know something. All right?" Another pause. "Though I'd be happy to hear news on the phone, too. Soon, I hope." Another voice came on.

"Miss Lillian is tired now. The phone does make her tired."

And then, for the rest of the day, I was humming a song from a beloved childhood movie, *American Tail*, which has a brave mouse hero named Feivel. That was a story of immigrants too. The mice sang about America, where there were no cats and the streets were paved with cheese. Maybe I should rent it and watch with Chris.

What would happen if I searched for Feivel instead of Frank? Of course there were multiple spellings of Feivel as well as Kravitz. I would do that as soon as I could. Then I returned for one more look at Savanna's Facebook page.

I was glad I did, because Zora sounded cautiously hopeful. The doctors would soon be seeing if Savanna could breathe on her own, a crucial milestone. Zora was breathing with her, she said. In. Out. In. Out. She asked for our good thoughts and prayers. I added my comment right away, that she had all my good thoughts, every day.

And then I read the other comments. Heartwarming and repetitive, they all said a version of what I had just written. And there was that StarrGurl again. Chris had explained to me how a fake name could be used and I didn't remember a word of it, but I remembered this name. She was the one who had posted venom earlier. She'd put this one up in the early hours of the morning.

HE WAS MINE. FROM THE START. LOVED HIS GREAT FUTURE. WANTED TO GIVE HIM A BABY. THEN SHE CAME ALONG F***NG HIS HEAD WITH NEW IDEAS.

Besides the fake name and the stunningly inappropriate post, there was a phrase that snagged my attention, "F***NG with his head." The real word would not get past filters but anyone who'd heard teens on the street knew what it was.

And where else had I seen it? I went back to what Chris had

found, Jackie boasting about something that might have been the attack on Savanna.

And there it was. "Someone was f***ng with my man's head." Did this mean anything at all? Nothing? Something?

I had no answers. I shut it down and went home.

Then Savanna's secret showed up, in the flesh

It began when I ran into Zora on the street. "Come see! I'm so glad to see someone I know." She'd never said that before. Her eyes were sparkling. "Come see what she is doing!" She held my arm and was already walking me back to the hospital. "I stepped out to get some supper. Come on! I have enough for two."

I learned long ago never to pass up a chance to hear good news. Bad news will always find you.

We instinctively lowered our voices as we got off the elevator on the Intensive Care floor. "They took the breathing tube out today." Her voice shook. "And she is breathing." Zora's grin grew wider as we approached Savanna's room. And then she gasped.

Someone was in the shadows beside Savanna's bed. We heard a murmuring voice. "Come on, girl. Come back. I need you bad. I know you hear me. You can do it. You can do anything. I know you can."

Zora flipped on the lights and said, most definitely not in a murmur, "Who the hell are you? And why you think you can be holding my baby's hand?"

The question I had, "And how did you get in here?" perhaps would come later.

He dropped the hand he was holding and stood up, a young man, but fully grown, tall and big and handsome. Broad shoulders but young enough to look nervous. Zora checked Savanna's monitors, breathing, tubes, saw nothing was changed and then stared at him, arms crossed, back straight, eyes darting to Savanna, and back to him.

I'd seen his photo on Brennan's wall.

Finally he seemed to find his courage and looked straight back at her. "Are you Savanna's mom? Miz Lafayette? I begged her to introduce us. I'm Tyler Isiahson."

"And I should care—why?"

"I am Savvie's boyfriend."

He was the boxer. Was that possible? That was what popped into my mind first, but not Zora's.

"No. She is not allowed to have a boyfriend until she finishes high school." She said it flatly, with no possibility of being contradicted. "None of that nonsense messing up her life."

He said softly, "Here I am anyway. And it ain't nonsense. It's for real."

"I am calling security." She didn't move or take her eyes off him. She reached out a hand and said, "Little E, please pass me the phone." She punched a button. "You don't have permission to be here. I'm giving them a piece of my mind, too. They supposed to be watching out."

A uniformed guard was already at the door.

"You see this boy? I found him here, after you all supposed to be watching out for anyone that's not me. What the hell is wrong with you all?"

He ignored the torrent of words. "Everything okay?"

"Hell, no, everything is not okay. This person—man, kid, whatever—was in here alone, when you all supposed to be taking care no one at all comes in. And after that other little creep?"

"What little creep is that?" Tyler did not speak so softly now.

"Kid named Jackie." Zora turned to him, furious. "Hanging around here. You know him? He a relative?"

Tyler didn't say a word, only nodded, but his expression hardened. I would not have wanted to be Jackie at that moment.

The guard said, "I'm calling my supervisor and see if we should call the police."

"What? I didn't do any damn thing." His voice kept getting louder. "No reason for police. I can't…that would be bad…I'd be in trouble…and Savvie too…" He stepped in, closer to the guard. Younger, taller and broader, he was a threatening presence. "You can't do that!"

"Can't?" Zora and the guard said it at once. "Can't?"

"You are telling me I can't do my job here?" The guard was in his face now. I was holding my breath.

Tyler's fists were clenched. Big fists. "I'm not going anywhere. No way. You want to try? You think you could make me?"

"Whoa!" The guard stepped back, hands up. "Just chill, man."

Zora stepped over to the supervisor who had just come in and poked him in the chest. "What the hell are you fools doing here, when someone is supposed to keep an eye out all the damn time?"

Then she shocked all of us by collapsing, bursting into tears and sitting down with a thump on the visitor chair.

"I don't believe it. Don't believe she been lying to me. Telling me she going to the library and really sneaking to meet him. Not her." But she did believe it. I was sure of that.

Everyone in the crowded room seemed paralyzed.

Finally she looked up, staring at young Tyler. "Okay. Now tell the damn truth. It's about time someone did."

He repeated his name and went on, "Savvie and me, we been seeing each other for awhile." His fists were still clenched. "Ms. Lafayette, I was never okay with lying to you. I know it's disrespectful and not how I was brought up, but she said you would never...so you forced us...if only you was more understanding..." His face lit up and his voice grew stronger. "She is not like any girl I know. She is...she believes she can do anything and she makes me think I could too. Be anyone." He looked at Zora. "Not much scares me, but I'm running scared now about losing her."

One of the guards said, "Ain't you the boxer? You already someone. Man, I saw your last fight."

He nodded.

"So if you love her so much, where you been this last week? I never heard a peep from you."

"I was in South Carolina, away at a training camp. Coach is real strict. No TV, no computer, no phone. It's all train, train, train. I didn't know a thing till I got home yesterday." He shook his head. "Who could...? Why...? I'm gonna hurt them bad when I find them. Believe that."

Zora took a deep breath. "There's a few people who left me real vicious messages."

He shrugged. "They jealous, most likely. Me, her, both of us." He thought a moment. "I got an old girl friend who won't give up, but I split from her before Savvie came along."

StarrGurl. I didn't even realize I said it out loud until his head snapped around to me.

"That's her. Her made-up name. She like to say it a lot. Real name is Tammy. Anyway, she didn't do this, she's a little thing." He seemed to think for a minute. "Whoever, they going to be sorry real soon. I keep thinking, if I was with her instead of in Carolina doing my stupid workouts, this couldn't happen. You know what I'm saying? What does it matter if I can't even protect my own girl?" He emphasized his anger with a punch to the back of a chair.

Pretty articulate, I thought. And nice manners too. I was starting to see the attraction for Savvie. Beyond the obvious, of course.

"Ms. Lafayette, what do you want us to do here? Can't hold him, really."

"You couldn't hold me anyway." His voice rose. "You think? You think I am standing still and letting you? You think you could?"

Zora shook her head. "You all go away. I am so tired. I just want some time with my child. You." She pointed to him. "You stupid kid. The police will want to talk to you. You got to do that if they are ever going to find out who did this and lock them up."

"Not what I am planning to do." He stood even taller and his expression was scary. "I have some plans of my own about dealing with this. I'll be tearing up the neighborhood, sending a real clear message. Not dealing with cops. And no one can make me."

"No one? NO one? You ever want to see Savanna again, MY Savanna, you get yourself on the phone with the detectives. I know, I know. They are sometimes bad themselves, but these particular ones do mean business. I have a card somewhere."

She scrabbled around in her purse, still sniffling, but I had one too, and handed it over.

She stood. "You all go away and give me time here alone. You too, Erica, go home to your own girl but come by some other time to see how Savvie is doing. It's too damn much right now."

As they left, the two guards accompanying, or perhaps escorting, young Tyler, were asking him about an upcoming boxing match, whose chances were better, when was his own next event and how had training gone. Men, bonding. Unbelievable.

Wasn't anyone else putting two and two together? A professional boxer, a man who knows how to throw punches, plus a girl who was beaten? That adds up to—what?

Chapter Seventeen

Home at last, mind whirling, I explained my lateness to Chris.

"It's okay. I made us both some dinner."

"You did what?"

"Geez, Mom, you don't need to sound so surprised! I know where the food is. I can work a microwave."

I took a deep breath. "Very true. And what is on the menu tonight, monsieur?"

She smiled, insult forgotten. Or at least forgiven. "Elegant tuna salad with olives and chopped red onion in it. Broccoli from the freezer, microwaved by *moi*. Garlic bread, also made by *moi* with the leftover Italian bread. Lots of butter, lots of garlic. Chocolate pudding. From a box, but I added the milk and cooked it."

"What are we waiting for?"

Over dinner, I told her about my recent adventure and she hung on every word. I had her from the moment the mystery boyfriend appeared.

"I knew it. I totally knew it. There had to be a boyfriend in the mix." She thought a minute. "But Mom, he sounds so nice! Could you really, really believe he was the one? The attacker?" She shuddered. "He loves her."

"No idea. Honestly, he did seem like a sweet boy. But—and it's a big but—sometimes they are the very people who beat up loved ones."

"Yeah, I know." She sighed. "I've seen photos. YouTube clips too. The ones of, like, famous singers, all beaten black and blue."

She was suddenly very sober. "I don't get it. I would never, never, never. Not ever."

"Glad to hear it. Now let's get to work. You made dinner, I'll clean up and you can go back to homework."

She sat there, not moving, lost in thought. "I have an idea. What if I send out a question about this to all my contacts, everybody out there in the cloud. Not an accidental connection, but on purpose. Let everybody pass it along and it will spread all over." She added, helpfully, "They call it going viral." She looked at me, uncertain if I would go for it. "I did a lot of homework before you got home."

"What can you do that the police department can't? They told me they have officers on this."

"Well, Mom, think about it. Teens like to gossip? You must remember that, even if you were young in the dark ages of talking on an actual phone."

And I did.

"Can you fix it so no one knows it's you? I don't want you involved. Seriously."

"Seriously? Of course I can."

So I had to say okay.

I was barely finished with kitchen cleanup when I got the call I had been half expecting.

"Ms. Donato? It's Sergeant Asher."

"I had a hunch."

"We had a very interesting call from Ms. Lafayette tonight. She said you were there and we thought it would be useful to have another report on what happened. Can you do that? And do we have permission to record it?"

So I told her what I had observed, as accurately as I could. She was not interested in my impressions, only in what I could report as fact. Mostly, it was who said what.

When we were done, and she stopped the recording, she sighed.

"I hope this was helpful."

"Oh, everything is helpful. But nothing gets us there." She stopped suddenly and then went on, "I didn't say that and you didn't hear it."

"I didn't hear you say anything at all."

"Thanks for your time. We may get back to you for clarification, okay?"

"Wait! Wait. I want to ask you something."

"Go ahead." Her tone was cautious.

"Are you also working on the murder of Deandra Willis?"

"Not exactly. We are keeping in touch, though."

"Are they getting anywhere? I just, I don't know, I just wondered. Savanna has so many people speaking for her. Deandra doesn't seem to..."

"Not so much. That's true. But that does not mean the officers are not doing their job, you know. It's a murder and... you have kids?"

"One. A fifteen year old daughter."

"Then you know. All victims matter, but one like this, just a kid..." She went on briskly, "Anyway, they're good ones, the team on that. They will do their job." She stopped. "No matter what people think of us, if it can be solved, it will be. What's your interest here, anyway?"

"I found her." My voice started shaking. "In that trash can. And I had met her, Deandra, just a few days before."

"Oh! Then I apologize. I did not make that connection from the crime scene."

"We talked a little, that day. She was very young and very nervous."

"Do you know anything that could be useful?"

"Doubt it, but she did talk about Savanna."

"Oh? Do tell."

So I did, that tiny moment, and asked if it was of any use.

"Well, we know about the boyfriend now anyway, but I'll pass this on to the guys on Deandra, too. They're taking everything they can find right now."

"I had one more question."

"Oh? I do have other…"

"I'll make it as quick as I can. Something strange happened to me, there in Brownsville, not about this, and I wondered if you could tell me if I should tell anyone. I know you all have more pressing things, so I didn't do anything then."

"Let me hear it." She sounded resigned.

So I told her about my encounter, still questioning myself. What was there to report? No harm, no foul, as my dad often says.

She was silent for what seemed like a long time. Then she said, "You are sure, testimony in court sure, they were the same boys who were pestering the victim, and you identified in a lineup?"

"Definitely."

"Okay. In the scale of what we deal with everyday here, that is very small potatoes, hardly worth the time to process a complaint."

"Is there a but coming?"

"In this case, yes. Because they have been in trouble before. Because we have a gang unit that, among other things, tries to keep on top of troublemakers. Because—unofficially—they are not clear of being Savanna's attackers. You know?"

"I thought they had alibis."

She snorted. "Pure rubbish, those alibis. Knucklehead friends swore they were all at a party that night. Every single one was lying, and we all know it, but we just can't prove it. Yet. So your story goes into the mix. I'll pass it on."

"Okay."

"And thanks."

I'd cleaned up the kitchen as we talked. Now I could get back to work. I had just enough functioning mind left to take a look at the Municipal Archives files. Put the different pieces in the right places so I could find them again.

I kept going back to the random candid shots that had popped up in the files from time to time. "Alleged mobsters, unworried, clowning on the courthouse steps." "Alleged members of the notorious Murder Inc, on a big night out with their wives." Silly, unimportant, but I was still trying to grasp who the hell these guys were. Was the night out photo from before or after they took a close friend for a ride in a stolen car and strangled him?

The poor photo quality was annoying but I remembered I had one of Leary's magnifying glasses. It had accidentally come home with me, dropped into my backpack along with some files. Aha! That helped a lot. I went back over all of them, and saw more details. Fun and games in some. A twinkle in the eye as someone tilted a new hat or brandished a cigar.

At that point I told myself to go to bed. I was way past being productive. I just wanted to look at one more, the lone photo that included Lil's brother. There he was, young and handsome, only a few years older than Chris. He had the smiling, open face of a nice kid.

And as I had just pointed out to Chris, that did not mean he couldn't also be a violent criminal.

I barely saw the tiny letters under the photo, as I was putting it away. K. Schwartz, Espy's long-abandoned real name. Did he know Lil's brother? Did he know all these guys, Brownsville's worst?

I was starting to feel like he was popping up everywhere and I needed to pay attention to that. The only question was whether he was a true guide or a false one.

Oh, really. When I start thinking in fairy tale language about mystic guides it is definitely time for bed. I am a historian, not a Brother Grimm.

Next morning I would have to make another trip to the wilds of Riverdale to talk to Lillian and probably Ruby too. I would have the photos right there, handy, on my old laptop, and I could blow them up to a size they could see easily. There was something I was missing, just out of reach. Maybe they could help.

Chris and I chatted over breakfast. Her classes started late today, so it was not the usual mad rush. She had nothing she was ready to share from her all points question last night, but she had something to say—of course—about my plans.

"Mom, is that work? Or just fooling around?"

"*What* did you say?"

She seemed to hear her own words a moment too late. Or maybe it was my expression. "Uhh, sorry? But that's what you would say to me! If it's a distraction from work, don't do it. And you have homework too." She smiled.

"Go to school."

She giggled and began collecting her gear. Of course she was right. I was just madly curious.

A smart child is a mixed blessing. Did my parents ever feel that way? I certainly didn't plan to ask my dad.

Yes, it turned out Ruby had some free time in the late morning, a good time for Lillian also. I would have to hustle. I had enough time, but barely, and only if I did not get lost on the way.

Riverdale confuses me. I navigated Brooklyn by dead reckoning. A collection of once-separate towns, it makes no sense really. Second Street, North Second Street and East Second Street have no relationship to each other and are in completely different neighborhoods. But I know this, I know the major avenues, I can find my way from any place to any other. Plus my dad, the cab driver, had expected me to master all of this when I began driving.

And on Manhattan's grid system it is impossible to get lost, walking or driving.

But put me in other parts of the city, where there are winding roads, cul-de-sacs, and unfamiliar parkways, and getting lost is always a possibility. Or even likely. I had the directions in my GPS, I threw on some semi-respectable clothing, checked to make sure all the info was easy to find on my laptop and I was off.

As instructed, I met Ruby in the usual spot. As usual, she looked stylish and alert, nicely made up, dressed in a smart wool dress and pearls, suitable for a daytime meeting. Except for the orthopedic oxfords.

Her face lit up when she saw me and hurried over to give me a two-handed shake.

"My dear! How good it is to see a young face. Really, I look around at all these old people and think I must be old myself." She smiled. "I thought you might like to see my little home, so Lil's aide will bring her over there."

She led the way to another building, carrying her cane and not using it, walking briskly, and talking non-stop as she pointed out the various buildings. She ushered me into a bright apartment filled with modern furniture. I don't know what I expected but it was not that.

She waved her hand in an all-encompassing gesture. "New décor, bright and sunny for a bright and sunny apartment. Just look out there."

It was worth a look, a large window framing the Hudson, a view so spectacular it had inspired a whole school of painters.

"I never get tired of it. Never." She moved a huge shabby leather chair to allow us to get closer. "This chair came from the old place, of course. My husband's, the one thing I could not part with." She sighed, then brightened. "I even junked the Rosenthal china, all those silly rosebuds, and bought a new modern set."

She pointed at the small table, already laid out with, yes, plain white china with a geometric border in pale green. "So come, sit down. I set up a little tea party. And yes, this is my old silver. One other thing I could not give away. I was so very proud when I got it."

Her voice dropped. "We socialists weren't supposed to want nice things. It distracted us from the struggle and it was immoral when others had nothing. But you know? I kind of did."

Her hand shook a little as she poured the tea, but before I could offer to do it, she had her other hand on the pot to steady it. Crisis averted by her own coping. And there was the doorbell.

Lil came in with a walker and an aide. Ruby arranged for the aide to return in an hour. Hmm. So she had the agenda of this interview all set up?

Lil looked worse than the last time, pale almost gray skin, darker circles under her eyes, thinner. It was a beautiful spring day but she wore a long, misshapen sweater over her orange velour running suit.

"What is on your feet, Lil dear? Bedroom slippers? I mean, we are all past high heels, but slippers?"

She shrugged. "Who cares? My feet hurt a lot these days, and they are easy to put on." She smiled and turned to me. "In my apartment, I have all my smart shoes, heels and evening shoes and spectator pumps. Bet you don't know what those are?"

"Bet I do. I've seen them in old magazines. White with another color on heel and toe and little perforations.

"Good for you! A plus. So I take them out and display them sometimes. My shoe museum. You should come and see."

"Why, Lil, I didn't know about this. You never invited me to come see them." Lil shrugged, unconcerned by the hurt tone in Ruby's voice. "It was thrilling to you too, when we could finally have nice things, wasn't it? What did you love most?"

"Those shoes, of course. And real silk negligees. And travel. Who would have thought, when we were girls, that one day we'd travel on the *Queen Elizabeth*? Just like the movie stars?"

"Yes, indeed. Unimaginable for little Brownsville girls. My husband gave lectures in Hawaii and Barcelona and I went along. Of course," she quickly assured both Lil and me, "Barcelona was after Franco. We certainly would not have gone while those Fascists were in power."

"I gave a talk at a conference at Oxford. Oxford! I had to wear my academic robe."

Ruby laughed. "I bet you wore nice shoes with it."

"I certainly did. Belgian pumps, ivory linen and oxblood leather. Matching bag, too. From Saks, no less!"

"Well, of course. I mean, it was Oxford!"

She and Ruby laughed when she added, "Of course I can't remember what I had for breakfast!"

They were laughing but I was ready to snap. How could I get them to focus? We had a small amount of time, and they were all over the place this morning.

Lil deftly pulled the tray of mini-Danishes closer and picked out several. Ruby lightly smacked her hand and said, "What are you doing, dear? Your diabetes…"

Lil sat back, still holding the tray.

"Ruby, don't be ridiculous. One, you are not my nurse. Or my doctor or my mother, heaven forbid. Two, they cover it with extra insulin now. And three, who the hell cares? The best part of stage 4 cancer, let me tell you, is I do what I want now."

Ruby responded by making her spine a little straighter. "I am only trying to watch out for your health."

"What health? I'm a sick person but not a child. Remember that." Her expression was unsmiling and unapologetic.

It looked like a good moment for me to jump in.

Chapter Eighteen

"I love chatting with you ladies and any morning with pastry is a treat but—and please forgive me—I am here to do some work. I don't have the time today to do the recorded interview that we discussed, but I do have some questions."

"Of course you do!" Ruby sat up straight. "Lil, focus. You can keep the pastry for later. If you must."

She was oblivious to both Lil's hard stare and her deliberate reach for one more.

"You've found something?" Lil's cloudy eyes lit up. "You have. I can feel it."

"Yes and no. I've found a few things but I don't know what they mean. I'm hoping one of you might be able to help." I brought onto the screen the enlarged photo that included someone identified as F. Krawitz and turned it to face them. "Who is this?"

Ruby gave it her considered attention, but Lillian had tears in her eyes. "Frank. That is my brother Frank. It really looks like him, not like what you showed me before. I've never seen this photo." It took a moment before she could speak. She gently touched the screen. "My parents didn't have photos at home, like people do now. No one had cameras. There was no money for even a cheap photo studio. So I haven't seen a photo of Frank in…it's been decades. It's been a whole lifetime." She looked at me. "Can I have this one? To have in my room with me?"

"I'll get one printed for you. And framed."

"Yes, that's Frank, certainly. But who are these other people?" Ruby leaned over to read the blurry caption. "Oh. Oh. Why, Lil, what was he doing with them? They didn't associate with these criminals, our brothers. They had the good sense to just ignore them. Most of the boys did."

She tapped the computer screen. "Lil, dear, you are not focused. Erica has questions for us about this photo. I assume she does?"

Lil blinked a few times. "I'm ready now. Ask away."

"I know something." Ruby was too dignified to wave her hand up in the air, but she had that look of Ooh, ooh, call on me. "I know where this was taken. Come on, Lil, you could figure it out too."

Lil stared at the screen again as I made the photo a little bigger.

"I'll be damned! That's our building. They were hanging around the front of our building."

Ruby patted her hand. "Good work. And we know it's our building because even though the street numbers faded away, that window right there—" She jabbed the screen—"*that* window was where I slept, and you can see some of my clothes folded up on the windowsill. Hot summer nights when I couldn't sleep I used to sit by the open window and watch the world go by."

"The world? Ha. Well, it was all the world we knew back then. But I expect what you want is not old ladies waxing nostalgic. You want to know what they were doing there, and why is Frank with them? And I don't know! That is the mystery."

"Probably no one still alive knows. Lil, I believe you are wasting Erica's time, asking her to look for information about Frank. It's impossible. She's a busy person, as we were, making her way in the world." There was some heat in her voice, scolding and something else. Before I had a chance to pursue that, we started to lose Lil's attention.

She smiled softly, and her eyes closed.

"You are not obligated." Now Ruby was laying down the law to me. She glanced at Lil, then whispered, "You have a life, and work to do. This is no more than a whim of a very old lady who has neither. No need for you to indulge her."

"But if I can, I will. And I have another question."

"Lil!" Ruby leaned over and tapped her friend's arm with a sharp, polished nail. "No drifting. We have more work to do." She opened her eyes. "I wasn't asleep. Just resting my eyes."

"Thank you both. There is a name on the photo. K. Schwartz. It's a long shot, but just in case it means something to you?"

"But it does." Lil was not fully back with us but she was trying. "I believe it does. There was this kid, a skinny, annoying kid, really only a little older than us, who got hold of a camera from somewhere. Probably stole it."

"Yes! He was always shoving it into people's faces, snapping away, like he was playing make-believe, the hotshot newspaperman in a movie. He should live so long!"

Lillian started laughing. "I haven't heard you use an expression like that in, oh, must be a lifetime!"

"It's all this talking about the old days." She shook her head. "I sounded like my mother just then, didn't I, instead of scary Dr. Boyle. So that kid? I remember him too. They called him... what? What was it?"

"Kallie."

"Kelly?"

"No. Kallie. Or Kal." Lil's whole face lit up. "Or Bug! That was because he was so annoying. He used to follow Frank around."

"That's right. Kal. Kalman, probably. But why do you want to know?"

"I'm not sure why I do. There might be one more connection I'm not seeing. But I'm glad you are sitting down. Ready for this? He did become someone famous. Sort of famous, anyway, in his day."

"Really?"

"Seriously? That annoying Bug?"

"Yes indeed, under his nickname Espy."

"For ESP?" Lil was still a sharp one when she focused.

"Exactly. Because he was so good at finding crime scenes to photograph, they said he must have ESP."

"Well, I'll be damned."

"Lil! Language!"

"Oh, stop. When did you become so proper? After you married the Yale professor?" Ruby turned pink. "Honey, I remember the days we used much worse language, showing off how bohemian we had become." She turned back to me. "I remember his photos, even used some in a class, and I never knew I knew him. So to speak."

"I'm still not connecting the name. He was a crime photographer? Probably for the kind of tabloid I wouldn't dream of reading." Ruby was still miffed.

"But there were times when you couldn't walk past a newsstand without seeing some of his work. Here. Take a look." I handed over the book I had brought, open to a row of papers with the same screaming headline and the same front page photo.

The two white heads bent over the pages, irritation forgotten for now.

They flipped, gasped at some, and finally Ruby patted one and said, "I remember this. This very picture. Lil, remember?"

"Oh, lord, I do. Yes, I do. They tried to keep it from us…"

"Protecting us. We were still kids. But we sneaked looks at the newsstand…"

"Of course As any smart kid would have."

It was in front of a bar, just down the block from Moonlight Min's Candy Store. A body sprawled on the sidewalk. It was a crowded scene, with cops, ambulance, medics, and many, many bystanders. The caption said this was the photo that got Espy his first real newspaper job. He was fifteen and dropped out of school to work chasing the news.

It was the shooting of Bernie Rosenblatt, the local hero of his time, the champion boxer killed in a robbery.

"Frank's friend, Bernie was," Lil said softly. "Of course I was bound to know about this."

"You and me and everyone. The whole neighborhood was talking about it."

"It looks like the whole neighborhood saw it! Is that possible?"

They looked at each other and nodded.

"We didn't see it then—we were home in bed. In fact our parents always told us never to walk on that block, day or night."

"And did you? Never walk there?"

"Of course we did. Even I did, and I was a real good girl. Not like some who always broke rules." She nodded her head toward Lil, but Lil's attention was turned inward.

She gasped. "Frank was there. I just remembered that. Is that possible, to remember after a whole lifetime of forgetting?" She sighed. "Maybe I'm imagining it, that he was there. That I heard him tell my parents. He was crying, my big, strong brother." She nodded emphatically. "Nope, not making up that detail. It happened."

She went on slowly. "They were friends."

"Yes, we got that already. Get to the point."

Lil paid exactly no attention to Ruby's comment. I myself was listening hard, and madly taking notes too.

"They were friends, and it was a busy ordinary evening. A street full of people going about their business."

"And hanging around, too. Lots of people were out of work and hanging around was their only business." Ruby tossed her head. "And getting into trouble."

"Yes, all of that. And Bernie was really well known. He had dinner with us a few times. Did you know that, Ruby? He and Frank went way back. He used to bring something to contribute, cold cuts, something. Because some times, we did not have enough to share with a guest. And then my mother would give up her meal." She blinked a few times.

"So he was famous, an athlete in all the papers."

She shrugged. "What did I know? I was a kid. I knew he always brought me candy."

"And that day?"

She arched an eyebrow at me. "Don't the history books tell you?"

"Yes they do. And the old newspapers. That shot..." I patted the page. "...that shot was in every paper in New York. But the books disagree a little."

"So what can we possibly add to the story? You probably know more than we do."

"What we can add, Ruby, is how it felt to be there. Everyone was crying, not only Frank, that's for sure. But like I started to say, I think Frank was there. They were out together and there was a robbery. Not at Min's." She pointed to the candy store in the photo. "There was a real Min, you know. Scary woman. No one would have dared to knock off her place. The robbery was a bar, I think." She pointed to it. "There. And he jumped in. And got killed. Just like that."

"That is what the history books say, pretty much. There is some disagreement about which place was getting robbed, and why someone would rob a bar in the daytime. Why did he jump in?"

"I suppose he thought he was tougher than anyone."

I nodded.

"But Frank. Frank was next to him when he fell. He tried to stop the bleeding, he said. To Mom and Pop, not to me. I was listening from behind the door."

"He must have seen blood before. We saw plenty of street fighting."

"Ruby, for God's sake, this wasn't a broken nose! Poor Bernie bled out in the ambulance. He was there—my brother going to the hospital with his friend. I think I remember that." She stopped, overcome.

Ruby stood up so quickly her chair scraped the floor. "Lil, you are tired. They said not too much activity. I am taking you back. No, Erica, I don't need help."

"I'm not tired. Not a bit." Actually, she looked exhausted. "If you are bored, you can take yourself off."

"Lillian, why would you say that to me? I am only trying looking after you. Your nurse said."

She looked back at her friend with hard eyes. "I am sick but I am not senile. Not yet, anyway. You were always a bossy kid even when we were children. 'No, no, draw the potsy squares this way.' 'Wear your matching socks.' 'That boy isn't good enough for you.'"

"After all these years? That's what you remember?" Ruby was still standing, face an angry red, voice shaking. "And when was I not right? Never, that's when. He wasn't good enough for you, as you learned the hard way. And your socks don't match now."

With that parting shot, she turned as if to walk into another room but Lil's chilly voice stopped her. "You always want to end the conversation when we talk about crime in the old days. Why is that? Was your brother maybe more involved than you want to say?"

"*My* brother? Who never took his head out of a book? Ridiculous. Now *your* brother..." She stopped with a gasp and covered her mouth.

"Never." Lil seemed to get a little smaller in her chair, deflating. "Or maybe. Who the hell knows? I'd like to know, but maybe I won't find out in time." She looked up. "Oh, Ruby, for god's sake, sit down. Enough drama for one morning."

This was deteriorating into a schoolyard spat. Someone needed to be the grownup here. It would have to be me.

"You are delightful and charming mature women." I summoned up a level of gracious hostess I did not know I possessed. "Ruby, let me fill your cup again." She handed it over, mechanically, eyes looking past us. "And why don't you take that last piece of cheese Danish?" I turned to Lillian. "You do look a little tired." She looked a lot tired. "Would you like another cup too? You like it with lots of sugar?"

She nodded, slowly. "Yes, I'm ready to go back and rest. And I'll take the Danish, too, in case I am peckish later."

She turned to me. "Now you know the truth about us. We are only pretending to be sweet old ladies. White hair notwithstanding, we're as evil as when we were drawing with chalk on the sidewalk, full of piss and vinegar."

"You always had a vulgar streak."

Lillian said flatly, "We've proven that, right, Erica?"

Her aide turned up to take her back.

"I'll stay here and finish my tea," Ruby said. "I am a little tired too. I need to sit quietly and sort out all these memories."

On my mind all the way home was the knowledge that Lil didn't have much longer. I wondered if Ruby had faced up to that.

And I wondered about the murder they had described. I knew the killer was never found. Wouldn't anyone wonder what really happened? Or was I just getting weird, writing this difficult chapter about crime? I thought about that on the way home, too.

It was a small miracle I did not get lost.

Chapter Nineteen

"Chris!" I called it up the stairs. "I'm home."

"Heard you come in." Her voice floated down. "What's for dinner?"

"Clean out all the leftovers in the refrigerator. You can have first choice. Five minutes."

"Again?" She groaned.

I covered the table with an array of plastic and paper takeout containers. It was a far cry from Ruby's elegant tea service, but I added real plates.

Tonight my child would have to live with it.

She made a face but then started opening everything. "Ooh, is that pad Thai? I didn't know we had some of that. And peanut chicken? Dibbies on these. I'm good."

Two containers down. I claimed a slice of lasagna and the last of a supermarket roast chicken. Two more down.

"And not out of containers. Real plates, at least."

"Oh, Mom, are you having a guilt attack? Honest, I don't mind this kind of meal when there's so much deliciousness."

"You were the one complaining."

"Silly Mom. Why do you listen to me?" She made a funny face. "You know I am being a mouthy teen."

She had a point.

"Anyway, you have to listen about this. Not more important than dinner, but a little more interesting than this one. So as soon as we are done…" She tapped her laptop with a significant look in her eyes.

"You found something?"

"Oh, yeah." Her smile was both triumphant and mocking. "But of course we don't have gadgets at dinner."

"You're being a smart aleck again. Give it up. We'll look together."

"But peanut sauce might get on my keyboard…you always say…" She was whining for fun, not for real, but she wisely stopped when she saw my expression.

"Okay, so what I did…no, you don't want to know how, right? Only results?" I nodded. "So here, I ran across this. Here's video of this Tyler, walking around the neighborhood."

The video was jumpy, and none too clear, but it was definitely him.

"People were following him around. See? Those kids are getting autographs. Is he kind of famous?"

"Evidently. At least in the neighborhood."

Tyler looked up, right into the camera, probably someone's phone, and the video stopped abruptly.

Chris changed the screen. "This is where it came from. See? The guy who filmed it is talking about how cool it is to see Tyler back in the projects, walking the home streets and stuff."

The street slang was dense, but that did seem to be the point.

"And here is someone else, with some snaps."

Tyler talking to old people in front of a building, genially shaking hands all around. Tyler with a little posse of small children, all smiles and fist bumps. Tyler not smiling at all as he talks to a group of boys his own age. And here was Tyler holding someone in a shoulder lock and definitely not smiling. He was shaking the boy, holding him against a wall, and then it stopped.

"There's another one, though. See?"

Someone else was there too, filming from further away, showing the first recorder—or so I assumed—being approached by a much larger guy, and walking away. Fast. That explained the abrupt end of the previous video. And this one showed Tyler saying something to the guy he had pinned to the wall with one arm. With the other, Tyler held his chin, forcing his head up to Tyler's eyes. Then Tyler let him go and they walked away in opposite directions, Tyler ambling, not even flustered, and the other one moving away as fast as he could.

"This is incredible, Chris. How on earth?"

"You like it? I found one more."

A few clicks and there was a page I had seen before, Tyler's brother Jackie.

Probably his brother. He had written:

> <<My man home at last. I know he out looking for me but he ain't find me yet. I can handle him. I believe we got him back on right road now. Road to famous and rich, rich, rich. Bitch was a distraction. >>

"He wrote that? And put it up in public? Can he be that stupid?"

"The answer to that would be 'yes.' He sounds dumb, overall, but, I don't know, it's hard not to just let it flow when you're typing in random thoughts. So look here." A strategic distraction.

She pulled something up that was from Tyler himself. Leaving out the slang, it said his relationship with Savanna was not a secret now, and he was asking for help about what happened to her. If someone stepped up, he'd owe him big. And if he learned one of his crew knew and didn't tell him, there would be a big price, worse than they could even think about in their worst nightmare. And it ended with,

> Yo, Jackie, you little worm. What you know? You gon give it up? Ain't you heard? You can run but you can't hide. Mom can't help this time.

"How did you find all this? It's amazing."

"Thanks but it wasn't even that hard, just too 21st century for you, right?"

"Okay. Sort of true though I can do without the sarcasm."

"Hold on. There's more. I mean info, not sarcasm."

She scrolled down through comments, most of them offering support and respect to "my man" Tyler and his honey. Then someone else popped up.

Bad spelling, bad typing, but the meaning was right out of a teen songbook of my youth, or anyone's. StarrGurl was back.

> Why you not DUMPIN that skinny skank and get back wit me? You know we ment to be together. You go change all those status back to IN RELA-TIONSHIP with me. Starr!

And the other commenters piled on, stomping on her for harassing their man. And she posted back:

> "Y'all haters? Can go f**k self. Free country last I heard. I can say whatev."

On one of the sources—by this time, I had lost track—graphics popped up next to the entries, a personal photo or an animal or a cartoon. Avatars, that's what they were called. And there was Starr Gurl herself looking seriously into the camera. She wore a low cut top, a frayed turquoise leather jacket and huge, gold, hollow-square earrings. Not a flattering style for her, but they sure did make a statement.

Oh, wait. With Chris' help I went back to the little videos, and there she was in one, in the background, not close to Tyler but watching. Watching with tears running down her face.

Finally Tyler came on and wrote:

> We were done before I met Savanna. It wasn't her, it was you and me not being good together. We're over. And you are blocked from every way to reach me.
>
> So done with you.

This was not sad teen songs; this was a grand opera, playing out in real time on a phone screen.

"If I wanted to send this out? I'm not even sure what to do with it, but if I did?"

"Already sent you the links. So what do you think?"

I stood up and hugged her. "Terrific. Brilliant. Thank you. Thank you twice. I see a great career ahead of you as a detective."

"A cop? Don't think so. You know I'm more like an artsy person. And I'll take the brilliant, but most any kid could have done this. Is it time to talk about those new boots?"

"I'll see what I can do. Honestly, you've earned them." She stood and surveyed the messy table. "Cool part about leftovers is the takeout containers go right into the garbage. Fast cleanup."

"You're sprung. Cleanup is on me."

As soon as I was done, I sent Sergeant Asher a note, telling her what Chris had found and asking what I should do with it. And even though it was already eight o'clock, I had a response almost instantly. "Yes. Send all to me immediately and other addresses I cc'd. There's always a chance she found something new."

I sat down with the newspaper and a cup of cocoa and it became one of those moments when the world throws us a little gift. It was delivered by PBS.

I glanced idly at the television section of the paper. Tonight I wanted to turn everything off, and TV is pretty good for that. And there it was, on public television, a new episode of a series about the making of modern New York. Tonight it would be about the mid-century intellectual life, "The Making of Ideas."

Really, I was hoping for reruns of *Full House*, escape not education, but the name Maurice Cohen popped out at me. Maurice Cohen, the writer and former Brownsville resident. My guide to old Brownsville. And not least, Ruby's brother.

In a fast minute, my cocoa and I were settled in front of the television. Because it was 20th century history, these people had been filmed in interviews over the years and bits of those moments were included. Gestures, voices, how they saw themselves, all in their very own words. A historian's dream.

It was large group of people with much in common and active in the worlds of both literature and politics. They worked together, socialized together, and were friends. Or enemies. That depended on the most recent intense political argument or who was sneaking around with whose wife. Lofty dedication to the realm of ideas, well-mixed with ego, ambition and sex. Human nature at war with high-minded intellect.

After awhile I may have drifted, lost in the details of long ago political feuds and love affairs, but I sat up again when Maurice Cohen first appeared on the screen.

What? He'd been dead a long time. It took a sleepy moment before I realized this was an old interview.

He was very short, but broad. Burly, even. Mostly bald. Dressed like a professor from central casting, down to the tweed jacket with leather elbow patches and a pipe.

He didn't sound like a stereotyped professor, though. He had a Brooklyn accent that came though even in the most arcane lit crit terms.

And he had an attitude. It took me a few minutes to realize I see it every day on the street. It said, "I'm too tough to mess with."

The interviewer wanted to talk about the early, ground-breaking works that made him famous. Well, not Frank Sinatra famous, but certainly famous in the literary world.

And he did not want to talk about them at all. "All you young smartasses want to ask me about Brownsville. I've lived a whole life since then! Did you even do your homework? I've written fifteen more books, all well reviewed, and I edited a major journal. I didn't write some great works and die young, for crying out loud!" He leaned forward, aggressively staring into the interviewer's eyes. "I've been here all along."

He leaned back, folded his arms and seemed to be saying, "Dare you."

The interviewer was a pro, not easily intimidated, and had the interview back on track in no time but I wondered if Cohen was always that prickly. He refused, in a few choice words, to talk about old scandals. However, he was scathing about old friends who became conservative political writers in later years.

I was alert to any mention of the old neighborhood, his childhood, and his family. His sister was in the midst of her own productive life at the time of the interview. Not one word. He made it very clear that he was there to talk only about himself and his ideas.

When my phone rang I jumped. It was Ruby, asking me, no telling me, to watch television immediately.

"I saw it, just by good luck."

"What did you think?"

"Was he always like that?"

"Like what? Self-centered? Conceited? Combative? Yes, he was. Did you notice, he never even mentioned our parents or any family?"

"Did I ever! And that large chip on his shoulder?"

"Always! I think it was…" She slowed down. "I think it was growing up where we did. Kids fought all the time, especially the boys. You had to be tough."

I thought it was the first time she had admitted that.

Near the end of that segment, Cohen was back on, in an even older interview. When he said, "Crime?" I started taking notes. "People were desperately poor. Some thought they had to do anything they could. In fact, a friend disappeared." His voice slowed and grew softer. "Poof! Just like that. And he was a good guy. We knew…well, we believed…he got on the wrong side of some very bad people." For a moment, the tough guy was gone and his voice dropped to a whisper. "I never saw him again." He turned away from the camera and I saw a handkerchief come out.

What? Had I heard that right? He was talking about Lillian's brother? Damn, they only took a clip from an old, longer recording. Could I find the whole thing?

I puttered around, still thinking about what I had seen, and finally called the one person I knew who would understand my excitement. It didn't matter that it was so late. His sleeping habits were never the same as normal people.

"Hey, Leary. Want to hear an interesting story?"

"Always, kiddo. It's what I live for."

"I might be on the trail of something."

He listened while I told about meeting Ruby and Lil, and Lil's request, and what I had seen tonight.

"So that's it. I just wanted to tell someone about maybe, finally, getting some answers. Or am I completely crazy?"

"It's not impossible to be both, ya know, hot on the trail AND crazy."

"Not the reaction I was going for."

"Aw. Did I hurt your little girl feelings?"

"Shut up. Or say something useful. Choose one."

"Awright, awright. Yeah, you had some luck tonight. What else you doing to find out?"

I told him about the Municipal Archives and how I knew I'd have to go back. I hadn't known it until that moment when the words came out of my mouth. What I had copied was good but there were considerable sections I had not copied.

"Ah, court papers. They can be a long slog, but sometimes there's that little nugget. You're reading about some crazy bastards there."

"Yeah. It's all kind of interesting, and I'm pulling out some info for my dissertation for sure. But for Lil, I'm not quite getting there. And it feels like the answer is almost there in front of me, but then it isn't." I stopped and thought it over. "Yikes. That sounds kind of crazy, even to me."

"Not at all. You've got that nose for a story. Kiddo, you should have been a reporter."

"Newspapers are dying. Haven't you heard? And I need a paycheck."

"So your goal is to become an underpaid college teacher? You think there might be a flaw in this plan?"

"It's way too late for a deep discussion about my career plans."

"Late at night? Or late in your life?"

"Both. And I know you're just pulling my chain now."

"So if I stop, you want to come over for a late night snort or two?"

"Oh, ha-ha. You gave it up, and I wouldn't drive home after drinking with you. What would be the point of my coming over?"

"I get a kick out of seeing other people enjoying what I can't." Oh sure he did. Not. He was lonely, perhaps. "Now that is even crazier than anything you asked about." He chuckled. "Good night, doll. Some of us have to be up and about early tomorrow. Not me, but some of us."

"Good night, Leary."

Chapter Twenty

Chris said, "What's up today? Are you at home?"

"Why?" Grumble, grumble.

"I was only making conversation."

"Too early. Eyes not open."

She looked me over and said cautiously, "Okay, Mom. I'm heading off to school. I can be reached in the usual ways."

What was she doing, being cheerful this early?

I was grouchy because I didn't want to go back to the Municipal Archives. And if I had done the research differently in the first place, I wouldn't have to.

Even in my grumpiness I knew that was being unreasonable. I could not bring home all the contents of all the boxes. I picked what seemed useful, and it was useful, but I had learned something new and now I needed another group of documents. Jennifer said no problem, they were already in use and I could have them later.

The ten-minute walk to the subway, plus a very large coffee, cleared my head. I texted Chris to let her know I would be unreachable by phone and where I would be.

It wasn't until I was leaving the subway station that I thought about why they were already in use. Again. Was someone else still caught up in this topic? And if so, why was he as persistent as I was?

I had emerged to a true spring day, sunny and mild. Later, I could eat lunch in City Hall Park or go for a walk, playing hooky for a short time. My spirits lifted.

The prospect of a walk around Battery Park or a look across the harbor, watching the ferries, kept them lifted even when an idiot talking on his phone bumped into me as I went in the building and he came out. The last of my coffee spilled down the front of my pants. He was gone by the time I turned around to let him know what I thought of him. I only had a glimpse of him as he walked away. Average height, blondish hair, raincoat-colored raincoat.

I mopped up the spill and went on about my day. Jennifer was there. We did some low-voiced catching up, and confirmed a date for more. Then she said, "Is something about this in the news? It would be useful for us to know why there is this flurry, so we can be prepared for more demands."

"Not that I know about. For me, it's about a dissertation chapter. That could not be less in the news."

"The real news will be when you finish it, right?"

She laughed. I didn't.

"But I still would like to know who else is looking. Maybe we should be talking to each other."

"Ah, no. I went out on a limb for you already. That's as far as I can go."

"Not even a word? Not even a description, in case I run into him? And then I could introduce myself and we could connect about all this."

"Not one word." She pointed to a table with stacked boxes. "Go work."

So I did. This time I could be efficient. I wasn't browsing for whatever academic treasure caught my eye. I was looking for anything that pertained to the death of Bernie Rosenblatt, on the chance it included his friend Frank Kravitz. Or more photos. The finding aids told me where to look. I flipped carefully through the files, pulled what looked useful, copied it, put it back. In two hours, I was done. Also hungry and in need of natural sunlight after working under the fluorescents.

I said good-bye to Jen and she thanked me for my care in handling the material. "Not at all like the colleague before you." She had a devilish smile.

"What? A colleague? Do you mean that's what he is?"

She laughed. "No. I'm kidding you. I have no idea."

I didn't think much of her joke, but perhaps I was losing my perspective. The outside world beckoned.

I left, looked around, saw there were no interesting places to eat, only an old-school hot dog cart. City Hall Park, though, across the street, had a small farmer's market today. With luck I could find a decent lunch. There would be lines, I thought, as I stepped through the sidewalk crowds. It's lunchtime; it's a nice day; everyone is out.

It was a few minutes before I realized that someone kept bumping into me. The same someone. The street was crowded but not that crowded. My first instinct was to drop my arm over my purse. Good. It was still zipped and all the usual bulges were there.

Second instinct was to cross the street, not at the light but through cars stalled in traffic.

Third was to stop somewhere out of the crowd and check my backpack. I had learned the hard way that a stranger hovering in a crowd might mean someone—me—was about to have a valuable possession lifted.

I sensed him still near me. Good. That meant he hadn't gotten anything. Bad. That meant he hadn't given up. Maybe I should stop and glare at him? Perhaps it would scare him away? How scary could I be? If I tried hard?

Before I decided, I felt a hand grab my arm, hard, and silently pull me away from the crowd and into the quieter park.

I pulled back. "What the hell?" Loud enough to sound strong, not loud enough to cause a major disturbance. I was ready to run, but his grip was too tight.

He whispered "Shhh. Shhh. I've got to talk to you. Just talk."

City Hall Park is well-populated. I was not being dragged somewhere with dark, deserted woods. Therefore I was not in danger. All that flashed through my mind in a second.

With one last jerk I pulled my arm free and turned to face him. And I had seen him before. This time he was clean, hair brushed, face shaved. He wore a lightweight, raincoat-colored raincoat.

"One step closer and I scream my head off. Cops are right over there."

He held up his hands. "I'm not doing anything. I just want to talk to you."

I was breathing hard. We both were.

"Why are you following me? What the hell are you doing?"

"That's what I want to know about you." He put his hands up again. "Not doing anything. But I saw you when I was leaving the building and I waited outside all morning, until you came out."

"You did what? You waited? Are you some kind of stalker?" But he looked more scared than I was now. And I wanted to know, too.

"We sit." I pointed to a park bench. "You at one end and me at the other."

He nodded and we both moved there, cautiously. First thing I did was check the contents of my backpack. All there.

I glared at him. "Now you talk. Or else."

"You're kidding, right?" His smile was close to a sneer. "Or else what?"

I stood up, ready to walk away—in the direction of City Hall police officers—immediately.

He jumped up. "Aw, come on, come on. I didn't mean anything." I sat down again, still keeping my distance.

"You were at the archives today, and so was I. And I think you've been there before. And me and my boys found you in Brownsville too, lurking around what used to be Moonlight Min's. So what the hell are you looking for? If it's not what I am looking for? I got to know."

"I don't have to tell you." Not that it was a secret, but he was annoying me. "I was scared and almost assaulted by those so-called boys of yours. And how did you hook up with those gangbangers anyway? What game are you playing? You look like a homeless drunk one day and a regular citizen type the next."

I looked him up and down, slowly and not with approval. "I don't think you're an undercover cop." I ticked off the possibilities on my fingers. "And I'm pretty sure you aren't an academic, which is what I am." A crazy thought struck. "Don't tell me you're an actor looking for 'authenticity' for a part."

"Ha. That's funny. Nope, that's not it, but I do have a real good reason for what I'm doing. Real good and real personal. I want to know what *you're* doing. You following me? Seems like you turn up every time I turn around."

"Following you? Me, following you? Hell no. Why would I do that?"

"Don't you know who I am?" He preened. "You should. I'm not a nobody, especially if you are looking at the boys from Brooklyn."

"All I know is that you seem to have an unhealthy interest in the Brownsville mob, a bunch of psychopaths if ever there was one." Now his attitude was really, seriously annoying me.

"Hey! One of those guys was my grandfather." He posed again. "They say I look a lot like him."

"Say that again."

"A lot like him."

"No! The rest…"

"Yeah. 'Liv' Nathan was my granddad. I got a legacy."

Liv was a boss, someone they all worked for, a sort of big name. I'd never seen anything about descendents.

"How could I possibly know you? I don't even know your name. And you seem young to be his grandson."

"My real name is Gersh Nathan, like him. I use James. His nickname, Liv, came from Livonia Avenue. And I'm young because my dad had me when he was old." He paused. "Young wife of course, my mom was."

I was still annoyed, but I was also cautiously, reluctantly, somewhat intrigued. He was a direct connection to a vanished past, like the reason people spend a fortune on a baseball Babe Ruth signed or Princess Diana's clothes.

"You are? Really? Did you ever know him?" If he had, how could I download his memories into my computer? And do it without having to deal with him?

"Nope. Long gone when I was born but my dad used to talk about him. And there are home movies, too. Plus I have older half-brothers who remember him."

He stopped and shrugged. "The mothers hate each other but we boys get along okay." He stopped again. "What I got from them is that the old man was a pretty good guy."

Not much leaves me speechless. That did.

"You don't believe it? He always behaved like a gent, didn't curse, had good manners. Respected his wife and his parents. Voted Republican!" He saw my face. "For real. You don't know everything even if you are some kind of student. Ya know what I'm saying?"

"Okay." I said it cautiously. It crossed my mind that he was not merely eccentric but delusional. I was glad to be in an open, public space surrounded by other people.

"They had reasons, those guys, they had good reasons to make money any way they could. And they only killed other crooks, you know."

"We only kill each other."

"Yes!" He nodded vigorously. "That is it in a nutshell. You get it."

He did not seem to recognize that it was a quote from Benjamin 'Bugsy' Siegel, another delusional crook. And that it was not exactly the truth.

"Now let's get down to business." He squared his shoulders and his jaw. "I need to know what you are after. You are getting in my way and I can't allow that to happen."

I still didn't like his attitude, but what I was doing was so innocuous, boring even—a doctoral dissertation!—that I told him.

"Yeah? Ha-ha. Very funny. You hang around a tough neighborhood, lots of gangs, just to do research? For grad school? Now how about telling me the truth."

"You haven't told me what you are doing either." At this point I really wanted to know. And I really wanted him to stop asking me questions.

"Grandpa Liv died poor." His expression became sly, the face I remembered from our encounter in a Brownsville alley. "So they said. But he made a fortune in his life. What happened to it?" He paused dramatically, as if he expected a response from me.

"Lost it all on slow horses and fast women?"

"Hey, watch it. That's my grandpop you're badmouthing."

Sure. Cause none of the mob had gambling habits or girls on the side.

"Spent it on lawyers? His associates stole it when he died? I never thought about it, but I'm guessing you have some of your own ideas."

"You bet I do." His chest went out and his spine straightened with pride. "He hid it. He hid it and I am going to find it."

After all these years? Right. But I stopped myself from saying that, just in time, because he had more to say.

"My brothers said no way, but I found something. Cleaning out my mom's old place I found a locked box, way up on a high closet shelf. Never saw it before, ever." He leaned toward me and I moved back a few more inches. He whispered. "It was my dad's. They were grandpa's papers. The real things. He had a notebook. And letters."

"I don't believe it."

He leaned in again more aggressively, and I added quickly, "I mean, I'm surprised, not that I think you are not telling the truth."

I took a deep breath. "You know, material like that, original sources, might have great historical value. Huge value. And maybe other kinds of value too. People collect these things. A library, or a museum, or…"

"Oh, they are valuable all right. They are. And for a lot more than a dusty library."

"Like the archives you were using today?" I half hoped he would hear the sarcasm but he took me seriously.

"Yeah, yeah, that place is useful but what I found isn't going there. It's the pot at the end of the rainbow. Yeah, you won't believe it."

"So don't tell me." I had had enough. "Or do tell me, but don't take forever." I tapped my watch.

"I know where my grandpop's fortune is hidden."

"What?"

"I do. His papers told me. They were in code but I cracked it. Of course everything looks different around there now, so it's a little hard to figure out. That's why I hooked up with that little posse. They are working for me. I hung around for awhile, disguised, until I found some guys who wanted to make some money and knew the ins and outs of the old neighborhood. My granddad didn't have no fools for grandchildren."

Now I knew he was a few aces short of a deck. Today, here, normally dressed, he had the façade of a normal person, but no one in his right mind would trust those thugs. However, saying, "Are you out of your freaking mind?" would probably not be the smart move.

Instead I said, carefully, carefully, "Has anyone else seen these papers? Someone who could, like, evaluate them to see if they are real? Or if they really do mean what you think?"

"No one sees them. Not even my own guys who work for me. That's how I make sure they don't go looking without me." His face lit up. "Now I get it. You'd like to be the one to do that, wouldn't you? Look for it? And get a cut, when we find it? Or even get there first?" He stood up and leaned in close to me. "Not a chance, lady. Not a freaking chance."

He gripped my arm and continued in a stage whisper, darting his eyes around to make sure no one was watching us. "Stay away from where we are working, near Min's, and stay away from the whole freakin' subject. I'll know what you're doing. And you will be sorry if you don't stop. I promise that."

He punctuated his tirade with a painful punch to my arm and walked away. In no time he had disappeared again into a crowd of tourists and I was too stunned to try to follow. And punch him back. Or at least, yell at him.

I didn't know if my arm hurt more, or my brain, because most of what he said made no sense. I didn't believe there was a treasure. And I didn't care if there was. And I was no threat to him. Or anybody.

Breathe, I told myself. Breathe. And then find coffee and gulp a few ibuprofen for what I was sure would soon be a dramatic bruise on my upper arm. And go back to finding some lunch.

Or maybe sit here for a bit. Breathe, and enjoy the normal spring sunshine and the normal tulips; the normal people walking around taking photos in front of quaint old City Hall; even the normal pigeons softly cooing and the normal garlic smell from the hot dog truck.

My phone rang. Oh, crap. Which pocket? Jacket or pack? I thought, oh, crap again when I saw it was my dad. And then I saw it was a text. My dad knows how to text?

It said: Downtown too meet me?

I called him back.

"Hi, Dad. What's up?"

"I am near City Hall today, taking care of some business, and heard you were in the same neighborhood?"

"What?" This was not making sense. Or maybe my mind was still on the previous encounter. "You heard about me?"

"Chris, honey. Chris. I do talk to my grandkid from time to time."

"Oh."

"So where are you? Thought I'd take you to lunch if we're nearby."

"Ah. City Hall Park. On a bench. Getting ready to head home."

"Eat yet?"

"No."

"I'll be there in two minutes. Don't move."

And there he was, all smiles, before I'd even had time to see what the market offered.

"Chris said you'd be at the Municipal Archives, so I thought I'd surprise you. I walked right in, but you already left."

I just looked at him, questioning. "You learned that...how?"

"Cause I recognized your old friend Jennifer, of course. We had a nice visit. She said I hadn't changed a bit."

"Come on. She didn't."

"Sure she did. She was at our house plenty of times when you were in school together."

I had two people stalking me today? But this one was buying lunch.

"You all right? You look a little weird." He quickly added, "Not weird. Fine. Pretty. But..."

"I'll tell you all about it. But lunch first." I pointed to the market and we wandered over.

It was too early in the season for much produce, but there was a booth with hand pies of different flavors, bland but hearty Cornish and spicy West Indian. A truck making waffles with a choice of sweet or savory toppings. The bakery booth had giant cookies and pie by the slice and tarts with vegetables and cheese. Lunch for me. Dad came back with two waffles in a box, one with maple syrup and one with thick, dark Dutch chocolate sauce.

"I see you went straight to dessert."

"Yeah. Life is short."

He had some struggles with his delicious but messy meal. I know it was delicious because he encouraged me to have a few bites.

So it took us awhile before I could tell him about my way beyond strange encounter.

"He threatened you?" I didn't like Dad's tone of voice. Even his body stance changed. The former Brooklyn scrapper was ready to go again.

"No, not really, dad." I wasn't encouraging that, not at his age. "He told me to stop following him around. Which I wasn't doing anyway."

"Or else." He sounded grim.

"Dad! Try to follow along here. One, I. Am. Not. Following. Him. Around. He is, um, somewhat delusional, I think. And two, if I don't show up where he is he will think I have stopped."

"Stopped what?"

"Following him and spying. Which I am not doing anyway. I am working on something completely different."

"And you are going to stop?"

"Hell, no. Are you kidding?" I saw his expression and quickly added, "Don't say one word. It's research I need to do. I don't care about his grandfather. And his legendary lost millions. As if."

His eyes lit up. "Liv Nathan, he said? There were stories. Let me rephrase. More like rumors than stories. He was big." He stopped. "Big locally. Not as big as the real big guys. But there should have been money and there wasn't. His girl friend found a new sugar daddy pretty fast but his widow was on welfare for a while. That's the way I heard it, anyway."

"Details, Dad. I need more."

He shrugged. "It was, like, a legend when I was a kid. Ya know? Liv's lost fortune. Way before my time. And I can tell you truthfully, I haven't thought of it in maybe fifty years." He was busy mopping up the last of the syrup. "Seems like there might have been a public screaming fight between his widow and his floozy about the money. Too bad your grandparents aren't around. They might have remembered more." He stopped and considered. "If they would talk about it. Which I'm pretty sure they wouldn't, ever."

It wasn't until we were walking to Dad's car that I thought to ask him about what he was doing there, far from his usual turf. I suddenly remembered that the marriage license office was around here. Had he gotten back with that woman? Heart beating hard and mouth dry, I asked him what his business was today.

"I went in to the Taxi Commission to see about reactivating my license."

"What? Why? I don't think that's a great idea, Dad. You were sick..."

"I'm better. I feel fine. I'm bored. I could use the money."

"You're not serious. You're not." Would saying it make it true? "I am. Why not?" I gave him the parental look he gives me. "And you can simmer down. I have to have health clearance before. So there's that."

"Okay." Of course he would do what he wanted no matter what I said. He has, from time to time, had the same complaint about me. Pretty often, actually.

At his car, I quickly created a reason I was not going home yet. I knew if I rode with him we would get into an argument about his going back to work. I knew that because there was a lot I wanted to say about it. Or we would fight about something else, as a proxy for that one. Idiotic but true. But not today.

The truth, the real truth, was that it felt awfully good to have my dad watching my back today.

Chapter Twenty-one

That night, I went back to the information my little home-grown spy had found for me. I needed to send the films and pictures to Zora, or at the very least, tell her about them. Phone, text, e-mail? Her blog? Facebook? Do I feel over-connected? Sometimes.

I went old school and e-mailed her. If she was catching a nap, I did not want to wake her. A few hours of rest are hard to come by in a hospital room, and this was too complicated to put in a text. At least it was for me.

My phone was ringing almost instantly.

"I don't sleep much. Yes, send them to me. You should have known I'd want them."

"And good evening to you, too. And how is everyone?"

She didn't take offense. In fact she made a sound that was halfway to laughter.

"Yes, I'm so excited I forgot my manners. Savanna is maybe—maybe!—having an improvement. Maybe. Something to take my mind off while I'm waiting to see would be a miracle. And how are you this fine night?"

"Okay, okay. I'll send it right out. I don't know if you will be disappointed." Suddenly I was unsure. "The little videos are fascinating to watch, yes, but they aren't very clear and the sound is bad. I don't know. Maybe you'll recognize people that I don't?"

"I have a better idea. How about we meet up tomorrow and watch them together? You bring your computer here or maybe

I come over to you? I mean…" Her voice dropped a little. "I don't like to leave Savvie but they tell me, the doctors and nurses tell me, I need a change of scene once in a while."

"I have a crazier idea. Do you want to do this right now?" I was wide-awake and didn't know who that was, that wimp nodding out on the sofa a few minutes ago. "I'm just a few minutes from the hospital."

"I'll come to you. Like I said, change of scene."

Quickly, I picked up random papers in the living room, stacked books, folded the afghan on the sofa. I scrambled for the makings of a snack

She was at the door in no time. Long legs will do that.

"Would you like anything? Bad wine? Sorry, it's all I have. Or good coffee? I scrounged up some cookies."

"Don't be silly. I am not here for a party."

We settled the laptop on the kitchen table and we looked, together, at everything Chris had done.

"Lord, lord, lord. I know some of those kids. Oh, that one there? I know him all right. But I never allow Savvie to spend time with that bunch." She turned to me. "I don't want you to think she never had fun. She had some very nice girls from the 'hood, ones she grew up with, and some decent boys too. And a ton of friends from school. She is on debate team and track and chorus. All those kids."

She stopped the tiny movie. "Wait, I missed something." She ran it again. It included a few seconds on a group of girls. "Ha. I know that one there. I do." She pointed to a girl who was gesturing fiercely. "She and Savvie were little girl friends, playing with dolls, but then they drifted, Savvie being all into school, and this one not at all. She dropped out entirely somewhere along the way." She sighed. "Damn. Can't quite get her name. Used to see her hanging around outside with some of those lay-about boys. That name will come to me in a minute." She shook her head hard. "Now, let me see that boy Jackie's messages again."

"Here it is. He is related to the boxer after all, I believe."

She stared at the screen. "Then, liar and stupid, both. I'm not making a mistake here, am I? He's as much as said he was involved somehow, right? Oh! If only I had him here, right now." Her fingers clenched. If Jackie were here, I wouldn't bet ten cents on him leaving in one piece. And I won't lie. I'd be tempted to help.

"Tammy! I got it. That girl's name."

"Tammy? But that's Tyler's ex? He said that, didn't he? She likes to be called Starr but she's really Tammy."

"Believe so. I didn't make the connection before." Her attention was elsewhere. She clicked back to the little films of Tyler and watched them several times.

"I want to hate him. I do. Him and Savanna together. She lied to me because of him. And now…and now…all those hopes stuck in a hospital room…maybe forever."

I didn't know what to say. There were no right words.

"Sorry, my mouth is running away. I meant to say, I intended to say, ah, crap." She swore a few times, fluently. That was not her usual style. "I get the attraction. He seems nice." She swore again. "Nice! He's a boy from the 'hood who beats people up for a living. How nice could he be?"

I smiled a little, I hope sympathetically. "You sound kind of…"

She jumped in. "Confused? Conflicted??" She rubbed her temples as if she could smooth out the conflicts in her head. "That's me these days. And it's not like the usual me, that is for sure." She looked up and gave me a tiny, wry smile. "There are folks who think I am a pushy attention whore. Imagine that!"

I wasn't sure if I should agree or say it wasn't true.

"Aw, come on, Little E! You can see I am joking. I don't care what folks think of me. All that matters to me is my baby getting better."

She turned her eyes back to the screen, looked at some things again, kept tapping the keys.

"Well, it seems obvious to me I need to talk to a few folks. Possibly including a slaps upside their heads. Want to come?"

"What, now?"

"No! Have you lost your mind? Even I am not tough enough to roam around the projects at...what time is it?...midnight. Let's not be stupid. We'd go tomorrow."

"You really want me along?" What did I have to bring to this plan?

"Well, I dunno. It was an impulse, but I'm liking it. You'll help me remember everything. And it will surprise people. You know what I mean? Throw them off a little. And you're not a cop so maybe they won't freeze up."

"I'm in." How could I not be? I had been pulled into this by a series of accidents but now I wanted to know. I wanted to know about Savanna and I wanted to know about Deandra's murder. I wanted that. It wouldn't contribute anything to my job life, or my academic life, and there are those who would say it wasn't safe. That would be, realistically, almost everyone in my life. But Zora was more than street smart. She was street brilliant. This was her home turf.

Besides, I was pretty sure no one picked on her, ever, from grade school on. Yes, I was in, most definitely.

In the morning, Chris was too busy herself to have any interest in my day. It was a relief, as I don't like lying to her. Today I would have.

Zora came by after breakfast and checked me out.

"You left a farewell letter behind? In case you don't come back from the Get-Toe?"

"Now you're needling me. I've been there before, you know."

"Sorry. Just goofing on you. Let's roll."

In my car, she explained her plan. It wasn't much of a plan. We would go to the project where she lived, look for people coming and going, and ask about Jackie.

And keep an eye out for Tammy, Tyler's ex-girlfriend, Savanna's ex-playmate. I had a moment of sympathy for her, everyone's ex. Was that why she was so bitchy in her digital world?

Zora sighed, a huge, heartfelt sigh. "I'm gonna have to accept him, right? If Savanna gets better? No, no, no. *When* she gets better. I'm going to have to give in on this, aren't I?"

"If she gets better, isn't there going to be a long recovery? Would you do anything to upset her? You wouldn't!"

"That's a given. Anything she wants. Even if it means some boy is always under foot, holding her hand and whatnot."

"Probably you are most worried about the whatnot."

"Ain't that the truth! Why did we do it? Go and have babies?"

I didn't respond. The reason for Chris was not the same as the reason for Savanna. She went on, "You know I don't mean it. You know that, right?"

I knew.

We were there. Time to park and get started.

"Is this a good idea?" I wasn't unlocking the car yet. "Seriously. Are we out of our minds?"

Her face hardened. "There is a possibility I am out of my mind, between grief and worry and exhaustion. That doesn't mean it is not worth a shot. I want to find the animals who did that and help their sorry asses go to jail forever. You can come with me, or not."

She hustled off, spotting someone she knew, an old man nicely dressed in a too-big topcoat. He put his shopping bags down, they hugged, they talked, all before I caught up. Zora took his bags and carried them to the door of his building, chatting the whole time.

"This is my friend Erica who came along to help me remember every detail. This is my neighbor Brother James, who knows lots of people."

"Please to make your acquaintance." He turned back to Zora. "Now that Jackie boy, I don't know a-tall, but that girl? That girl you asking about? Tammy? I do know her, but I haven't seen her lately. Doesn't her grandma live where you do? Maybe someone over there might know more." He put his hands on Zora. "And you tell your Savanna we are all saying our prayers for her." Then he patted her arm. "Savanna will hear what you say to her. Don't you doubt it." Zora helped him get the bags into the building and then motioned to me that we should walk.

"Now what?"

"Now we practice some more of the fine art of hanging around." She saw my expression. "Feeling just the same. We are the go get'em types, not the hanging around types. But we wait for someone to go in or out and then I pounce. But in a nice way, so they will be relieved when they see I just want to talk. Then maybe I can get them to tell me something useful. Maybe not. It's a fine line between gossip and giving it up to the wrong person."

A mother came out with two little girls in tow, rushing and yelling at them. Zora didn't even try to stop her. A couple of young men said "Good morning, Ms. Z," but insisted they knew nothing. An elderly lady came along. She had a cane and walked with great caution.

"I know her," she whispered. "Can't hardly see to get her door key in the lock and won't take any help. No point in asking her anything."

People came and went, people she did not know, and Zora tried to approach them with questions. Brush-offs were immediate. Some stopped to listen for a moment, some hurried away without even hearing her out.

Growing bored, I wandered around. Tall brick buildings. Open front doors, an obvious security issue. Grassy areas with no grass. Graffiti here and there, dark sprays of paint on the beige brick.

And then I spotted Jackie.

I was so surprised that I didn't react, and then I realized I shouldn't react. I very casually stepped back to Zora.

"Be cool. Jackie is right there, around that building corner. I think he might be watching us."

She nodded, pretended to look around, held her phone up for pictures, and slowly turned so she could use it to view him.

We moved around a building that hid us, and approached him from behind. Those tall, unfriendly project buildings had their good points.

"Good morning, Jackie."

He swiveled to see us, and then stepped back, ready to turn and run.

Zora grabbed his jacket by the collar.

"Don't you even think it." She was a big woman and now she had his arm bent behind his back. He looked scared. He should. I would have been.

"No running, you lying little worm. You Tyler's brother? You said no relation. You hanging around my daughter's room. Spit it out, what you know, before I turn you right over to him."

She moved his arm a little, and he gasped.

"I do believe I could break your arm right now if I felt like it. You are a scrawny little thing."

She sounded perfectly in control and cold as ice. He couldn't see her face but I could, sweat on her forehead and mouth a grim line.

"Little E."

"Right here."

"Paying attention?"

"Of course." I was all eyes and ears, holding my breath.

"Get a snap to show he was here today. Okay? Wait! Not showing me manhandling him." She yanked him upright and faked a friendly pose. I snapped away.

With her free hand, she shook him.

"What do you know about Savanna? Now!"

"Her...her and Tyler...they all deep into each other...love, love, love. Sickening."

"So what's it to you?"

"He's my big bro, my man. Big future. She a distraction. Bossy little bitch."

She jerked his arm, hard, and he cried out.

"My baby you talking about. Don't do it again."

"She talking to him about going back to school. Putting dumb dreams in his head. I'm right about this. We already got a good dream for him. People counting on it. We always said... rich and famous...and I go right along with him, taking care of things, heading up his posse."

"I know you didn't beat up my girl. You a shrimp compared to her." She shook him again. "So what do you know?"

"Nothing. Nothing worth knowing. They said…they said… just scare her. Come on. Let me go." He was crying now. "Praying for her every day."

"Really?" She used her free hand to pin him to the building. "You praying? Sure you are. For the girl you this minute called a bossy bitch?"

"Ahh, that just talking trash. I didn't mean nothing by it. You got to believe it!"

She looked about to bang his head against the brick, and he looked terrified.

I had no role here, but I was rooted to the sidewalk. I would not have left for a million bucks. I watched while my mind also raced, thinking about what Jackie said. They wanted to scare her? Who did? After him, who else would be most unhappy about distracting Tyler from his career? Maybe I knew who to ask about that. But not now. Now I could not tear my eyes from the drama right in front of me.

Then Tyler showed up.

"Yo, Jackie." He was confident, almost casual. "Why you been hiding from me?" As he approached, he turned to Zora. "Thank you, Miz Lafayette. I got it from here." He peered into the boy's face. "You ain't answer my question yet, little brother."

Zora let go and stepped back to me, breathing hard.

"Come on, Jackie." Tyler shook him. "You know I could beat you down into the sidewalk without breaking a sweat. Or having a second thought. Done it before. So give it up and save yourself a world of hurt."

Jackie shook his head. "Beat me if you have to. You going to beat me if I tell and beat me if don't tell."

Tyler slapped his face. Hard. The sound rang out into the air. "Why don't you save me the trouble?"

"I'm your little brother. You thinking about hurting me? We brothers, man!"

"Should have thought of that before you messed up hurting my girl!" Tyler's cool was slipping now. "And we only half-brothers. Mom givin' me your dad's name don't make us kin. You just like him, too, sneaking around."

At that, Jackie tried to kick Tyler but Tyler never lost his grip.

A crowd was gathering. A low hum of "Look! Look!" and "Yo, Tyler's over there." A few encouraging shouts, soon followed by more, louder, closer, meaner.

A girl's voice came screaming out of the crowd. "Tyler, you get your hands off." A short, round dynamo in a turquoise jacket launched herself at Tyler, fists pounding. "You. Let. Go."

He held Jackie with one hand and grabbed the girl's neck with his other. "You ready to stop now? You know you ain't gonna win in a fight with me."

"Let her go, bro! She just being a stand-up girlfriend."

Zora grabbed me. "That's Tammy. I'd like to have a few words with her myself, but looks like Tyler got it for now. I feel like I am going crazy here."

"You called it. Me too."

I turned just enough to see the crowd behind us and it scared me more than the fighting. It was surging closer.

"Fight!" they shouted. "Fight him!" "Show him! Show us!"

When Tyler realized his life was becoming entertainment, he dropped his hands, looking a little shocked. "You? Come on! With him?"

Tammy wrapped her arms around the younger boy.

"Hey!" Jackie shouted it. "Why the hell not?" He stood up straight, but he still looked like a child next to his brother. "She sees something here she wants."

"That so?" He pushed his face into Tammy's. "Then why you keep bothering me? Drunk texting? Sending me those snaps? Girl, ain't you got no shame?"

Jackie shouted, "What? What you been doing? You whoring around behind my back?"

Tyler whirled back to him. "She still meaning to get back

with me. What the hell matter with you, taking up with my sloppy seconds?"

Tammy shoved off cursing and yelling. "I ain't nobody's sloppy second. I do what I want, when I want, for myself. And you don't even care? Aw, Ty, you know you the one. I'm hooking up with your brother and you don't even care?"

I was shaking. We had gone from watching *The Wire* to watching *Game of Thrones*. A smack on the head reminder that these violent young adults were, after all, still kids.

He eyed her up and down for a long minute. She looked rough, her flashy jacket wrinkled, her hair messy. The giant earrings were too big for her short neck.

He finally said, "I keep telling you we are done. Been done a long time. Jackie, you want her, she's all yours. Good luck with that."

"Now I been disrespected right here in public." Jackie squared his shoulders. "Girl, if you want to stay hooked up with me, some things got to change." He was trying to seem manly, but the growing black eye and the way he cradled a wrist in his other hand undercut his effort.

She slapped his face. "I don't give two cents for you, stupid little moron. Never did. Trying to make my Ty jealous." She kicked him and then started to sob. "After all I did...after all I did...bad things to keep you..."

Tyler grabbed her by the arms. Jackie slid down to the ground, hands over his face.

"YOU did? You did? What did you do? I can put a lot of hurt on you, here and now. And ain't nobody here think it's wrong either."

Just the opposite. The shouts from the crowd were encouraging him to teach her a lesson. Vile words described Tammy and what he should do.

Tammy kicked Tyler and pounded on him with her free fist. He didn't even seem to feel it, putting her in a hammer lock till she finally stopped moving.

He didn't let go, but he loosened his hold.

"What you know about Savanna? Spit it out."

"Everybody know. Some men showed here and beat her up." She radiated resentment like a hot stove. "I didn't do a thing to that skinny skank. Not her." I felt Zora, still holding my arm, tighten her fingers. She froze, as the battling teens yelled at each other.

"She had nothing to do with her." Jackie spoke as he pushed up from the ground. He faced his brother. He even put his hands on Tyler's jacket, but quickly pulled back, seeing his hostility. "You got it all wrong. She didn't do nothing, Ty-bro."

"Don't call me that."

"Okay, okay. But you been getting it all wrong. Savanna bad for you. We all got big dreams waiting on you. Mama counting on you to make life better."

"Don't you bring mama into this."

"Okay, okay, okay." It was a nervous stutter. "But see what I'm saying? You looked like throwing it all away, talking about school and whatnot. Over what? She just a girl. Dime a dozen. You can have your pick. Have the whole dozen at once if you want to."

Tammy gasped at that, smacked Jackie one last time and walked away, a little unsteady but determined. As she went, with her back to all of us, she threw her hand above her head and lifted her middle finger in contempt.

Beside me, Zora was shaking. I was too. In front of me, Tyler crunched his brother in headlock again.

"Tell. Me. Now."

"Let me go."

"You think you got anything to bargain with? I could tear your arm off right now. Beat you over the head with it. Enjoy doing it, too. "

"How you explain that to Mama?"

"I told you to leave her out of this." He gave an extra shake. "Since when you caring about her anyway? She up all night, worrying about where you at?" The hold tightened. "I'd be doing her a favor."

"I'll tell you. Let go."

Jackie sneaked a look, calculating what his chances were if he ran. He went limp when he saw they were zero.

"I see you going down the wrong road. So I told some people...told them...where they could find her...they said, they said, only scare her away."

Tyler punched him in the face, so hard Jackie's body vibrated before crumbling. Tyler kept at it until Jackie broke free and ran, limping. Tyler was on him in a minute. He threw Jackie to the pavement and straddled him. He pummeled him like a punching bag, rhythmically, with a focus that made his fury even scarier. I thought he might kill Jackie right there in front of us.

By then the two boys were sprawled on the ground, surrounded by a circle of other young men—and some not so young and some not men—cheering them on.

Then the cops showed up.

Chapter Twenty-two

They had to pull the boys apart and hold them. They shouted to the bystanders "Break it up! Move on!" No one moved until more cops arrived and waded into the crowd shouting and shoving. Myself, I could not take my eyes away from the brothers.

"We need to be there." Zora had a firm grip on my arm. "Let's go." She whispered, "And not get stuck in this crowd."

"You boys got to break it up." A cop was shouting it. "If we let go, you gonna behave?"

"I'm gon' tear his head off, that's what I'm fixing to do." Jackie was thrashing around, trying to get free.

"On your best day, your BEST one ever, you little cockroach, you couldn't get close to me."

Jackie's struggles became even more frenzied as we got closer. Sergeant Asher, radiating authority, approached from the street. She glared at all of us.

"Get these two baby gangsters subdued. Now." She turned to us. "You have more to say about my case? That you didn't already tell me? I don't like having my time wasted." She turned back to the uniformed cops. "Cuff the boys if necessary but bring them in."

"No, no, no." Jackie was still twisting and turning. "I can say it here. Ain't much but my big shot big bro needs to hear it."

Asher made a "hold off" gesture to her men. Zora and I stopped dead in our tracks.

"I told some men where they could find Savanna." He staggered to his feet, his face oozing blood and eye already swelling and purple. "I told them. That's all. Didn't mean no real harm." He looked at Tyler. "In your interest, man, that's all it was. They your people, not mine. They didn't say it would be a beat down."

You could have heard Zora all the way to Manhattan. "What did you say?" She broke through the little knot of cops and was right in Jackie's face. At that moment I wouldn't have given him any chance at all against her. "You led those monsters to my baby? And you still are not saying who they are? I could rip you apart." She was panting. "I would like to."

"No, no, leave him to me, Miz Lafayette," Tyler said. "My half-brother, my girl. That's my job."

"No, it is not." When Sergeant Asher spoke she somehow became the person in charge. Just like that. How did she do that? "It's *my* job, you young fools. See that?" She pointed to her shield. "That says so."

"You spit it out, Jackie boy." Tyler ignored her. "Who these men you keep calling mine? I got no gang, only my home boys, and none of them would even think to lay a finger..."

Jackie smiled, swollen eye and all. It was a vindictive grin, both evil and pathetic.

"You so busy being the good boy, you don't know who your own people are. Never knew their names, but they sent from people paying for your training. You think it comes for free? Cause they like your pretty face? See, they saw same as me—she distracting you and they worried about their investment."

Under his smooth tan skin, Tyler flushed an angry dark color. Zora turned on him. "You made this happen?" She looked ready to give him his own medicine.

"No." He shook his head. "Hell, no. Not possible they would do that. Knowing she means everything to me?"

"You still the cause. Your life." She poked him in his chest with each word. "Your friends."

"Stand down, Ms. Lafayette. And I mean now." Asher was signaling to her men.

"Not my friends. They are not. Not now. Not ever, really. They are…they are kind of…."

Sergeant Asher grabbed Jackie by the back of his neck. "Explain. Now. Or we are taking a ride you won't enjoy."

Seeing with only one eye, and bleeding, Jackie said "They had a lot of money in you. The beaters work for them. Sent to give a message to her, like, stay away, and to you too, like, keep your eyes on the prize." He spat a mouthful of blood. "You not going back to school, boy, no matter what honey she whisper in your ear. You sticking to your training and you gonna make big money for them. And us all."

"Oh, for crying out loud!" Asher looked to be at the end of her rope. "Take this idiot in." She turned to Jackie. "And no more problems from you, either. Hear me? You are in big trouble." Back to the uniformed cops. "Use cuffs. And give him an ice pack. I want him able to talk. I have a whole lot of questions for him."

She looked at Tyler. "You. You are coming along. I have plenty of questions for you too." She snapped her head back to the cops. "In a different car, not anywhere near each other. I want them alive and conscious."

She looked us over. "Ms. Lafayette, you need to go away now. None of this concerns you."

"None of this concerns me?" She could have singed Asher with her glare. "Who else you know is *more* concerned than me? I am not letting those two little SOBs out of my sight until someone is behind bars."

Then I learned that Sergeant Asher was a smart cop.

"Ms. Lafayette," she said softly, "I know when it comes to involvement, no one cares more than you, not even close. But we are taking these two knuckleheads and we are going to get everything they know. I do mean everything—they're going nowhere until they give it all up and Jackie's not going even after that. No way. I promise. With each word, her voice grew softer but more emphatic.

By the time we are done we will know what the thugs had for breakfast and what car the boss drives. And we'll be right on top of every single detail, I promise." She stopped. "After you, we are the people who most want to nail the bastards. And we might finally be on that road. Sounds good?"

"Yes, but..."

"Why don't you go hug your daughter and tell her we are making some progress here?"

The lieutenant shouted at the last stragglers to move on now, and headed for her car.

Zora suddenly looked a few inches smaller and thoroughly exhausted. Myself, I was still shaking. She shocked me by putting her head on my shoulder.

"I can hardly take it all in," she whispered. "I don't even know who to be most mad at now." She stood up and looked at me. "What do you think? Can I trust that woman to go after them like she said?"

"Her? Oh, yeah."

Zora pulled herself straight and gave a little shake.

"Lord, lord, what now?" She looked all around, not seeming to see anything. She closed her eyes. "I believe I do need to take her advice and just go hold my baby. You going in that direction?"

"Yes, I'm going home. I'm exhausted, just watching all that. All that...all that..."

"Craziness?" Zora's voice shook. "But their stupid drama almost got my baby killed." She took some deep breaths and stood up straighter. "I don't feel like saying they're just stupid kids and stopping there."

We were out of the project by then. She pointed down the city block to a doughnut shop.

We fueled up, drowning the shakes in comfort food—coffee all around, a chocolate glazed doughnut for me, and Boston cream stuffed for Zora.

"Make it a double." Zora said. "One for now, one for the road. Caffeine and sugar, two of my favorite food groups."

My smile trembled, heartfelt. My pulse slowed, my breath evened out. I was calming down from the shakes from the burst of violence.

She said, "I'm serious. They are. Savvie loves the doughnut holes. She could eat a whole bag in a flash."

"Someday soon you'll be buying her some." I patted her arm.

"Your mouth to God's ears. When that day comes, I plan to buy the whole party size box, all for her."

A woman in layers of dirty sweats pushed past us as we were leaving.

Zora stopped and turned around. "I do believe that is Deandra's mother. I haven't seen in her in forever. She looks in a bad way."

We went back in, me following Zora's lead as I had all morning. Her world, not mine. The woman stood at the counter, wheedling. No, the right word is begging.

Her speech was slurred as she tried to persuade the older woman behind the counter to give her a doughnut.

"I am so hungry and I ain't got no money today. I'll pay you back when I get some. That's a promise, me to you."

"Ma'am, I can't. I'd lose my job."

"You can just pour me a coffee then. I'll fix it up with a whole lot of sugar."

"Ma'am?" The woman looked desperate. "Please. I have to ask…"

Zora stepped to the counter. "Give me a small bag of doughnut holes and a coffee." She turned to the woman next to her. "Why, Alice Ann, is that you? It's Zora. You know, Savanna's mother."

The other woman's eyes filled with tears. "They took my baby. Did you know that? You have Savanna but my girl is gone. Gone." She started rocking back and forth. "Never gon' see her again."

Zora guided her to one of the few seats. She promptly put her head down on the table and didn't move.

"My order is ready, Erica. Bring it here?" Zora was shaking the woman's shoulder. "Come on, Alice. Wake up. We've got doughnut treats for you and smell that coffee."

"Ha. Wake up and smell the coffee. Ah." She wrapped her hands around the warm cup. "Still cold out. Spring but not warming. I been up most of the night, wandering around. Cold."

"Drink up. You still have a home?"

She glared at Zora. "I ain't living on the street! But I don't like being home now. Never did, really. Even before…before… walking at night kept the devil away. It's a comfort to be out and around."

"I know. But now you need to go home and shower and then get some sleep. Take the doughnuts."

She was holding a doughnut hole as if she hadn't seen one before. She licked her sugary fingers and then ate the munchkin in one bite. And ate another. She was not ready to move.

"My sweet little Didi. Did you know her?" She peered at Zora but I'm the one who answered.

"Yes, ma'am. I met her a couple of times. She was…she did seem…very sweet. And nervous? Like something on her mind?" I stopped myself before I blurted out that I had found her body. Not an image I wanted to lay on this woman. Instead I said, irrelevantly, "I liked her sneakers."

She smiled sadly. "She loved those pink sneakers. She did." A pause. "I don't remember how she got them." Another two munchkins and she sighed. "Yes, she was a nervous little girl. But more now. One time…one time, a nighttime, she came to find me when I was wandering, my sweet girl, and she was real upset. Something she saw… she wasn't supposed to see…and I didn't listen. Wasn't quite myself that night." She was crying again. She stood up, hugging her coffee and putting the bag into a pocket.

The woman at the counter opened the door for her to stumble out.

"You know her? She comes in a lot looking for free food. Sometimes I have day olds I can give away." She shook her head. "She must have some demons chasing her."

We watched her shuffle across the street, mid-block, ignoring the traffic. She stopped to eat a doughnut hole from the bag, then walked off aimlessly in the wrong direction. She stopped to talk to someone. Would she ever get to her home?

"Yeah, those demons have got her good." Zora rubbed her eyes. "No way to get her help if she doesn't want it. Haven't slept much myself lately."

That was the truth. She fell asleep in the car. I woke her when we reached the hospital.

"We're here? Already?" Before she went in, she added, "Thank you. Good to have you along today." She smiled the faintest of smiles. "Later today I'll start harassing those cops for some results."

"What are you going to do if Tyler comes back to the hospital?"

"Cross that bridge when I need to. What I am hoping is, he is too afraid of me to try it."

"Afraid? Really? He gets beat up for a living."

"Yes, but he's still a kid. And there is nothing as scary as an angry momma with attitude. Don't you know that?"

I thought about it the whole rest of the way home. Could I learn that from Zora? As Chris moved ever deeper into teenager-hood, it could come in handy.

For a little while, it displaced the other question I had been running in my head. Tammy. She said, "After all I've done." I was sure of it.

What did it mean? When she said it, it looked to me like something more significant than loving Tyler. That she had actually done something.

And as I thought about it, I realized the cops had not arrived yet, when she was ranting, so they didn't hear it.

When I finally got home I found mail from my advisor, both e-mail and a paper letter. At the sight, all conflicts from this morning flew out of my mind. I only wondered how much trouble I might be in, how far behind in my academic work I was.

I didn't open either of them. Not yet. The argument in my head split me right down the middle. Half of my brain said, "I don't care. I need a break. I don't care." Okay, maybe that was not my brain talking. The other half said, "So many people have helped you with jobs, fellowships, and encouragement. You owe it to them to be responsible and dedicated." I had no idea who was talking there, but I didn't want to listen.

This called for chocolate. I suspected Chris had some stashed away.

How much snooping could I legitimately do in her room? Ah, probably none. And if I did it anyway, would I find things I don't want to know? Risky.

So I texted:

Chocolate emergency. Got some?

Ten minutes later, she was back with:

Shelf next to bed. Touch NOTHING else! I'll know!!!!

A bag of M&Ms, all for me. After a handful, I had the courage to open my advisor's e-mail. She was changing her phone number. That was it? That's all? And the letter merely confirmed the same and explained the overall building communications upgrade. Like I cared.

All that angst for nothing. Although I did get the M&Ms out of it.

After the flurry of panic about the official mail, I went back to the events of the morning. It was not only the drama that I couldn't get out of my mind. Or the tragedy. It was Tyler and Savanna. They had hope, in a corner of the city where there was very little of that to be found. They believed they could write a different story for themselves. It would take a heart of stone not to be touched by them.

Then again, was all of this the truth? We only had his story about Savanna and himself, deeply in love and supporting each other. What would Savanna say, if she could talk to us? Chris was in her first romance and I myself wasn't taking it very seriously. She's only a kid. Savanna and Tyler were a little older, and lived far less protected lives, but that still did not make them adults.

Chris' words came back to haunt me. "I'm a year younger than you were when you met dad. And you were old enough to know."

Somewhere in that moment, for a second, I was that girl again, dancing at a party with a new boy and feeling like my life was forever changed. As it was.

Making myself move on, I considered Jackie. He was a nasty piece of work, looking to his half-brother for fame and fortune. And he did say someone else was behind the attack on Savanna, the mysterious people he had helped.

Long ago, I learned something useful from Leary.

"Don't you believe it is churchy la femme, no matter what those Frenchies say. It is churchy la francs. Following the money always gets you somewhere."

So. After Jackie, who would be most unhappy to have Tyler quit boxing? Who had the serious money in the game?

Boxing trainer Brennan would not tell me, and claimed he did not know. Yeah, right. Tyler and Jackie could not tell me, as they were busy telling everything to Asher. They did not appear to know, themselves, who pulled the strings. Maybe they were telling the truth, maybe not.

But now I knew someone myself. Joe's friend Archie. The lawyer who loved boxing.

I e-mailed. <Could I ask you one more boxing question?> <Call me.> So I did.

He sounded impatient so I got right to it.

"Besides his trainer, who would be most unhappy about a promising young boxer quitting? Would it be the people who are investing in his career?"

"If there is a lot of money out? You bet. The big money supporters would be controlling as much of his life as they can. All for his own good, they would say."

"How far would they go?"

"Hey. You are getting into some deep waters. Is this really about grad school? Maybe you need to tell me why you want to know?"

"Don't think so."

There was a long silence.

"Then this is as far as I can go with an answer. If it was someone like me, say—and I have made those investments—I'd just talk his ear off until he got back in the game. If it was some, ah, less polished persons? They might exert pressure." Over the phone line, I could hear him thinking.

"For an example, because I met his trainer? That young Tyler Isiahson?" I was trying to be devious. "What about him?" I held my breath.

There was silence. Then he said, "There are rumors. Just rumors and gossip. Remember that's all it is. That his backers are...let's say, not the most respectable businessmen. Does that help?"

"Yes, I think it does. Thank you very much."

"No problem. But be careful, okay?"

So there was gossip about Tyler. And if there was gossip? Then it had to be out there somewhere. These days, every kind of gossip is out there somewhere. And while I couldn't interrogate or threaten or arrest anyone, I could sure as hell research.

Chris came home after dinner at Mel's, knocked on my door, said she was going to bed.

Two grueling hours later, way into the night, I had followed every hyperlink, skimmed an enormous amount of celebrity gossip, browsed obscure webzines and listservs about sports, boxing, and Brooklyn. And I knew something.

It was a tiny article from an obscure boxing fan newsletter. Obscure to me, anyway. There was a photo. A winning boxer, not Tyler, posing with some "very big fans." They had arms around him, huge grins and an overflowing bottle of champagne. The caption had names. And it mattered because I had seen two of them before. In a parking lot.

Those photos I had taken so impulsively in Williamsburg, trying hard not to include them in the evocative scene? When I opened my phone for the first time since, there they were. It was a bad photo, odd angle, irrelevant people, and car in one corner. My failure to keep them out of the photo had become a success for information. I almost laughed as I keyed the names into my search bar.

There weren't a lot of hits but all were shady. Lots of words like "alleged" and "organized crime" and "dubious". In fact, it reminded me of the captions on the photos from the archives, the Murder Inc trial files. Only the names had changed.

I made a neat little digital package for Sergeant Asher—boxing article, my photo, the background articles and labeled it "Merry Christmas." With a smiley emoticon. Inappropriate, but by then I was giddy with exhaustion. I fell into bed in my clothes.

Chapter Twenty-three

I slept late into the morning. Chris had gone to school. I forced myself to do normal, everyday, boring things. On automatic pilot, I looked in the refrigerator for the makings of breakfast. Somehow I had missed dinner last night. I opened the mail I had ignored yesterday.

Bills. I set them aside. I had an invitation for a concert at the Hudson Home, and reception following, signed in perfect penmanship by Ruby. "I will be playing, and Lillian too if she is well enough. We'd love to have you as our guest. Bring friends!"

No matter what I did, I couldn't stop thinking about Deandra. And Tammy too. Did Sergeant Asher know that Tammy had been part of the fight, before Asher arrived? Should I tell her? Or should Zora? I sent Zora a quick note and her response was, "You do it. I am busy watching my baby breathing. On her own! It is beautiful."

That was the best thing I had heard in several days.

I finally called Sergeant Asher.

She said, "Ms. Donato, are we going steady? Not that I don't enjoy talking to you but I am quite busy."

Exactly the embarrassing response I was dreading, but I knew that what I had to say, that Tammy was in this mix, was important. Maybe. Of course Asher already knew about it.

"People might not want to talk to us, one to one, but out of that whole crowd, you think there was no one who wanted to gossip or feel important or be eager to tell a tale on someone they did not like? You can be sure we heard about Tammy."

"What about Deandra? I met her mother yesterday."

"Ah, Deandra's mother." She sighed. "Yes indeed. But there are detectives working hard on that one. Trust that. Ms. Donato… ah, thank you for the information you sent me earlier." Did I hear a little warmth in her voice? "We would have found it in time. I believe we would have, but you shortened the process." She paused, then continued.

"Look. I need you not to interfere, but, well, if people talk to you? And you happen to pick up something? Send it my way. You never know." Did I hear a little warmth in her voice before she said, "Back to work now."

In the night I had dreamed about Deandra's mother, standing across the street, bag of doughnuts in her hand, talking to someone. And the someone was Tammy. I was sure of that.

In the morning I was not sure. I was sure Zora and I had seen Deandra's mother talking to someone after she left us. I didn't get a good look and wasn't really trying to from across the street, but something in my memory was telling me it was Tammy. Hairstyle? Clothes? Shoes?

Hollow squares of gold dangling from her ears. I'd seen it without seeing it. And turquoise clothing.

Well, damn. Why? Why was she talking to Deandra's mom? Why wasn't she home, nursing her wounds and writing crazy posts? I took a deep breath. Was she a friend of Deandra?

I thought about Deandra as I found her in the trashcan. Deandra being lifted out, so thin, with bits of garbage caught in her hair. And Deandra in my car, wanting to talk and practically shaking with fear of what she was going to say.

I should have kept her there, made her tell me the rest. Keeping her secrets had not kept her alive.

Damn again. It looked like I would be going back to Brownsville. I didn't want to. Now I just wanted to finish my chapter, get right with my adviser, and be done with that place, but I was not going to be able to banish Deandra.

I could try to find Tammy and ask some big questions.

It was a dumb plan. I knew it was even as I double-checked the location of Zora's building where Tammy also lived. I looked for the school she no longer attended. Dropouts, against all logic, sometimes hang around looking for their friends. Maybe most important, the spot where I had seen Tammy, across the avenue from the doughnut shop. A public street, under the elevated train tracks. A commercial strip in its own depressed way.

I took the subway. I didn't want to deal with finding parking, getting back to the car from wherever I ended up, didn't want to worry about it. My stop was out toward the end of the line, when the subway cars become spookily empty. I got on a middle car, the most crowded, but by the time I got off, there were only a couple of other passengers. They were all minding their own business, just as I was, all of us not seeing and not noticing. And hoping not to be noticed.

I started at the doughnut shop. The woman behind the counter remembered me. Why was I surprised? I could guess she didn't have many white women customers who weren't regulars, people working in the area.

She certainly remembered Deandra's mother. When I asked her about Tammy, she nodded. "Yeah, yeah. I know her. Likes a cinnamon twist. Mouthy little girl with those silly-looking earrings." She stroked her own sparkly drops. "And soon as summer comes, tops down to here. I mean, way down."

I had my list of questions, a mental list not on paper. I asked if she'd ever seen another girl with her, small for her age, with flashy clothes and bright pink sneakers. No, not one of the ones who hung around with Tammy.

I bought a whole box of doughnuts to thank her—and because I love doughnuts myself—and as I was leaving she said thoughtfully, "Pink sneakers? You asking about that girl got shot last week?"

I nodded. "Her mother's the woman asking for free doughnuts."

"Oh, my lord. I had no idea. No idea. And I do think I seen her girl. Not here, but somewhere. Let me think on it."

"Care to share my doughnuts with me while you do?"

"Oh, hell no. I'm around them all day. All that sugar makes me sick now." After a minute, she said, "I am thinking I saw her, this dead girl, rest her soul, with that Tammy somewhere. That little store over there?" She pointed across the street. "They sell socks and gloves and underpants and like that, and some jewelry too." She closed her eyes, remembering. "Seems like that girl—Tammy?—was buying her something. And I noticed only because I recognized that Tammy." She smiled apologetically. "That's all. Must be last time, maybe only time, I saw that other girl." A customer came in, and our conversation ended but I had my next stop.

The cramped shop had items piled on tables and hanging from the wall. The two people in it, an older woman and a young man with a flashy jacket both ignored me. Pointedly. I didn't feel at all welcome, but I selected a pair of cheap, stretchy gloves anyway in hot pink and went to the register.

"You want those?"

"Yes, and I'd take two pair if you have another in this color." I smiled and confided, "My daughter loses them all the time."

The woman was not charmed. "You think we have lots of gloves left? It's spring! We are getting them out to make room for summer things."

I nodded strong agreement. "Hard to remember when it's still so chilly. Think it will warm up to spring weather soon?"

That was as innocuous a remark as I could think of. She only stared and put her hand out for the money I held. I made one last try.

"I know a girl who lives around here and loves this color. Did she ever shop here? Just wondering what else I could get for her. Maybe was with another girl who liked great big earrings? The kind that make my ears hurt thinking about them?"

"We got girls like that here all the time. You buying anything else?"

"Uh, no." I couldn't wait to leave, but just as I was pulling the door, the young man spoke up.

"The girl with the earrings? Who wants to know? You some kind of welfare worker?"

"No. I knew the younger girl."

"You a cop?"

"Do I look like a cop?" I straightened up to my full sixty-inch height.

He stared me down.

I gave in. "No, I'm not a cop. Not any kind of official."

"I might know who you mean." He shrugged. "Sorry, Mom, but you know some of these girls come here to see me. They get all giggly practicing how to flirt. So, yeah, I seen her here lots of times. One time, maybe, another girl with her, a kid. She was buying her pink gloves, yes, and some big pink hairdo things."

I tried to say thank you nicely but he had turned away. Time to make my next stop. Now I wanted to talk to Tammy more than ever. Her brutal romantic life was Lieutenant Asher's problem, but it seemed pretty certain that she knew Deandra. They were friends. Or something like that.

I started in the direction of her building. As I had learned from Zora, I would sort of wander, sticking to the places where there was some foot traffic, and see what I might find. Maybe Tammy herself. I crossed my fingers and wondered what I would do with hot pink gloves.

Going in the right direction—at least I hoped so—I realized I was close to the little impromptu memorial for Deandra. I swerved, looked around, headed onto the path that connected the project's apartment buildings.

It was still there, days later. A lot of the flowers were turning brown and the toys had been destroyed by rain, but there were new flowers too. She was not forgotten. It made me sad and angry, both at once, to wish these people had been watching out for her when she was alive. Including me. I didn't know which people or who to be angry at. I just was.

I would never be able to explain this but I hung the pink gloves on the branches of the scraggly bush that was there. I saw there were buds. It would be blooming soon.

If there is an afterlife, my Jeff would have been in touch. I was sure of that. So I am not a believer. This little shrine was not for her but for the living people who made it. I guess I was one of them.

I walked away, eyes blurred, and then turned around for one last look. I would not be back here. Someone else was there. From the distance it looked like Tammy.

I went back, softly, softly as I could. I did not want to give her a chance to run. Halfway there, I heard her talking. To herself? To a phone? Dear lord, to Deandra?

She looked around, hugged herself, and looked around some more. She snapped off one of the flowers and tucked it in her hair.

"Stupid bitch, you know you don't need gloves where you are at now. What fool left them here?" She ripped them off the bush and stuck them in her pocket.

By then I had texted Asher about what I saw. I wasn't letting Tammy out of my sight. She walked away and I walked after her.

When she suddenly sat on a bench and took out a candy bar, I did not stop behind her soon enough. She saw me, looked me up and down with contempt.

"Bitch, you following me?"

"Excuse me???" I gave her an equally aggressive stare.

She was not impressed. "If you following me, get lost. I don't know you and you in my place here."

"I knew Deandra."

"Oh, yeah. You the white lady who found her? Stupid little twitchy kid." Tough words, tough voice, but her expression had changed. Just a little. At least I thought so. "No sense at all. Big mouth."

Ugly attitude about a dead child. I took a few steps toward her.

"You knew her? Were you friends?"

"Who's asking?" She stood up. "I got places to go, white lady. Get out of my face."

"Not till you tell me what you know about her." The words left my mouth before I could think about them.

"You kidding me?" She looked me up and down again, "You and who else stop me?"

"Was it about Savanna? Deandra knew something that scared her." A light went on. "Were the secrets about you? I was here yesterday. I saw and heard everything."

She came running at me. It's been a lot of years since my last schoolyard fight but I saw it coming and was able to keep my feet firmly planted. I don't know how. Unable to knock me down, she shook me so hard I bit my tongue.

"What you know, stupid white bitch? You don't know a thing. Not one thing."

She never let go of me, but she began to sob. She hit me in the face, hard, and ran away. I ran too. Fueled by my own anger, I caught her, grabbed her jacket, and pulled. We both went down and she was crying so hard, I was able to pin her.

"What. Did. She. Know."

"Me and Tyler. She knew about that."

"Who didn't?"

"She saw me. That night. She was out looking for her crazy mom."

"What? The night Savvie was attacked?"

She struggled, trying to get up. Had I hit a nerve? Sitting on her, I was barely heavy enough to hold her down. Not for long, but for now.

"I was there that night. Saw it all. Cheered, too. I don't care one bit, but she saw me, where I shouldn't have been."

"She saw you? She would have told Tyler, is that it?"

"He'd hate me if he knew. I'd never get him back, my own Tyler, never, ever, even if that evil bitch died. And I knew Dee would blab. I knew, even after I bought her presents. I knew she was bursting to tell."

She wasn't trying to get away anymore. Her face in the gravel, she was gasping for breath.

"Did you kill her?' My own words sounded unbelievable even as I spoke them. "You? Because you thought she might tell Tyler?"

She went completely still, frozen and silent.

I got up and hauled her to her feet. I looked straight into her eyes, holding her arms as tight as I could. "What happened to her?"

"I did what I had to do, just making sure she never told a soul. Took my brother's gun and dumped it after. All her own stupid fault cause I couldn't trust her. And I don't care. Ain't it a shame?" She had stopped crying. "Never had no choice."

"You killed her in a crowd? I don't believe that's possible."

"Not right there. Across the street. No one near and I waited till there was lots of noise so no one heard. I had walked with her near a place I could dump her. After. She was heavier than she looked. It was hard. Harder than I thought. I never catch a break."

She collapsed into an unmoving and silent ball, right on the gravel walk. I saw two cops coming from the street, and I kept a tight grip on her until they arrived. I answered their questions, they cuffed her, and she didn't even put up a fight. I was not entirely sure she knew what was happening.

Then I walked away. Their boss had my number. They could contact me if they needed to.

I wanted to get home and stay there.

Chapter Twenty-four

A few weeks later we went to the spring concert at the Hudson Homes. "We" included Chris, who surprised me by asking to come when she saw the invitation. It took me a full twenty-four hours to connect the location with her boyfriend. I have no explanation for this.

She looked sheepish when I asked, and admitted that one of his grandmothers was in residence there too. He would like to join us. She added hastily, "If it's okay."

It was a perfect spring day, sunny and mild. The tulips were blooming in bright colors everywhere, swaying slightly in the breeze from the river. I remembered with a pang Lil's comment that she might not see the flowers from the bulbs she watched being planted in the fall. Would she be playing her flute today?

No. The orchestra came in, all white hair and festive outfits, and Ruby was seated last, an honor for the first violinist. I know that from public television. I did not see Lil among the flutes. The conductor disconcertingly looked like a music student, young enough to be someone's grandson. I flipped through the program. Yes, it turned out he was the grandson of a resident and he donated his time to the orchestra. One very proud grandma, I thought.

I don't know anything about classical music. I grew up on rock 'n' roll and Mom's show tunes—I used to complain about Rogers & Hammerstein on car rides—and that's about it for me.

Chris has had to take music classes in school, though. She pointed to the list of pieces and whispered, "We studied some."

She patted my hand. "Don't worry. Nice music. You will like them." And I did. I especially liked the only one I recognized, excerpts from *The Nutcracker*.

Jared, the boyfriend, turned up at the reception, a beaming white-haired lady on his arm. He's a cute kid in a goofy sort of way. Chris turned pink when he introduced her to his grandmother as his girlfriend.

Ruby found me before I found her and she gave me a hug. She looked surprised at that herself. "I am sorry if I was pushy. I'm still so excited from the music. And the applause! You know we have some real retired musicians here. Fully trained, real pros." She whispered to me, "I only got to be first violin because there isn't someone here who is better. But don't tell anyone." She smiled graciously at our little group.

"I thought it was wonderful! You all played with so much, uh, so much enthusiasm."

"Brio, Mom." Chris turned away from Jared and his grandmother. "Brio is the word you want."

"Why, who is this?"

"This is my daughter Chris. Chris, please say hello to Dr. Boyle. And this is Chris' friend Jared and his grandmother, Evie Levine."

Ruby said with a smile, "I know Evie from the orchestra. Nice clarinet work on the Mozart."

"Why, thank you. Of course I am much too young to have a handsome grandson this grown up." She winked and it was Jared's turn to go pink. "But where is your sidekick? The lady who wears the track suits?"

"Ah. You know…" Ruby fluttered a hand toward the clinic. "Not so well…"

"So sorry. Come, Jared, escort me to get some punch and let these people visit. You can come back later."

"What is going on with Lil?"

Ruby's face turned to stone. "She is in hospice now and mostly sleeps. I always push her to wake up and talk, to keep her mind alive, but it works less and less."

She turned to Chris abruptly and demanded, "Tell me about yourself. Are you interested in music? Or did your mother drag you here? Are you interested in history, like your mom?"

"I'm into creating, not studying." She added quickly, seeing my face, "Not that I'm not a good student! But making things is what really interests me."

"Ah. So you are an artist. And you know it early. Excellent. And what medium do you like best?"

"I went to art camp and we got to try everything! That was so cool. My photography won a prize. And my painting is only so-so, but my sketching improved a lot."

"Come walk with me," Ruby began, as she took Chris' arm. "I've known a number of artists, some quite famous. Would you like to meet a working artist? Perhaps a summer job? Now I have to warn you…" They walked off together, talking away, Chris confiding her dreams to a complete stranger.

I was surprised. No, flabbergasted. I turned to Joe, who was amused by my reaction.

Yes, Joe had come with us. He invited himself, just like Chris. In fact, I suspected Chris had something to do with it. His only explanation was, "I get along great with old ladies. And I can sit through a concert as well as the next guy."

I abandoned both Chris and Joe for a little while, to go see Lillian by myself. I wanted to see her and I was scared to see her. If she was awake, I would have to tell her I had failed at solving the mystery of her brother. And if she was not awake, I should probably still tell her. They say even unconscious people can hear voices—Zora talked to Savanna as much as she could—and I needed to talk to Lil. Or she needed me to.

She was awake and sitting up by the window, looking out. I was so surprised I checked to make sure it was the right room.

She turned a little when I called her name. "You see. There are the tulips. I watched the bulbs going in, in the fall, and here they are now, all that pink and red. Do you know the lovely poem about needing darkness for birth and light for flowering? I've been thinking about that lately." She sighed.

"Anyway, here I am to enjoy them. For a little while, at least."
I walked in, standing near her at the window and leaning
over to shake her hand. Impulsively, I turned it into a kiss on
her soft, wrinkled cheek. She smelled of lotion and cologne and
something else, underneath, that was not so sweet.

"We missed you at the concert but I sneaked some cookies
for you."

"Why, thank you dear. I'll be happy to have a cookie or two.
I am partial to the ones with the swirl of chocolate frosting."
She ate it in two bites. "And what concert was that, dear? Was
I supposed to go?"

This was worse than I expected. She didn't remember being in
the orchestra. Her enunciation was blurred and so were her eyes.

"Lil, do you know me? It's Erica Donato."

"Come stand here, where I can see you better. Why of course
it's Erica! The sun was in my eyes so I couldn't see you clearly."

Nice save. I pulled a small stool over so I could sit at her
level. I held her hand and said, "You wanted me to find you
some information."

She smiled gently. "And did you?"

"Not really. I am so sorry. I found a tiny handful of refer-
ences to your brother but that's all. Nothing that told us what
happened."

"My brother? Frank? That's all right. He talks to me now. I
suppose he will tell me himself in due time."

How many drugs was she on? A lot, it seemed. I knew the
goal was to keep her comfortable and pain-free now. I wasn't
sure she understood anything I said, but did it matter? She was
smiling, not worried about a thing.

"I did bring you this, though. I thought you'd get a kick out
of it."

It was copies of the census pages that showed her and her
family, the originals and some I'd blown up to allow her to read
the hand-written lines that had the Krawitz family data.

"You see, there you are, and your parents and your other
brothers."

"There I am! Little Lillian, the first baby with an American name." She put a finger out and stabbed one of the boxes. "And my Feivel at the top, because he was the oldest. So someone knew about us? What was this, the secret police?"

It said US Census at the top of the page in clear letters. I explained and she said, "Really? All our names are here, written in these books, forever?" In a minute, she was gently snoring.

I left and I won't lie. I had to stop and get control of myself before I returned to our table.

Joe looked up and he knew everything and saw everything. He stood and put his arms around me and I stayed there for a long time. It helped.

I took the fourth seat at the table, and he handed me a glass and pushed the plate of cookies my way. Chris and Jared were there too, sharing their own plate. I wondered if I was on a double date with my daughter and her boyfriend. And Joe. How was this possible?

Under the table, Joe picked up my hand. I curled my fingers around his and held on tight. He whispered into my ear, "Let's ditch the kids and have a nice dinner out. Chris plans to go to Jared's and his parents will bring her home."

So it was a date after all. I had been conned. It didn't bother me at all.

That was the last time I saw Lil. She died a few days later. Ruby called to tell me, and I wondered how small their circle had become, if I was important enough to be told. There would be a memorial service later, and I promised to go.

Ruby did arrange for Chris to meet a famous artist, son of a painter who had been a close friend. Chris' mouth dropped open when she heard the name. She wrote a note to Ruby, thanking her, without any prompting from me and they have continued to keep in touch.

Zora and I stayed in touch too but she was busy with Savanna now. The doctors are cautiously saying full recovery is possible but she has surgery ahead and many long months of physical therapy. Knowing Zora, I was sure there would be no slacking on the hard work. Wellesley would defer her admittance and her scholarship for a year. Tyler continued boxing, with Savanna's name in big letters on the back of his warm-up jacket.

Some months later, I had a message from Sergeant Asher. "News tonight. Just beginning!" It was a brief story: the state was indicting prominent boxing promoters on charges of racketeering, bribery, money laundering and more. Tax fraud, too. Among the boxers under management was Tyler Isiahson. Savanna was not mentioned then, and the case remained officially open, but two of the men repeating "No comment" had been talking to Tommy Brennan in a parking lot one spring day. Brennan retired abruptly, for real this time, and moved to Florida. And Joe's friend Archie told us over dinner one night that Tyler had a whole new management team.

James Nathan never found his treasure, or at least, not that I ever heard about it. I found one, though.

Before the Stone Avenue library closed for renovation, when it was already closed for packing, I had an invitation from Ms. Talbot.

"Would you like to come by this week, while we are still here working? We found something you might like to see. We usually take a break about three and I bring in a treat."

I wasn't going to miss that. I brought baklava from one of the Syrian groceries.

The inside of the building looked so different, stripped of all contents and crowded with cartons. The emptiness made the stained paint and pitted wooden bookcases and cracked flooring far more noticeable. Yes, it was time for a facelift. Like Ms. Talbot, I hoped they would not destroy the original charm.

Ms. Talbot, Mr. Wilson, and a small crew of clerks and teenagers were there. We ate cupcakes and baklava and fruit juice, and shared news of Savanna. They would all be scattering next week, the full time staff to different branches, and the teenagers to the nearest other branch, a couple of subway stops down the line.

When everyone went back to packing, Ms. Talbot brought me into her office. It too was mostly stripped, except for the furniture the movers would take to storage, but there were stacks of books and files on the desk.

"These are the valuable items. I pack and mark them myself so there is no question about how they need to be handled." She handed me a cardboard folder, faded red and tied with attached string. "This is what I thought you'd like to see."

It was photographs, old, cracked, peeling. Black and white.

"We found it way in the back of an old closet behind cartons of supplies. This place hasn't been cleaned out in decades!" She saw my questioning look, and added, "Nothing with it, no explanation of any kind. But you can tell where they were taken."

I surely could, the streets surrounding the very place where we were standing, and a long time ago, judging by the cars and the clothes and the absence of apartment towers. I turned them over, and there was a name scrawled on the back. "K. Schwartz."

Three guys in street clothes of the day, double-breasted suits, talking intensely in front of a car, standing in what looked like a vacant lot. These were not poses; they seemed oblivious that they were being photographed. Was Espy hidden? Behind a car, perhaps?

In the next photo, another man had joined them. Lillian's brother Frank. I nearly stopped breathing as I turned over the rest. In the next there was wrestling. Was it for real or for fun? The one after gave me the answer. Frank was unconscious. They were loading him into the trunk of their car.

I lost my breath when I saw it. Then I looked again a few times, to make sure it showed what I thought at first. It did.

This was the answer for Lil, too late. There were no names and no dates, but an expert could add some of that. Had Espy hidden these because they were too dangerous? Or had he lost them? Or was he holding them for some other purpose? Blackmail, or to trade with the authorities? He would have been so young then, too young for that kind of thinking. Then again, he was on his own in a tough world. How did I know what he was capable of?

"These are, well, they might be quite valuable."

"So I thought. It looks to me like a crime in real time."

"What happens to them?"

"They go right to the Brooklyn Collection. They'll know what to do. I'm going to take them over myself along with some other folders I found, library history and such." She smiled. "So you think this was worth a visit?"

"You have no idea. I can't even tell you…"

And then I did tell her.

She had a set of photocopies for me and she gave me a name, the person who would be handling the originals.

Then she said, "I have one more for you."

It was a casual snapshot in bright color, right here at this library, with Christmas decorations. Tall, elegant Savanna was in the back and tiny Deandra stood in the front row, wearing an outfit in startling colors.

"Staff holiday party, last year. I thought you might like to have a copy."

I almost couldn't get the words out to say thank you.

"I'm holding on to one for Dee's mother, if we can ever find her."

Ruby and I finally did the interview about girls in Brownsville. Ruby began, "I miss Lillian a lot. My job today is to speak for both of us. I know what she would have said, and I will say it for her." That was brave of her and it was a great interview, vividly describing the teachers and writers who opened new worlds for these girls, the barriers along the way, the parents who meant well but only encouraged the boys, the fights about staying school or going to work in a factory, the group of girl friends who so bravely supported each other's dreams. I got a lot of kudos for it at work, but to be honest, it was all Ruby.

When we were done recording I turned it off and showed her the lost Espy photos from the library. I thought she would be interested.

She turned alarmingly red and dropped the cup in her hand.

I jumped up, asking if I should call emergency service, but she covered her face, breathing hard, shook her head and finally was able to look up at me.

"Sit down. I have something to tell you. I suppose it's time. No, it's way past time. I never told anyone, not even Lil." She stopped, gathering her strength. "I should have told her. I was too..." She smiled bitterly. "I was too something."

"Can I help?"

"No. Only listen. Do you remember we looked at photos and one showed the window where I used to sleep? When I was a girl?"

I nodded. "You said on nights it was too hot to sleep you'd stay up and look out."

"Yes. So one night, I was up and my brother and Lil's were hanging around on the steps, talking and smoking. I knew Frank more because of Lil than my brother. They weren't so close, but knew each other forever. They sounded comfortable that night."

"Like old friends?"

"Yes. Just like that. They talked about the Dodgers and about girls. And this is what I can't forget. Frank talked to him, to Maury, about the meat cutters union. Some bad people were cranking up the pressure. That's how he said it. And he said he wanted to say no, to fight back, but was that possible? I remembered it, but I didn't understand it then. It sounded serious."

"And did you figure it out, later?"

"Years later, when I learned some history of labor racketeering. And my brother said to Frank, 'Good for you. You're tough enough to fight back. We've got to stand up for what's right,' he said. He and Frank saw just the same on that."

"But your brother, Maurice, was he involved too?"

"Not at all. He wasn't a union man himself, he was a college boy. But Frank liked what he said, and laughed and said 'They can all go to hell, those crooks. And I plan to tell them so.' And I remembered that because he said hell, a very bad word." She stopped and caught her breath. "I was only nine. And they said good night, and Frank said, 'Thanks old buddy. I just needed to hear it out loud. Yeah. My road is clear.'"

I looked at her and waited.

"Frank disappeared two days later." She patted the photos. "Now we know what happened. And Lil was sent away soon after. Maury would cross the street to avoid her and her parents."

"Did he ever talk about it?"

"Not to me. I was only a kid. What did I matter? But it was impossible to keep secrets in that crummy little apartment. My parents were nagging him to go call on Lil's family. It was the right thing to do, they said. He lost his temper and shouted at them. He felt guilty, I guess." She sighed. "You understand, some of this is what I pieced together later, trying to make sense of what I knew but didn't understand."

She stood up then, nervously, and stared out the window. "Well, hell, Lillian, do you think it mattered? That I didn't tell you? What would it have changed?" She turned to me. "She's out there you know."

"What?"

"Oh, don't look so shocked. I didn't mean it literally! I don't believe in ghosts and neither did Lil. That is for sure." She paused. "Some of our parents might have."

"But she would say to me…"

"Meds, darling, just meds talking. Lil herself didn't believe in a thing. A long life does that to lots of us. But! But, she said she wanted her ashes where she could see some flowers. I sneaked out one night and scattered them in that big flower bed right out there. I owed it to her. She's got tulips now and lilacs soon. She's got a nice view of the Palisades too."

Then she did laugh.

"When you finish that exhibit? Put a picture of her up on a wall. She would have loved that. Frank, too. And me. And even my brother Maury. Why not?"

I promised I would and I did. And I persuaded the museum director to send a car for Ruby the day it opened.

Afterword

Brooklyn Secrets, like my other Brooklyn books, is a blend of actual history, possible history, and complete fiction.

Like Erica, I was drawn into present day Brownsville by my interest in historic Brownsville. Unlike Erica, it is not entirely new territory for me, as I worked at the Stone Avenue branch library many years ago. None of the characters in those scenes is based on an actual person, though there are a few incidents that come directly from my own experience.

This is not intended to be a full portrait of Brownsville, nor could it be. I am seeing it through the eyes of Erica, an observant outsider, but still an outsider. I hope the small part of the picture described here is an honest and fair one.

In the dialogue, I have tried to suggest, rather than duplicate, street slang. It changes too quickly to catch in a book, has too much obscenity to be published here, and further, only a local teen could be sure of how a local teen should sound.

Some people whose names are mentioned are obviously historical figures. The basic facts of 1930s Brownsville life, and the history of the organization nicknamed Murder Inc, are as accurate as I could make them. I was surprised several times by people I know telling me they had old family connections to Brownsville and the mob.

Beyond that, this is a work of fiction. The historical facts inspired a number of fictional characters and incidents, as some readers will recognize, but they have been re-imagined to suit the story I was telling.

For readers who are especially interested in the history: the Brooklyn Collection at the Brooklyn Public Library was a great source of information. Some of the books that offered useful facts, perspectives or anecdotes were: *The Girls: Jewish Women of Brownsville, 1940-1995*, by Carole Bell Ford; *Tough Jews: Fathers, Sons and Gangster Dreams* by Rich Cohen; *Our Gang: Jewish Crime and the New York Jewish Community, 1900-1940* by Jenna Weissman Joselit, and *Brownsville* by Alter F. Landesman. The photographs in *New York City Gangland* by Arthur Nash, and in Weegee's *Naked City*, nourished my imagination.

Like Erica, I began with a book: Alfred Kazin's great *Walker in the City*, first read decades ago, as vivid now as it was then.

To receive a free catalog of Poisoned Pen Press titles, please provide your name and address in one of the following ways:

Phone: 1-800-421-3976
Facsimile: 1-480-949-1707
Email: info@poisonedpenpress.com
Website: www.poisonedpenpress.com

Poisoned Pen Press
6962 E. First Ave. Ste 103
Scottsdale, AZ 85251